SA
D0093122

Nightingale

Also by Amy Lukavics:

Daughters unto Devils
The Women in the Walls
The Ravenous

Nightingale

AMY LUKAVICS

Recycling programs
for this product may
not exist in your area.

ISBN-13: 978-1-335-01234-0

Nightingale

Copyright © 2018 by Amy Lukavics

All rights reserved. Except for use in any review, the reproduction or utilization of this work in whole or in part in any form by any electronic, mechanical or other means, now known or hereafter invented, including xerography, photocopying and recording, or in any information storage or retrieval system, is forbidden without the written permission of the publisher, Harlequin Enterprises Limited, 22 Adelaide St. West, 40th Floor, Toronto, Ontario M5H 4E3, Canada.

This is a work of fiction. Names, characters, places and incidents are either the product of the author's imagination or are used fictitiously, and any resemblance to actual persons, living or dead, business establishments, events or locales is entirely coincidental.

This edition published by arrangement with Harlequin Books S.A.

For questions and comments about the quality of this book, please contact us at CustomerService@Harlequin.com.

® and TM are trademarks of Harlequin Enterprises Limited or its corporate affiliates. Trademarks indicated with ® are registered in the United States Patent and Trademark Office, the Canadian Intellectual Property Office and in other countries.

www.HarlequinTEEN.com

Printed in U.S.A.

dedicated to all the weird girls

-1951-
the institution

THERE WAS A DEAD GIRL IN THE BED NEXT TO June's.

The corpse was giggling uncontrollably into her pillow, muffling the sound, making it much quieter than the shrieks and cackles coming from behind the closed door leading to the hallway, a wicked harmony of pain and grief and fear.

Hysteria.

June knew that she wasn't *actually* dead. She just believed she was, and when June had first met her earlier that afternoon, she'd refused to give up her name and instead had insisted June simply think of her as "the dead girl." This was proving to be quite difficult, given how very loud this dead girl was. Shouldn't she have been still and quiet at least *some* of the time?

"I think we should go to sleep now," June said shakily

after licking her lips, feeling the least tired she'd ever been in her entire life, despite the fact that she hadn't slept for days. She was desperate for the dead girl to stop laughing at her. June was so exhausted from the events of the morning, and sleep felt impossible, just as it had in the days leading up to this.

What on earth would happen to her tomorrow?

"What's *sleep*?" the dead girl asked, the laughter completely gone now, her voice hollow and fearful instead. June heard her sit up suddenly in the dark, the mattress springs screaming in strain. "I remember sleep. It used to be comfortable. It used to be quiet. It used to just...*be*."

June nodded, even though her back was turned and the lights were out. She suspected it was only the first night she would lose significant amounts of sleep, *devastating* amounts, but deep in her heart of hearts, she knew right then, with her allegedly dead roommate bouncing up and down on the squeaking mattress and giggling again, that things were truly about to change in all of the very worst ways.

"Sorry," the girl said. "I'm kind of high right now—those damn nurses. This is not a great way to welcome somebody new. Nobody new ever comes, let alone comes to sleep in *my* room. It's exciting. It's actually quite difficult to remember what came before this excitement."

June poked at the memory of this morning in her brain like a hesitant tongue fearing blistering heat. Mom and Dad, at breakfast. The way they'd looked at her when she screamed at the sound of Mom's voice. *Good morning, Nightingale.* Then, the way they had acted, as though they had no idea what June was scared of, what she was shrieking about, what was the matter with her.

"We're your parents," they'd cooed desperately, as June

had backed up against the counter, taken the butcher knife from the drawer beside her and pointed it back and forth between them. "Of course we are! June, honey, what is wrong with you?"

Only it wasn't them. It wasn't them at all. They were liars.

They were something else.

Maybe I could be happy to be here, June thought suddenly, the silver lining showing itself at last. *At least here I won't have to continue living how I was. I won't have to break myself into pieces just to show them that I can.*

Maybe this place is my destiny.

Somewhere outside the locked door leading to the hallway, someone screamed the Lord's Prayer, getting half of the words wrong.

And—she continued to ruminate, as her roommate finally quieted down and settled into her bed because apparently even dead girls needed sleep despite acting as though they never did. How dramatic!—*at least whatever happened to Mom and Dad won't be able to happen to me. I'll be much safer locked in here.*

Part of June understood that she belonged in here, understood that *she* was the one who wasn't safe for others to be around. But most of that was buried by the emotions, wild and shrill, magnified by the insomnia, muddled by the desperate insistence that she was sane. She had to be, she had to be sane, she had to be safe.

Safe. The word echoed itself within the confines of June's skull, a desperate promise, a needed reality. *Safe safe safe safe safe.*

But then she remembered what she'd seen when she'd first walked through the common area and hallways of Burrow Place Asylum. Women shivering in shallow baths, begging for a towel, their teeth chattering and their body hairs sticking out from their goose-fleshed follicles like quills. Women wandering alone, mumbling under their breath, and the nurses occasionally barking for them to get away from other patients' doors. Women sitting with their backs to the wall, forgotten cigarettes smoking away between their fingers as they stared ahead, their eyes blank and staring into nothing, no doubt doped out of their minds.

June wondered about that. About her upcoming *treatments*, as they'd been so ominously alluded to her during check-in.

"Don't you worry, Tulip," the intake nurse had said to June with a wink, a terrifying glimmer in her eye. "You'll be right as rain after you go through your *treatments*. We're here to help."

Something seemed wrong about it, though. "Here to help" didn't fit what June had seen walking through the stone archway leading to the hospital's common room. This had been after changing into the plain blue housedress uniform, a straw-colored sweater worn open on top. And now the sun had fallen, and dinner had been eaten and all those women she had seen earlier were stuffed like mice into the boxlike rooms that lined each side of the single long hallway. *Safe* wasn't anywhere close to how June felt.

Nowhere was safe.

Nobody was trustworthy.

For all she knew, they could *all* be replaced, every person she'd seen since this morning, all of them walking, talking duplicates that would endlessly act as though June had lost her mind. A much worse thought bloomed within June, a thought that made her hands tingle beneath the scratchy covers of her bed.

What if, she thought slowly, biting her tongue behind closed lips, *Mom and Dad weren't actually replaced at all?*

What if I was?

No, no, no. June turned over onto her other side, now facing her roommate, asleep at last and snoring, one arm hanging limply off the side of her mattress. June had not been replaced. Of course not. Something in the *world* had changed, some time between going to sleep last night and waking this morning. Mom and Dad—*they* weren't themselves anymore. They'd been taken, and impostors had been put in their place.

Things haven't been right for a long time, a wicked voice whispered in her mind. *Your unraveling has just been too slow and steady to notice over time.*

She thought about all the things that had happened leading up to this: clues that had suggested the worst. The inability to control herself. The creatures that hid in her bedroom at night, peering at her in the dark, *expecting* things from her. The story she wrote.

June suddenly thought about Robert and of how he might have felt about what'd happened. Who cared about whatever Robert thought, though? It wasn't as though he was important to her, she told herself; she was simply used to having to pretend like he was. She could drop that now, especially after what had happened last night. She doubted he'd ever speak to her again after what she had done.

Besides, what if Robert was replaced, too, just like Mom and Dad had been?

Something is happening, she thought to herself, the pills the nurse made her swallow before bed finally coming into effect. She felt heavy, her ears still adjusting to the sound of the newly quieted hallway.

Something is coming for us all.

days past

"JUNE HARDIE!" HER MOTHER BELLOWED UP the stairs, twenty minutes after the alarm clock had gone off. "Breakfast, I said!"

Upstairs, June sat on the edge of her unmade bed, her short hair in a bird's nest of a mess around her ears. The room was unkempt, the air thick with the smell of morning breath, and she went over to the window to open it for some fresh air.

It was a Saturday, what should have been a warmly welcomed break from school, which June found tiring and worrisome, although deep down she had to admit to herself that the real source of the anxiety came from those damned mathematics. Whenever June was being talked through a math problem, she often couldn't even follow along with the first step, but the teacher would continue as though she clearly understood, and the idea of interrupting to admit that she didn't made her heart race and her palms sweat. If only every class was English!

Despite the potential for math sweats, June thought she'd rather be in school today.

Outside, her older brother, Fred, was mowing the lawn, his hair combed to the side, his slacks rolled up around his ankles. June stared blankly out the window, unblinking as she combed through the tangle of thoughts in her head, until she realized that Fred had stopped mowing the lawn and was now staring up at her in uneasy confusion. After a moment, she stepped away from the window, letting the delicate white curtain fall back into place.

Yesterday, June's mother had told her that by the time she came down to breakfast every morning, she needed to have already gotten dressed, with her hair brushed, her nose powdered and her lipstick applied.

"You need to learn to be a better young woman," Mom had said, her arms crossed over her butter-yellow dress, the one with the white buttons that she always wore the first day after wash. "This week I'm going to teach you how to make meat loaf and boil potatoes and keep the house clean."

June couldn't think of anything more disgusting than squeezing mounds of raw ground meat in between her fingers, the waxy fat coating her skin and gathering under her fingernails, embedded with salt and pepper and dicings of onion. She was a lousy cook—always had been. Mom had a hard time accepting that. So today June would be touching the raw meat, forming it into a loaf, baking it into a bubbling brown log and then slathering it with ketchup before cutting it up into slices for Dad and Fred and Robert.

But first, June knew, the day would be filled with all sorts of other lessons. Cleaning, keeping house, being a better young woman. *What* was *a "better young woman"?* June had wondered, not for the first time. She stared at herself in the mirror atop her unorganized vanity, her wild hair and frowning face an unpleasant sight to behold. *Someone who can bite her tongue during maddening conversations between men? Someone who can keep her house so it looks straight out of a magazine? Someone who can follow in the footsteps of Betty Crocker without mistakes or, God forbid, letting a curl fall hopelessly out of place?*

June supposed she had other thoughts about what would make a "better young woman," but she knew that her feelings on the subject didn't matter, or at the very least, they weren't supposed to. Still, she couldn't resist fantasizing about being the type of woman who lived unapologetically, who experienced and learned and applied the knowledge gathered along the way to enable herself to thrive. The type of woman who learned to navigate her way out of the impossible labyrinth of family history and tradition. One who unlearned the inherited toxic traits that were handed down to her and bound her to an unstable and wildly limited path like angry, unbreakable vines.

It wasn't about the cooking or the cleaning. The specifics were different for everybody. It was about the source of the expectation, what drove it. And in a world that seemed to constantly be going to shit, June thought, surely life was too short to spend it settling in the name of unthinking compliance.

"June!" The knock on the door was sharp, unrepentant. "For goodness' sake, didn't you hear me hollering for you? It's time for breakfast now. We have lots of chores to get through today, if you don't mind."

"Be down in a minute," June called back, shocked at how

level her voice sounded, how devoid of emotion. Usually, she'd feel irritated or sassy or ready for an argument over this, but today she felt different: calmer, more dead inside. It was like she'd understood fully, for the first time, that Mom and Dad were who they were and always would be, no matter what June thought or how she felt. They'd never be happy with the idea of letting her go study in a college somewhere far away. They'd never support her dreams of travel. They would accept one thing, and one thing only.

Be a better young woman.

She chose a dress, green to match how her stomach felt, and used her comb to fluff out the bob haircut she'd gotten a few weeks before. It was miraculous, June mused as she brushed her teeth in the en suite bathroom, how much she'd aged in the last two weeks. She was still seventeen but felt about forty. Is that how changing into an adult worked? Overnight, and with the weight of a million pounds? If so, June sorely wished somebody had warned her.

June came down the stairs and had a quick look around the house, which already looked to her like it'd been cleaned, but she knew Mom had different standards. The kitchen smelled like eggs and bacon. The table had three dirty plates in the places where Mom, Dad, and Fred usually sat. June's spot had a loaded plate waiting for her, with glasses of both orange juice and milk, as well as a small plate piled high with toast.

"Eat fast," Mom said without turning from the sink, where she scrubbed at a pan and set it gingerly in the mouth of the brand-new dishwasher. They'd had it for a little over a month now, ever since Dad had closed the big business deal with his new partner, Mr. Dennings.

Mr. Dennings, whose son, Robert, was twenty.

Robert, who June had been agreeing to see on dates ever since the business deal was just a plan in Dad's back pocket. What a tangled web *that* had been!

It had started one evening after dinner, a school night, and June had had her feet up on the couch while she read a textbook. Dad hadn't been parked in front of the television where he usually had his drink; instead, he had turned his armchair around to face Mom as she wiped down the kitchen table.

"I have something to tell the both of you," Dad had said. "I already talked to Fred about it this morning, since he has bowling practice tonight."

Mom put her cloth down, wiping her hands on her apron front as she stepped into the living room and scolded June for having her feet on the couch. June sat up, put her book on her lap, folded her hands out of habit. She studied Dad's face as he swirled his drink mindlessly in its short glass, but she had no inkling that something so serious was about to be broached. June and her mother sat silently side by side, waiting.

"There's a chance I can take my business to the next level," he finally announced, setting the drink down and leaning forward in the armchair. "You'll both help me to secure a partnership with Stewart Dennings. The economy is booming, and we're both ready to cash in on it. We talked all about it at Stan Reuben's poker night last week. Now I just have to convince Stewart to make the leap and invest."

The radio played in the background, some band playing live from New York City. June's mother shifted in her seat.

"That sounds wonderful, honey," she said softly. "But how are June and I supposed to help?"

"I'm getting to that," Dad said. His fingers tightened ever so slightly around his glass. "If you'd keep your mouth shut and let me, please."

Mom apologized and straightened her back. June fought not to roll her eyes.

"I'm going to start bringing Stewart around here for dinner some evenings," Dad continued. "As well as his son, Robert, who's just joined the family business. Stewart's wife passed away last year."

June was still waiting to hear the reason she was involved in any of this. Likely so she could assist Mom in whatever dinners were coming—not that she was any help with that sort of thing. Still, saying as much to Dad would be pointless, so June continued to listen.

"Oh, how tragic!" Mom said. "Those poor boys."

"I know they'll certainly enjoy being cooked for and fussed over, while they're here," Dad said. "It's very important that we schmooze them as much as we can. When we walk through the door, you will offer us scotch on ice. Have the house ready for guests. Have dinner ready to eat as soon as the drinks are done. We'll have two scotches each, then another at dinner."

"Yes—" Mom nodded as she took in her directions "—of course."

"As soon as the meal is finished, hurry to clean up the table and serve coffee and cake, and probably more scotch."

"Of course."

"Are you getting any of this, June?" Dad demanded suddenly. "Aren't you wondering what your role in all of this will be?"

Maybe he wasn't as thick as June often thought.

"I'm listening, Dad," June said, working to keep her

voice light and noncontrary. "I suppose you'd like me to help out Mom as much as I can, yes?"

"Your mom doesn't need help," Dad answered. "Although heaven knows you could certainly use the practice. No, I've got something more important for you to do."

June's stomach dropped, heavy inside her. What could he possibly want from her in all of this? "What is it, Dad?"

Dad finished the drink in his glass and handed it to Mom to take away. Understanding that her part in the conversation was done, Mom was quick to squirrel it away to the kitchen to be washed and dried and put away. By the time she returned, June was sitting there looking aghast.

"You want me to *what*?" June said.

"Don't get sassy with me," Dad said sharply, leaning forward in his chair a little bit more. "Robert is twenty years old, only three years older than you. There's no reason you can't go on a few dates with him. At your age, June, you should have boys lining up around the block to flatter me into letting them take you out. Feel lucky. Robert is an exceptional young man, the kind you want to look out for as a young woman."

June's cheeks had reddened considerably then. It was true, she'd never been asked out on a date. Never had much interest in it: she was always too busy reading, or working on her story, or taking the bus into town so she could go to the drugstore and look through travel magazines. Awful, horrible possibilities flashed through her mind: What if this Robert character was unkind or—worse—unfunny?

The only rule June had ever set for herself regarding a potential mate was that they'd need to be able to make her laugh, no exceptions. Laughter was all she had to get through life sometimes, and to lose it would be to lose everything.

"So it's settled," Dad went on without waiting for her to reply. "Tomorrow, I'll bring Stewart and Robert. Then again on Friday. This deal could change our lives, girls. Our family needs it. If we all work together, we'll achieve it."

And so it started: the chain of dinners, the meat loaves and roasted chickens and casseroles, coffees and cakes and pies and puddings, always cocktails and cigars in the den to follow. Robert was strikingly handsome but painfully boring; June rather liked him in a nonromantic sense but often grew tired with his ideas of fun, like walks in the park, coffee downtown, or long drives in his car while he talked about himself and never asked about her.

Once the business deal between Dad and Stewart Dennings had finally been closed, June got the courage to teach Robert a little bit more about her real self, as opposed to the dressed-up, tidy little thing that Mom had transformed her into before every one of their dates. Dad and Stewart were on their fifth scotch each and had gotten into a particularly animated conversation about politics, both on the same side and simply repeating the same three or four tenets to each other over and over.

"I want to show you something," June said, rising from where she sat on the couch and catching Robert's eye. "In my bedroom."

days past

THE IDEA FOR THE STORY HAD BLOOMED aggressively in June's brain in a single blinking instant. She'd been sitting in the dark at her bedroom window, looking down on the empty street, as well as up to the night above, which was filled to the brim with stars. Despite being a voracious reader for most of her life, June had never held any dreamy thoughts about writing. She'd never had a good enough idea of her own, or anything even close to one.

Too often, the rest of the household would fall asleep far too early for June's personal tastes, so she would sit at the window seat in her bedroom to dream and to ponder, usually unrealistic ideas about exciting things to do once high school ended. Sometimes a stray dog would wander down the street, and June would watch its every move, trying to figure out exactly what it was thinking, imagining exaggerated situations that could have ended with the dog being alone.

The night June's father had told her that she would be dating Robert, she had sat at the window and opened it for once, letting the cold air bite at her face, neck, and arms. She had shivered a little and pulled her knees to her chest, hugging her legs as she looked down like she usually did, reflecting.

What a strange situation, to have found her very first boyfriend in a circumstance that actually had little to nothing to do with herself! She imagined what might happen if Robert showed up the first time and found June viscerally appalling. What would Dad do then? How was he so sure this arrangement was a good idea? He wasn't, June knew; he was just greedy and willing to try anything he could to secure that money.

June couldn't blame him, she supposed as she watched a squirrel dart from mailbox to mailbox, hiding behind each post as though looking for something. More money would certainly make Mom happier and less likely to complain about all that she had to do on her own to run the house.

She was wondering how long she'd end up with this Robert fellow after all was said and done, when she noticed a flash of light in the sky, quick enough to distract her eye from the squirrel. A shooting star perhaps? June's hand flew over her heart as she began to whisper her deepest wish, but she stopped when she realized that the flash of light wasn't fading away or disappearing. It kept hovering in the same spot, but it was blinking, and before June could make sense of it, two identical lights appeared on either side of the first one. *Blink. Blink. Blink.*

Then, as quickly as they'd come, the lights were gone.

They must have been the result of an airplane or something, although even then June knew that airplanes didn't work like that. Why had the lights struck her so? It was as though they were familiar to her in some eerie sort of way. They made June feel thrilled and frightened at the same time.

Click.

The idea for the story filled June so quickly and massively she'd actually gasped out loud, her heart quickening at the strange feeling. She had no idea what would happen at the end of the story or even in the middle, but the beginning was so terrifyingly vivid that June actually feared what might happen if she didn't get it out of her mind and onto a page.

It didn't matter that her newfound project distracted her in a way that made her withdraw from the few friends she had at school, and that made her grades get even worse than they'd been. The night June started her book was the night she'd gone from having nothing solid to strive for to feeling like she may have actually stumbled across her destiny, her true self, self-evident at last. She started her story that very same night, and by the time she decided to bring Robert into her bedroom to show him a glimpse of her real mind, she already had a few chapters of the story written.

Ordinarily, such a thing would probably be considered to be inappropriate, but June knew her parents were so happy over the fact that she was dating anybody at all that they had set virtually no rules or limitations to her relationship with Robert. This became particularly helpful if she wanted to leave for a long drive on a weeknight, to clear her head and get away from Mom and Dad. It was helpful again now, on the odd Saturday night as Robert followed June up the stairs and into her bedroom, which Mom had cleaned to be neat as a pin like she always did when the Dennings men came for dinner. All of June's school books were neatly stacked, bound absurdly with a belt, which made her roll her eyes but chuckle at the same time. June's mother was so strange.

"What did you want to show me?" Robert asked now, his eyes sweeping over the bedroom as he settled on the bed. He took a long drink of his scotch. June pretended she didn't notice, making her way to the opposite side of the room, where her desk was. Her typewriter sat there in all its glory, no messy stacks of papers marked up with edits surrounding it like before.

Mom must have stuffed them into the drawers, June thought, and when she opened one she could see that she was right. Clearly, Mom had never imagined that Robert would see the inside of the desk drawers, so they had been stuffed with all the odds and ends that June usually kept out on her desk. She gathered the bound stack of papers closest to the top, the one with a title page that said nothing but *The Gift of the Stars* typed on it. Taking a deep breath, she pulled the rubber band from around the stack of papers and handed it to Robert.

"What's this?" he asked, looking dubiously at the papers in his hands. He appeared to have been inconvenienced as he set his drink down on the dresser and lifted the title page away to expose page one of the story beneath. It was then that June felt the first wave of doubt wash through her.

June watched Robert's eyes move uneasily over the text.

She was in the forest when they took her. She tried to scream, but they knocked her out. When she woke up, she was naked on a cold metal table. There were unseen straps holding her

*down, a strange smell in the air like nothing she'd ever expe-
rienced. Like formaldehyde and warm sea water. There was
a circular window near her; outside of it, she could only see
the deepest reaches of outer space.*

Robert's brow relaxed from its previous furrow; June
took this as a good sign, and her doubt receded. In its
place, she felt a wonderful and terrible rush of adrenaline
flood over her, the idea that finally somebody besides her
was reading over the words she'd crafted so carefully on
the page. June decided right then and there that if Robert
complimented her writing, she wouldn't be able to stop
herself from walking up to him and kissing him right on
the mouth.

They hadn't embraced or kissed or done anything more
than hold hands for five minutes at a time, but watching
him now, June could feel her body give in to the curios-
ity of what it might be like if he were to touch her, grab at
her, kiss her neck and slide his fingers into the place that
the rest of the world loved to pretend didn't exist. *Why
not make the best of the situation?* she thought as she watched
him read her story. *I may not love him, but he's nice enough.
I'm sure he wouldn't mind the physical exchange.*

"What do you think?" June said softly, but Robert didn't
answer, didn't even lift his gaze from the paper. *He must
be really into it*, she thought, unable to help the smile that
erupted over her face. *I'm so glad I decided to show him after all.*

"'The things came in through an electronically wired
door,'" Robert read out loud. "'They looked a little like
men, but not quite. Their skin was as gray as ash. Their
eyes were three inches apart, and all shining black.'"

He looked up from the paper finally, and June met his

gaze with more vulnerability than she'd ever allowed with him before. "I didn't know that you like to write," he said.

"I love to," June had answered, turning away so he couldn't see her flushed skin. There was no way she'd be able to stop herself from kissing him, she knew that now, her tongue anxious to explore his, her insides aching with want. She suddenly became hyperaware of the feeling of her cotton underwear stretched tightly over her skin. June turned back toward him, and his mouth opened just the tiniest bit at the look on her face, understanding fully her intent.

Robert set the manuscript down on the dresser beside his drink, then stepped to the bedroom door and shut it. June followed, reaching intimately around his side to lock it. "I never expected something like this from you," he said, and June swelled at the idea of being complex, interesting, a surprise. "I've really enjoyed the time we've spent together so far, June."

"So have I," June said in a near whisper, realizing that while it wasn't true in the same way he meant, it was true in a general sense. She stepped closer to Robert, their stomachs lightly pressing against one another, reached her hand to curl around the back of his head and pulled his mouth to hers.

They kissed deeply, mouths open, June's blood electric with excitement. She'd never fooled around with anybody but herself before, but she felt like she'd done it a million times, like she knew exactly what to do. *It's easy when you follow your body*, she thought, stepping away and breaking the kiss. He moaned slightly and reached his arms out for her, but she gently pushed him away. She took a step back and began to unbutton her dress. Shame was nonexistent.

He'd read her story. He'd thought it was wonderful, she could tell. He knew her insides now.

It felt so good to open the dress over her chest, to expose her skin to the open air and to his eyes. The thick housedress hadn't required a bra, and as he watched she rubbed her hands over herself, over her mounds of warm flesh, over their hardened tips. She could see the front of his pants bulging.

June didn't understand the intensity of the feelings that only got more desperate by the second. This was Robert, the boy from all those boring dates, content with sitting and doing nothing for hours. Now, at least, they were certainly doing something. She stepped out of the dress, and out of the underwear that felt confining and alien.

June lay down on the bed, on her back, writhing around a little bit, not letting herself think about what she was doing on a physical level but clinging to the feelings that came from sharing her writing with Robert and feeling like finally, *finally*, someone understood her. He watched her for just a moment before he reached up and loosened his tie, pulled it off, and wrestled with his belt buckle.

She pulled him toward her, pressed her bare chest on his, lifted her hips to grind greedily against his warmth. June knew she was surprising herself more than she was surprising Robert, which was really saying something—if his eyebrows pulled any higher, they'd certainly fly off his forehead. She briefly forgot how any of this had started, what had come over her to make her want this so badly, and remembered that Mom was downstairs with a drunk Dad and Stewart Dennings.

But the doubt lasted only until Robert kissed her again and pushed himself into her, and she let him, letting out a brief but strained moan at the sensation. They bucked against each other, each breathing hard in between the moments of kissing. She'd heard in the gossip groups at school that men were all talk when it came to the subject of stamina. By the way Robert was moving now, she believed it.

Finally, he gave out a final moan and then rolled off her, her clammy skin flourishing with goosebumps at the chill in the air. Their eyes met and they both smiled, but then there was a loud thumping sound downstairs that seemed to snap them out of their ease and back into nervousness. They dressed quickly, neither speaking, and while she leaned over the vanity to brush her hair and wipe the smeared lipstick from her face with a tissue, he took his drink from the top of the dresser and drained what little was left.

June stood up, her eyes falling to the manuscript beside the empty glass. "I'm glad you liked my writing," she said shyly, not understanding how she could ever be shy in front of him again, yet here she was. "I've always been afraid to show it to anybody."

"Well," he chuckled, making his way over to the bed to straighten the comforter they'd rumpled. "It was certainly something, darling. And so are you." He leaned forward, tenderly brushed a curl from her face, and kissed her on the cheek.

"I'd love to write stories for a living after I'm out of high school," she said brightly, taking the manuscript back to the desk, not bothering to stuff it back into the drawer. "This is my first one. And when I finish it, I'm going to submit it to publishers."

"Publishers? With an odd story about aliens from outer space?" Robert asked in a way that made June's heart fall with such a sudden crash that she had to be careful not to glare. "I don't know about that part, darling."

"Why not?" she asked, crossing her arms. "Why in the hell not?"

He looked at her, at the anger on her face, and let out a pitying smile. "You are so adorable," he said, leaning forward again, this time to kiss her forehead. "Honestly, I think that it's a great hobby for you to do in your spare time."

Hobby. She felt as though she could murder him. Didn't he know that this story had essentially caused her to completely withdraw from whatever form of social life she'd had before? It wasn't just a casual project based on a whim; it was her life, her *whole* life.

"You should go back downstairs," June said, stepping away from him, sore and irritated. "They'll be wondering where we've gone. Would you mind telling my mother that I've got a headache, if she asks? Tell her I've decided to lie down."

Robert nodded and went for the door, and she suspected he knew that the headache was both a lie and not a lie. "I... think I may be falling in love with you," he said, pausing with his hand on the knob. She wanted to laugh, but it was too depressing. When June didn't reply, Robert blushed and let himself out.

As soon as he was gone, June went into her closet, retrieved a shoe box hidden beneath some scarves, and took out the thin stack of papers that she'd placed in there just last week. On the papers were all sorts of questions about June, from basic information to longer, more thoughtful questions about writing and reading.

She'd taken the application from the library the last time

she was there. There had been a table set up to advertise a writing program out East. June had overheard the fellow manning the display explain all the details to another man who had inquired about it.

Hobby.

If you were selected, you got to attend a month-long writing retreat on scholarship, in upstate New York. You got to have your own private cottage that was within walking distance of a large building where you could eat and converse with other writers. You got to drink scotch and smoke cigarettes and spend as much time as you wanted holed up in your cottage writing.

You are so adorable.

June had not yet had the courage to fill out the application until now—hadn't even decided for sure that she wanted to try until tonight. She spent two hours poring over the application, making sure every hand-written answer was as perfect as she could get it, responding to essay questions and writing prompts on the lined paper space provided in the packet. June spoke every sentence out loud both before and after she wrote it on the paper, carefully considering it in combination with the ones that came prior before moving on.

Publishers? With an odd story about aliens from outer space?

She hoped her desperation came across without sounding unhinged. She hoped her talent showed itself in the voice she used to answer the questions. She hoped her idea of applying as *J. Hardie* instead of *June Hardie* would be enough to mask the fact that she was a woman. If they knew the truth, they'd never consider her for the final prize.

When she was finished, June slept through what little was left of the night and well into the afternoon. Mom and

Dad didn't even bother her about it, when she came into the kitchen for orange juice far past lunchtime. They must have still been pleased with her for another night of successful schmoozing. If only they knew! After she finished her juice, she got dressed and brushed her teeth and took the thick sealed envelope to the mailbox, lifting the little flag for the postman to notice.

She stayed in the living room until she saw the mail truck pull up and the white-uniformed man remove her application from the box. She watched through the window as he stuck it in a bin in the truck, and then it was off. She was able to relax then, knowing for sure nobody had intercepted the envelope.

Now all June had to do was keep on going as she had been, however they needed her to until she heard back. She knew she shouldn't have gotten her hopes up, but she had anyway. With one split-second decision, she'd taken control of her life.

And now, several months and many boring dates with Robert later, wearing the green dress that matched exactly how she felt inside, June Hardie ate her breakfast and thought all about that night with Robert, how they'd never talked about it again, how they'd never repeated it. Obviously, she never showed him, or anyone, pages from her story again. If she hadn't heard from the writing program people yet about her application, she doubted she ever would, but she could still try her luck with publishers once it was finished.

Now that the business partnership was a done deal, June thought she was probably going to break up with Robert, sooner rather than later. Mom and Dad would be upset, she knew, but what did they expect to come out of this arrangement long-term? High school graduation was approaching, and it was time for her life to begin.

"There's a sale on pork roasts," Mom said from where she stood, still washing dishes at the sink. "We should run in and buy a few for the deep freezer."

"Sure," June said, miserable at the idea of cooking and cleaning all day. "Whatever you say, Mom."

the institution

JUNE WASN'T SURE HOW MUCH SHE'D SLEPT, if at all. It seemed that a nurse opened the door to her room every ten seconds for "checks," causing June to nearly jump out of her skin and her dead roommate to grunt in her sleep. Why did they have to check in so damn often? As if she *or* the dead girl could somehow sneak away from this impenetrable fortress of iron and stone.

"Up and at 'em, girlies," the nurse bellowed from the doorway, her hair pinned into a bun that was far too small for her head. "Meds in five, new girl. Breakfast after."

June's roommate sat up and stretched, looking nervously over as if unsure whether or not she could trust June.

"Good morning," June said, still flat on her back. "You snored for literally the entire night."

"Sorry," the girl grumbled, looking over the edge of her bed for her slippers. After she swung her legs over and slipped the slippers on, she stayed sitting on the edge of the bed, clearly waiting for June. June couldn't tell if she liked or disliked this.

"You'll wait for me, but you won't tell me your name?" June asked, begrudgingly sitting up and getting her own slippers on. "Doesn't make much sense to me."

"Dead girls don't have names," the girl shot back, sputtering, much more upset than June expected or intended. "It doesn't fucking matter what my name used to be. Stop asking about it. You'll never know."

June frowned. "But I do know it. I just wanted you to be the one to say it to me."

The girl froze, and June could see the gears turning in her head as she tried to figure out if June was lying or not.

"It was on your chart, which was next to mine on the door," June said, not sure why she was picking the scab that was this obviously fragile and imbalanced girl. The words kept coming out, even though she wished she could just have the strength to shut up and get her nerves calmed some other way. "Your name is Eleanor."

Eleanor's face reddened then. "Yeah." She got up and made her way to the door, stopping to look over her shoulder at June. "Are you coming or what? They get really cranky if you don't show up for meds on time."

"I don't have any to take," June said, and Eleanor rolled her eyes and walked out.

It took June a moment to gather the courage to stand. Were they really supposed to go straight out there, without prettying themselves up first? It felt like the sort of thing that would make Mom fall over if she knew. At least in this place June wouldn't have to follow those standards anymore. It seemed to be the one silver lining out of the situation—no more pork roasts, no more lipstick, no more folding Fred's and Dad's laundry. Her mother would have to do it all by herself. Not that June had ever been much of a real help.

The thought of her mother made June's stomach pinch into a horrible knot. What had happened to her mother? Her *real* mother, not the eerie duplicate that had tried and failed to seamlessly take her place. June thought of the story she had written, thought about the aliens, always taking people away and changing them and trying to put them back as if nothing had happened. But nobody was ever quite right after coming back. Something had been taken away from them, permanently, something very important.

"Good morning, Nightingale," the thing who had been pretending to be her mother had practically sung out to June yesterday morning, when she had come down for breakfast.

And then June had screamed.

Outside the room, there were several women in a disjointed line that came to a head at a station protected by huge panes of thick fake glass. Behind the panes stood three nurses, their outfits so white, crisp, and perfect, their caps pinned in place over their carefully styled hair. June looked around at everyone outside of the glass, with their tangled hair and their sweat-stained garments and their grungy slippers. It didn't feel right that the nurses were so clean; it made June feel unworthy, unequal, animalistic.

This is all just one big zoo, June realized. *Those nurses don't care that we're humans. They're just herding us.*

A tiny flower of dread bloomed within June's stomach when the tallest nurse, the one in the middle with the low blond side bun and cherry-red lipstick, made direct eye contact with her and held it for what felt like thirty full seconds without blinking. There was something unsettling about the nurse; familiar, like June had seen her somewhere before. Then, as quick as the awkward moment had arisen, the nurse turned and disappeared into a hallway behind the station.

"Cadence," the monotone voice of one of the remaining nurses called from the window. A woman who looked to be about forty strode up to the window and took a small paper cup.

"Cypress," the nurse called out again, then, a few moments later, "Dominguez."

June watched as everyone claimed their medication. She was suddenly overwhelmed by the curious notion that none of these women were sick at all. They all looked so much more *normal* than they had when she had first arrived yesterday.

What even was *normal*, though?

And when June thought about it, everyone who had looked strange to her yesterday had done so as a direct result of the hospital: the shivering, naked women in the bathtub; the women who were leaned against the wall with cigarettes in between their fingers, looking doped beyond this world. As June remembered all these things, she spotted an older woman crouched beneath the counter of the nurses' station, peeling pieces of drywall away from a crumbling weak spot and eating them, her medication cup empty beside her on the floor.

Shame on you for judging any of it, June scolded herself as she waited patiently to see if her name would be called. *There's no such thing as normal, anyway. You can't tell by looking at someone if they're well or not.*

Was she herself *well*?

"Hardie," the nurse called, and June flinched as if being poked. "June Hardie."

June stepped up to the counter, spotting her roommate, Eleanor, looking at her with victory painted on her face. *Told you so*, she mouthed playfully, and June made an effort to ignore her. The pill was the strangest looking that June had ever seen: an extremely large, clear, smooth capsule filled with what appeared to be blood. Of course it wasn't blood, though, June thought as she shakily raised the paper cup to her mouth. *Your imagination is just on overdrive.*

Why was she being given medication without having seen a doctor first? Maybe the pills were more like vitamins?

She thought back, momentarily, to the time she'd let Robert read her story. How he'd sounded when he read the part about the aliens out loud. With shock and grotesque intrigue.

He hadn't even made it to the part where the girl's eyes were removed, suctioned harshly from their home and laid down to rest, by their roots, on her cheeks, hot and wet and heavier than she ever would have thought possible. The girl in the story was certain she was about to die, especially when she could hear the awful scraping of the space creatures' tools inside her orbital sockets.

June recalled writing the girl's internal monologue.

I felt a change happening. I thought that the change was death, but no end ever came, no darkness to welcome me, no release from the terror of knowing I would never see my home, my planet, again.

Once the sample of her brain was collected and her eyes were back where they belonged, everything had looked different.

"Hey." A whisper jolted June from her thoughts. Eleanor was standing near her, peering at her curiously. "What are you thinking about? Looks like it was something real bad."

June realized that the paper cup with the large red capsule was now empty. She frowned at the sight; she didn't remember taking the pill, only bringing the paper cup up to her mouth.

"They're big pills, but they go down easy enough," Eleanor said, following June's gaze. "It's only your first full day, and you're already swallowing it dry? Impressive."

So, that must have meant that June had swallowed the pill, even though no matter how hard she stretched her mind, she couldn't locate the memory of having done so. All she knew was that she had been lost in her story, again. Losing herself in her story was her favorite way of feeling better. And she would rather remember anything other than what had happened to land her in Burrow Place.

"Breakfast is this way," Eleanor said, linking her arm through June's and pulling her gently toward a room where all the other women were headed. "I keep telling them that dead people don't need to eat, but they keep making me. If I don't, they…" Her voice faded away, her breath quickening.

"It's okay," June said gently. "If you don't mind me asking, when did you, um…die?"

"Three years ago," Eleanor replied. "It was very sad."

The main room narrowed into a hallway, not nearly as wide as the one that connected all the bedrooms. Every table, every chair, was identical. There were already people sitting down to eat, all of them wearing the same house-dress and sweater as June. Across the room, standing in the corner with a clipboard, was the nurse who June had noticed earlier, with the side bun and the red lipstick, her cap still pinned in place. She'd stared at June then, and she was staring now.

"Have you ever noticed that these nurses look kind of fake?" June said, following Eleanor to the line. "I mean, they look like they're out of a film. It's strange. It's like they're wearing costumes."

Eleanor turned back to her, and in all seriousness, said: "They are."

June had to blink for a moment at that one. "What?"

"It's not a real hospital," Eleanor whispered. She nervously looked to the nurse with the red lipstick. "Not the kind it's supposed to be, anyway."

June stayed quiet for a moment, unsure how to respond. She realized she didn't know how much she could trust Eleanor—if her strange new roommate thought she was dead, how trustworthy could she be? She gathered a plastic bowl, filled with oatmeal and topped with raisins and nuts, and took a little paper cup filled with milk.

The tables were more crowded than June would prefer.

"Damn," Eleanor said, her eyes scanning the cafeteria. "My friends are surrounded with no empty seats. We'll have to eat over here and meet up with them afterward."

Across the room, a pretty girl with long hair bellowed to Eleanor to bring her a dirty gin martini. Eleanor laughed at the request and shot the girl a wink. June followed Eleanor to a table at the opposite end of the cafeteria, and they ate mostly in silence. After breakfast was finished, the girls went back to their room to find freshly folded clothing on their now-made beds.

"Shouldn't they have us make our own beds?" June wondered aloud. "This isn't a hotel."

"They always do little things like that," Eleanor said. "They like to keep watch over everything, make sure nobody's hiding any secrets."

June followed her roommate down the hall to a bathroom that looked like it was supposed to be all white but instead took on a sickly, buttery-yellow sheen. Grime gathered in between tiles that felt unpleasantly warm beneath June's thin, already worn slippers. There were no doors or any partitions to separate the toilets from one another, nor were there any shower curtains or bath mats. In the corner was a bucket that was filled with used sanitary pads.

"Should that be out?" June asked, eyeing the bucket, feeling her stomach turn at the mixture of the chlorine and old blood smells in the enormous, overheated bathroom. Eleanor shrugged and brushed her teeth at the long trough sink. Eventually, June followed suit.

"What do we do now?" she asked later, when they joined the chaos of the recreation room. "Where are all the doctors and nurses?"

"They only take us when they need us," Eleanor answered, making her way to a group of girls gathered in the back of the room. "Until then, we wait."

the institution

ELEANOR LEAD JUNE OVER TO A SET OF couches arranged in front of a television, where five other girls all sat.

"Be right back," she said, leaving June to fend for herself among the rest of the girls. June had a brief moment where she felt the stark social pressure that came with being the new addition to an already well-established group.

The girl sitting closest to June, the one with the long, soft-looking brown hair, introduced herself as Lauren.

"I'm here because I like eyes," she said. "I'd like to be an eye doctor someday."

June paused, unsure how to answer. Why would liking eyes land someone in Burrow Place?

"My own eyes can see things that aren't there," Lauren continued, and June understood then. "I can also tell by looking at someone what their eyes have seen. Sometimes, anyway."

June smiled, rather liking the idea of Lauren's supposed talent. "What have my eyes seen, then?"

Lauren smiled back and locked eyes with June, but almost immediately the smile faded into a pained grimace. "Something that I find strange," she mumbled, her fingers nervously lacing over themselves, "is that we've all seen the same impossible thing. Even you."

"'Impossible'?" June asked, but Lauren wrapped her sweater around herself more tightly and turned away.

"Sometimes I'm even able to tell what your eyes *will* see, even if they haven't seen it yet," Lauren answered, sounding troubled, looking at June once again but keeping her body turned away. "Don't worry. I won't tell them what's in store for you."

June shifted uncomfortably as Eleanor returned carrying a long, flat box: a board game.

"Let's play Monopoly," she suggested. "That way you can get to know everybody. It's the original version, too."

The last time June had played Monopoly, she had taken all of Fred's money, and he'd pretended that he'd let it happen on purpose, enraging June, and Dad had made her give some of the money back to him. She didn't particularly want to play right now, because to play a game in a place like this just felt wrong, but what else was she supposed to do?

"I always thought it was so silly that they didn't have a game piece shaped like glasses," Lauren said, choosing the top hat instead. "But, what can you do, I guess."

"I want to use the ship token," a small girl with white-blond hair insisted, placing the game piece on the starting square and sitting cross-legged beside Lauren. "And I want to buy a hotel on Boardwalk."

"Ambitious," Eleanor said, choosing the thimble for herself. "And of course you'd choose the ship. Would you like to tell June why you're here, Cassy?"

The girl wrinkled her nose. "Not really. Does *June* want to tell me why *she's* here?"

Cassy may have been small, June thought, but she was fierce. "Nobody has to tell me anything," June said, trying to sound nonchalant.

"Oh, but of course we do," Eleanor insisted, shooting June a reassuring grin. "We're all here for a reason, aren't we? Might as well get acquainted."

Eleanor had said last night that there were never any new girls admitted. Surely that couldn't have been true, but on the other hand, it was obvious that they were all fascinated by June. Cassy may have been playing it cool, but June could see it in her eyes, just like she could see it in the rest of their eyes: they were curious about her.

She felt her cheeks warm as she sat down opposite Cassy and chose the iron as her game piece. "I, uh…" She cleared her throat and tried again. "My parents got replaced. By duplicates that looked exactly like them. But it wasn't them."

"That sounds horrible," Eleanor said, sounding like she meant it, and the other girls nodded in support. It filled June's heart with unexpected gratitude. To have somebody believe you about something so *un*believable…June appreciated it very much. "I'm sorry."

"It's okay," June said casually, not wanting them to think that she was hogging all the attention. She wanted to get to know them just as much as they clearly wanted to get to know her.

"What's your name?" she asked one of the other girls from the group, the one who had told Eleanor that she wanted a gin martini at breakfast. The girl curled the ends of her long braid in her finger and regarded June.

"Jessica," she said. "And this one—" she wrapped her arm around the girl sitting next to her on the couch, the one with dark bangs that went straight across her forehead, like a flapper from the roaring twenties "—is Adie."

"It's nice to meet you," Adie said, offering June a tip of the head. "I could tell at breakfast that you were super nervous because your eyes were shifting around far too much. Don't let the nurses see you act that way, unless you want a dose of something awful."

June nodded back, grateful for the information. "Thanks for telling me."

"Of course." Adie seemed so warm, like one of those people that just radiated with motherly love and wisdom. She was comforting to be around. "Glad to have you on board, June." She winked.

June had now met all of Eleanor's friends, except for one—a girl who had been working furiously away in her sketchbook all this time.

"I'm Simpson," the girl said as if reading June's mind, too absorbed in her drawing to look up. "It's a pleasure to have you join us in this special little circle of Hell."

June looked around the room at all the other patients; many of them were chatting or reading or listening to the radio or watching television, but nobody else seemed to have access to any sort of art supplies such as a sketchbook.

"I know what you're thinking," Simpson said, and June noticed that the girl had raised her eyes from the paper for a brief moment. "I get to draw because it's part of my treatment. They're always encouraging me to draw as much as I can."

If one of the treatment options is drawing, June thought, *then maybe I'll be all right after all.*

Simpson went back to her sketchbook. Too curious to resist, June moved to try and catch a sneaky glimpse of what Simpson was working on. The girl noticed June leaning over and playfully pulled the sketchbook toward her chest to hide whatever was in it.

"Come on," June encouraged, a small smile pulling the side of her mouth up into a curl. "Whatever it is, I can guarantee you it's better than any stick-figure mess I'm capable of doing."

Simpson returned June's half smile and handed the sketchbook to June. As she flipped through the pages, she gave out a little gasp of delight.

The drawings were violent and thrilling and weird, blood splatters and butcher knives and long-haired women with enlarged, hairy limbs and wide eyes and red mouths. The images blended together, surrounded each other, multiple scenes playing out on single pages.

"So, what is it that *you* can do?" Simpson asked as June marveled over the drawings. The other girls seemed very keen on hearing the answer.

"What do you mean?" June looked around and then returned the book to Simpson, who immediately opened it up again and continued working on the newest picture, which showed a woman's severed head in a birdcage.

"Lauren told you all about her special talent," Simpson continued as she dragged the tip of her pen across the paper in smooth, wavy flicks to fill in the woman's hair. "And I can talk to dead people in my sleep."

"I can hear things that others can't," Adie added glumly. "It's like these weird, ticking noises that I can't figure out one bit. It's almost like it's some sort of language that I've never heard before. And it's always talking to me! If only I could understand it, maybe it'd tell me something useful."

"If you do start understanding it," June said, "tell it to let us know what the hell is going on around here."

"For real," Eleanor added.

"I'm a time traveler," Cassy blurted randomly from where she'd been sitting in silence. The other girls broke into smiles.

"At least, that's what we've all decided her talent is," Simpson said with a little laugh. "It's the only thing that makes sense, don't you know."

Her eyes flitted up—wanting to gauge June's reaction to her joke, no doubt.

"Oh, of course," June answered, grinning. "Oftentimes when something doesn't make sense, I realize that time travel must be to blame."

Eleanor laughed then, and June decided that she liked Eleanor so much more when she wasn't high on drugs and cackling at June in the dark. She seemed to have forgiven June for finding out her name. "Tell her, Cass," Eleanor said. "What happened to you."

"I was on the greatest ship in the world," Cassy said, her smile fading as her eyes unfocused into the memory. "And it sank. My parents were killed in the rush to get off. My baby sister, who was six, she and I were floating and holding on to debris and waiting for help." She paused. "She… ran out of strength. She drowned."

"Oh, geez," June said, suddenly feeling awful about making the joke. "I'm so sorry to hear that. Truly."

"That's not the kicker." Jessica pulled a cigarette from the pocket of her housedress, lifted it to her lips and lit it with the matches from a nearby coffee table. After a long drag, Jessica held the cigarette in front of Adie, who leaned forward and eagerly pulled on it herself. June was shocked that Jessica was speaking about such a tragedy so flippantly. "Tell her the kicker, Cass."

"The kicker—" Cassy said, then stopped to clear her throat "—was that while I was waiting for one of the damned lifeboats to come back and help, everything went black, just like that." She snapped her fingers. "And I could hear the sound of rushing water, but I didn't feel wet anymore. I felt dry, and when I opened my eyes, I was here in Burrow Place."

"That's *still* not the kicker," Jessica insisted impatiently, blowing out a huge puff of smoke and leaning forward to help organize the Monopoly money. "Stop holding out on her."

June couldn't believe there was more to the story. Already her heart was so heavy with pity for Cassy and her poor baby sister.

"The ship I was on," Cassy said. "It was the *Titanic*. In the year 1912."

June accidentally let out a nervous but sharp *Ha!* Cassy's face darkened, and June felt horrible. What if Eleanor had made that same sound when June was sharing about her parents?

"I'm so sorry," she rushed, but already Cassy was smiling again.

"Your face made it worth it, I guess," Cassy said. "Also, from what I can tell, my special talent is way cooler than yours."

"You're not wrong," June said. "But to me, the real question is: If we have all these wonderful secret talents, why aren't we using them to get out of here?"

She had meant it as another lighthearted remark to ease the tension from her gaffe, but the girls looked at her like she was stupid.

"You think we know how to control it?" Simpson smirked. "Don't we wish! Also, not sure how talking to a dead person could help anybody get out of here."

"And my thing only happened that one time," Cassy added, crossing her arms over her chest. "Even then, of course Nurse Joya and the doctor don't believe it really happened." She paused. "But at the same time, it's almost like...they *do* believe it. They just don't want me to think they do. Do you guys ever get that at all?"

The other girls nodded. "Yes!" Lauren said, finally letting her anxious hands drop to her sides. "And what's even more strange is that the more they want to know about it, and the more they prod for information about it...the less it happens."

"Yes!" Eleanor and Adie exclaimed in unison.

June couldn't understand how believing your parents were replaced by replicas was a *special talent* in any way. It's the only thing that had ever happened to June that could compare to the wild stories of these other girls. Maybe it was a good thing she'd been roomed with Eleanor—thinking you're dead wasn't much of a talent either.

"What's your talent, Jessica?" she asked, suddenly eager to start playing Monopoly. She was beginning to feel out of place again.

"Like I'll ever tell you!" Jessica said, and June couldn't tell if she was joking or not.

"She sculpts things," Simpson said, and Jessica shot her a glare. "With pieces of trash that she finds lying around. She sculpts body parts that aren't human. There's a whole bunch of them hidden under her bed, according to Cassy."

Now Jessica was glaring at Cassy, who June realized must be Jessica's roommate.

"Sorry," Cassy said, shrugging, then reached forward and rolled the dice.

Maybe writing was June's talent. It seemed boring compared to talking to dead people in your sleep or being able to hear someone speaking an unknown language in your head, but it had taken a peculiar and almost otherworldly grip on June back when she'd been in the thick of it. Oh, how she missed her story!

"Whatever you're thinking about right now," Jessica said to June, her cigarette hanging limply between her lips, "make sure never to tell them about it."

They may have been an unsettling bunch, but June herself could easily be considered just as unsettling, with her darting eyes and paranoia and tendency to get lost in her own mind. She decided that she liked the girls Eleanor hung around.

With the exception of Cassy's ridiculous *Titanic* story, none of the other girls talked about their lives before Burrow Place, nor did they mention what they wanted to do when they got out someday. Most patients did get out, right? They had to, June decided. They were all so young. There was no way this was it for any of them.

June considered with great sadness how long some of the other patients must have been at the institution, some of them as old as eighty. The building had been around since the late 1800s, if June wasn't mistaken, more than enough time for spans of lives to come and pass. Even Eleanor had said that she'd "died" three years ago... Had she been here that entire time? What had her life been like before?

"They tried to put one of those worms in me again," Simpson mumbled out of nowhere, while she was moving her piece along the edge of the board. She lifted her hand to her head gingerly, as if taking care around an injury, but her head looked fine. Slowly and gingerly, the girl's fingertips probed her scalp a few times before she stopped and wrapped her arms around herself. "They're hiding them in my bed, beneath the sheets. They're going to schedule me for a lobotomy. They're going to get it in then. I just know it." She began to cry.

"Lobotomy?" June burst out before she could help herself. "They don't do lobotomies in this facility. There's no way—"

All the girls looked at June then. Their faces said it all. This hospital was the kind that drilled holes into your head, shoved ice picks into your brain through your eye sockets to scramble things around until you were no longer yourself. To truly imagine going through it—*the feel of it! The sound of it!*—ignited a dizzying amount of fear in June that she could feel all the way down to her bones.

"I—" June's voice caught in her throat. She realized her hands were trembling. Simpson continued to cry. The girls all leaned over to pat her on the back before continuing with their game.

"Hey," Eleanor said, clearly anxious after Simpson's worm comment. "Can I ask you something?" Then, without waiting for a response: "Do I smell to you? Like decomposition?"

The other girls were not fazed by this. Eleanor waited for June's answer, eagerly, desperately, and June had no idea how to react. When a few seconds passed, Eleanor reached up and manically scratched a place behind her ear, then smelled her fingers.

"No," June said blankly. "Of course you don't. Come on, Eleanor. Surely you understand that you're alive?"

But Eleanor didn't answer, only gazed wistfully at the Monopoly board. This was only the beginning, June knew, and the more time she spent here, the more disconnected she was feeling from everything that had come before this.

Maybe it'd be better that way, for everyone.

There were two truths in June's head right now, but the thing about them was that one couldn't be true without the other being false. She couldn't figure out what was what.

The first truth was that she was in a hospital, a place built and intended to help her, improve her health, give her her life back, or at least what little of one she'd had before. If she was here, surely that meant that she *should* be here. This wasn't supposed to be a nightmare house: it was supposed to be a place built to make people feel better.

The second truth was that there was nothing wrong with June, and there was nothing in *this* place that was right. The nurses acted strange, the pills looked strange, the protocols and policies were strange. Maybe she just needed to talk to a doctor, let him see that what had happened was a mistake, that they shouldn't be inspecting June but rather her parents.

It was them that something was wrong with.

June realized she was shaking again. She remembered something from a newspaper months before that had left her feeling ill even at the time: an illustration depicting a lobotomy, and beside it, side-by-side photos depicting a woman before and after the procedure. Her face in the second photo was completely different. There was an eerie emptiness that dimmed her eyes, like something had been taken away that could never be given back.

Like she had been punished.

No, June thought, a lump forming in her throat. *That isn't going to happen to you. It isn't. Surely that kind of thing is saved for the more severe cases.* When she saw her doctor for the first time, June would make sure not to say anything that might lead him to think she was one of the more severe cases, nothing about time travel or brain worms. At the same time, she felt a yearning to be truthful, to properly convey to somebody else just how terrifying it had all been, make them learn it, make them *feel* it. Because whatever was going on, it was real, and it was big.

Then again, the girls had told June that it wasn't in her best interest to tell the doctor the truth. She didn't know what to do anymore.

Please, June begged of the universe, closing her burning eyes and bringing her knees to her chest, not caring if the other girls were all staring at her with their mouths open as she rocked gently back and forth. *Please just let someone help me.*

the institution

WHEN JUNE'S NAME WAS FINALLY CALLED TO see the doctor, everyone in the room got very quiet, watching her as she hurriedly scuffed her way across the massive recreation room. She wondered how much longer she could stand to wear the damned slippers. Her feet felt itchy and hot, and she was desperate to rip the slippers off, but the occasional smear or slick on the floor compelled her to leave them on.

June searched frantically for clues inside her head, grasping for anything that might explain how the steady decline of the past year could have possibly taken such a hairpin of a turn, away from the dark place in her head, where she'd once felt sure she'd be trapped forever, and into this sickly lit facility instead.

All that buildup she'd felt gathering since she'd started writing her story and dating Robert, that excruciating pressure that had promised something big was going to happen, that knowledge that there'd soon be an equally massive relief whenever she finished it—it simply could not have been leading to *this*, to her parents being replaced, to herself being locked away. June had been so sure there would be something great in store for her if she could just get out of that house, her destiny awaiting. Her story had been the thing that was supposed to lead her there.

There had to be a mistake of some kind.

She'd been the black sheep of the family since she was young, there was no doubt about that, and sure, she'd been a little blue for the past handful of years, but had there ever been any real warnings that either her mind was about to break or that reality was? Were what happened the night before she was admitted and her parents being replaced like they had been the next morning just symptoms of a mind that was actively breaking apart? *No.* In June's deepest gut, she knew she believed it was the other way around. Something had already been broken. Her parents being replaced was a warning that awful and unexplainable things were real. She had to be careful in this place. She had no idea what could actually be going on.

But there were *happenings*, a voice inside insisted, chilling her blood. *Unholy signs abound of a sick mind in tatters. Be honest with yourself...*

June grit her teeth and pushed certain details out of her head forcefully, details like how she'd stopped sleeping at a certain point while writing her story, and how she'd begun to see creatures in her room at night. She thought about that last year leading up to graduation. How she'd planned to break it off with Robert right away, how she never had, how she still hadn't, not officially anyway.

After what had happened the night before June was admitted, there was no way she and Robert were still together, right? She wondered where Robert was now. Still devastated from what he'd suffered? Angry at her for what had happened? (It had, after all, been her fault.) Perhaps Robert was even happy that June was here, locked away from the rest of the world, no longer a risk with all those *delusions* in her head.

It was surreal for June to know that despite the forced circumstances that had brought them together in the first place, Robert had always claimed to truly love her. But with that love came assumptions, expectations. And as hard as she did or didn't try, June couldn't bring herself to feel the same way about him. It drove her mad, really. So much so that, even now as she was making her way across the common room of the institution toward the nurse with the red lips and wicked grin, she looked wildly to the past for answers.

Robert had often talked to her blatantly about their future, exactly as he saw it to come, as though no other option was fathomable: someday they'd be married, and she would wait at home for him to return from work every day and they could enjoy each other "like we did in your bedroom that night, but also in other ways, like board games over scotch and hosting parties for friends," and how he would take her to casual business events, and she would charm all the old men silly, although of course she'd need to go to the beauty parlor beforehand so that she could be "spruced up a little."

Yes, he had really suggested that she'd need to spruce up her appearance once they were married. This was hilarious to June, considering the fact that she intended to marry

Robert about as much as she planned to become the president of the United States. And he would say all of it with such confidence, such *surety*, his neatly combed hair blowing delicately in the wind as he drove with one hand on the wheel in his convertible, leaning on his elbow and smiling at June but unable to see that she wasn't smiling back.

To have the confidence of such a pathetic type of man! June theorized that such power would gift her the world and all its possibilities.

But everyone at home had told June how lucky she was to have Robert. Her mom, her dad, her stupid older brother, Fred. "You're so *homely*," her mother had remarked one night over dinner, her head cocked to the side as a sloppy effect of the scotch June saw her sneak from Dad's cart before dinner. "Shoulders like a boy, big feet, hair on the back of your neck. Even when you were younger I worried about it."

Mom had seemed to realize then that she was staring and had pulled herself up straight again, moving her focus to the dismally white, unseasoned chicken cutlet on her plate. "And then your habits only followed. Writing, lazing around, and let's not talk about how big of a slob you are."

Yes, June's room was often a chaotic collection of all her belongings, strewn about just like her thoughts. There were clothes on the floor, papers on the desk, chocolate wrappers hidden hastily behind the headboard. She'd wear the same dress for days in a row, before it started to really stink and she couldn't deny that a new one was needed. The box of baby-pink plastic rollers that had been a birthday gift from her mother sat unopened on her dresser. A girdle, also unused, lay in a crumpled pile in the top drawer.

It wasn't that June didn't love herself as her mother had

once suggested; quite the contrary, she found herself *quite* interesting. It was that she just couldn't bring herself to *care* about the things that others expected her to. *Be yourself* was a great phrase to live by to a point, but when she approached the situation logically and factually, June knew that in order to be considered successful by anyone else's standards, she'd have to force the pieces to fit somehow.

If she were ever to do what she really wanted to do—travel around and write and meet new best friends all around the country and *experience life*—she'd be forever cast out from her family. Why on earth did she care if her family shunned her for no other reason than because she was simply being herself? Why couldn't she flip them the bird, ride off on her newly purchased motorcycle into the night, and never look back again?

Yet, June found that she *did* care, and she hated herself a little bit for that. It made her doubt her identity as a strong, confident girl with her own feelings, made her feel spineless and confused, someone who wanted to be in control and strong but just…wasn't.

June wondered: Was it possible that she was wrong about her parents being replaced by impostors? She had set her brain on how she felt when she'd first been overcome by terror, trying to remember every single thing that had gone through her mind in that horrifying moment the Mom-thing had turned to her and said, *Good morning, Nightingale.*

Something felt funny in her stomach when she did this; it was like the memory was out of focus. She couldn't really remember why she'd felt the way she did, how she'd known something else had taken her mother's and father's places. All she remembered was the cold handle of the knife in her palm, the crash of the plate that she'd accidentally knocked onto the floor when she'd backed into the corner, the look in her parents' eyes when she'd pointed the knife back and forth between them.

June realized that she'd stopped walking across the big recreation room, had been simply staring at the ground ahead of her, and that the nurse who'd called her name was watching her carefully. June quickly made her way across the remaining distance, her hands stuffed into the pockets of her frayed sweater.

"Sorry," June mumbled at the sight of the nurse's face. "I...I thought I saw a roach on the floor."

"No, you didn't," the nurse said curtly, turning on her heel to lead June to the big door at the very end of the residential hallway. "That was a lie."

June immediately felt her cheeks warm. What kind of nurse was this woman? June noticed now that she was the strange nurse who'd stared at her before, the one who looked like she was wearing a costume. Those red lips, that magazine-worthy blond hair with a cap pinned perfectly on top, that wicked curl in the corner of her mouth. Nurses were supposed to be...not *warm* exactly—June would never expect to be coddled—but still, at least *willing* to reflect that mutual wish for wellness, right?

"Excuse me?" June said shakily, proud of herself for not letting the silence take over. "What did you say?"

The nurse looked over her shoulder to meet June's eye for just a second, one eyebrow slightly raised. "The doctor will see you now."

The door at the end of the hallway was huge: both door and hall were unnaturally wide and tall, painted a solid and startling black. There was a worn brass knob. It chilled June a bit to stand before it: she felt like it was trying to swallow her. How had she not noticed before how big it was? Maybe it was just because from her room at the other end of the hallway it looked much smaller. Yes, she decided with a nervous clearing of the throat, that must have been it.

The nurse raised a dainty fist and knocked a lively little beat on the face of the door. Without waiting for an answer, she grasped the old brass knob and pushed. Disbelief immediately washed over June as she caught sight of the room on the other side of the door.

While the rest of the institution seemed to be all a worn white and even a little shabby, this room was immaculately decorated. A yellow and brown carpet that featured a long, recurring triangle design was a stark contrast to the flooring outside the black door. Furniture of dark cherry oak loomed tall, casting shadows over the carpet. An enormous, unframed oval mirror hung directly over a desk centered to the back wall.

Behind the desk sat an old man. His wrinkles were so severe it reminded June of one of those bulldogs from the dog park Robert loved so much to go sit at and do nothing. The man was looking her over in a way that made her stomach turn—she could see his eyes wash over her slowly from her head to her feet.

The nurse cleared her throat, and June noticed that she was pointing to the empty chair in front of the old man's desk. The chair was wooden and painted white, very out of place with the rest of the furniture. The nurse didn't lower her sharply pointed finger until June had sat down on the rickety chair.

"Thank you, Joya," the man said. The nurse gave a silent nod and made her way to stand behind him. June expected the doctor to do the talking and was surprised when Joya spoke up instead.

"So," the nurse said, her thick lashes lowering as she glanced at the chart she held before her. "June Hardie."

"Yes," June said, feeling a little silly. Why wasn't the doctor doing anything except staring at her?

"You're here because you believe that your parents have been killed, when they're indeed alive."

"No," June said, a little defensively. "Not killed. Replaced."

Again came the flicker of doubt in her mind. That was exactly the sort of thing she shouldn't have said out loud, but she couldn't help herself. It was real. It had happened. Saying it out loud made it seem so nonsensical. *Don't get yourself lobotomized.* But June figured that something as intensive as a lobotomy could never be the first course of action; there'd be plenty of time for her to dial back if she needed to. They would try other things on her first. Right?

Joya scribbled something on her chart, rubbing her crimson lips together. "Replaced by what?"

June shifted uncomfortably in her seat. She avoided the old doctor's gaze and tried desperately to force the nurse to reassure her in some way, but no reassurance came, just that same cold stare, full of expectation, impatience even.

"Replaced by—" June's breath caught in her chest. "I don't know. Maybe...maybe aliens?"

This made the old man's eyebrows rise for just a moment. But he didn't look perplexed, or disgusted, or like he wanted to laugh at June for saying such a thing. He looked *curious*.

"Why do you think that?" Joya asked, and June was struck with the hysterical notion that Joya was reading the doctor's thoughts and voicing them for him. *Stop*, she scolded herself, her eyebrows furrowed. *Stop, stop, stop it!*

"I don't know." June was trying not to cry now. She felt disoriented.

"Well, you must know," Joya insisted, her expression unchanged by June's upset. "It says here that you couldn't be reasoned with. That you were out of touch with reality."

And I am, June thought wildly. *I am, I am, I am.*

"Yes," she mumbled, not sure of what else to say. "I suppose that may be right. I mean, I don't understand what's happening. I don't want to believe they've been replaced. I just…knew somehow."

Joya was writing furiously as June spoke, as if copying her words into the file verbatim. "Go on."

"They didn't look any different." June forced herself to forget the strangeness of the institution, of this very loud room and the odd silence of her doctor. In order to move past all of this, to get out and continue living her life, no matter how dull it may have been, June knew that she'd need to cooperate. "But the thing—" She stopped herself. "My mother, I mean. She smiled at me when I came down. She called me *Nightingale*."

"And that struck you as odd?" Joya asked, raising a perfectly groomed eyebrow. "That your mother smiled at you, called you a pet name?"

"Yes," June confirmed, knowing already how ridiculous it sounded. "I know that sounds wrong, but believe me. With the way the night before went—" she took a deep breath, trying to calm the rising panic in her chest at the memory "—she wouldn't have been happy to see me. She wouldn't have called me *Nightingale*. She's never even called me that before. It didn't make sense."

"And what happened the night before the incident?" Joya asked, and the doctor leaned forward on his elbows, clearly interested. June wished so badly that he'd open his big fat mouth and say something, anything. She didn't want to be treated by Joya. That wasn't how it should have been happening.

"I—" June found that she was short of breath. Wouldn't they have known the story already somehow? "I don't think it matters, really, the details. I just meant to say my mother shouldn't have been happy to see me that morning. And yet she was. It couldn't have been her."

Already she was sorely regretting bringing up the night before her parents were replaced. It hadn't been the only thing that made June believe her mother had been replaced. Of course not. It had been a feeling when she saw the Mom-thing standing in the kitchen, everything about her perfectly identical to the real thing, except for a slight variation of the eyes. A daughter knows her own mother. This wasn't her.

"Well, June," Joya said shortly, closing the file with a smack and tonguing the corner of her red painted mouth. "I regret to inform you that those details do matter. Very, very much."

June said nothing. She picked at her nails, banged her heel against the leg of the chair, bounced her knee up and down without even thinking about it. She would not be talking to Joya about what happened. She truly didn't believe it mattered, but even more so, she didn't want to remember it herself.

"Let me tell you how this is going to go." Joya moved away from behind the desk and sat on a front corner of it, as the doctor shamelessly let his eyes linger on the plump of her behind. It made June's stomach sick to see. "We're going to help you work through this. It may take a few tries and a few different methods, but believe me, we are fully equipped to handle you."

June didn't like being told she was something to be *handled*. It filled her with a newfound sense of fearlessness and irritation that had been quelled by trepidation up until now. She wasn't lesser than this stuck-up bitch, she told herself sourly, even though deep down she didn't quite believe that was true. "Why did I receive medication before having my first appointment?" she asked boldly.

If this doctor wasn't going to do anything but gawk at her and Joya's bodies, maybe she could make him talk, provoke him into it. "That doesn't seem very legitimate to me. It's *this* place that isn't being *handled* right. You've got women sharing nasty bathwater that's cold and stagnant. You've got a pail filled with bloody rags from our periods in the corner of the bathroom."

She turned her attention to the doctor now, choosing to stare as intensely as she could straight into his eyes. "You're treating us like animals, yet you expect to make us better? How exactly are you planning on helping me *work through this*, as you'd say? By doping me up until I can't do anything but drool all over myself? By cutting into my brain?"

"Yes," Joya responded simply, with a glowing grin that made goosebumps run down June's back. "If that's what it takes, we most certainly will."

The doctor gave a small nod. June stiffened in her seat, the wonderful and weirdly soothing bout of anger gone as quick as it had come. *Be more careful, damn it!*

"That'll be all for today, June Hardie," Joya said. She lightly dropped the file on the desk in front of the doctor, who rested his hand on top of it and drew a little circle with his finger over and over. "We'll be starting your first treatment immediately."

An unconscionable wave of fear washed over June. *They're going to kill you.* She didn't know why she thought so, and she couldn't control what the fear made her do in response. Apparently in her fight-or-flight response, June's survival method of choice was flight.

She scrambled out of the seat as quickly as she could, forgetting to pull the door open and initially trying to push it instead. The nurse and the doctor didn't move to go after her, didn't try to calm her down, didn't do anything but watch quietly. June fled and while she was scurrying away, she could have sworn she heard the sound of Joya and the doctor laughing.

days past

SHE HAD HOPED HER MOTHER WOULD FORGET about dragging her along to the supermarket to check out the pork roasts on sale, but by the time June was finished with her breakfast that morning, Mom was already wearing her black leather pumps and pink lipstick and making sure her pocketbook was full of coupons before snapping it shut.

"Is that what you're wearing?" Mom said when it was time to go, looking at June's green dress with a curled lip. "Didn't you wear that yesterday?"

"It's clean," June answered, rolling her eyes as she wriggled her feet into her flats. "And you're the one who bought this dress for me."

"I can't imagine why I'd buy such a thing." Mom turned and clicked her way across the hardwood floor to the front door. "That color reminds me of baby spit-up."

June didn't take it too personally. She'd learned by now

that most of the things that fell out her mother's mouth were not so much malicious as they were careless and thoughtless. She doubted that her mother thought about anything before she said it, especially when it came to her daughter. Also, June was the one who had really bought the dress, at the Goodwill one afternoon when the family had gone together to look for housewares.

She wasn't supposed to have been looking at clothes, but the green dress had struck her as delightfully simple and comfortable looking. She'd known her mother would hate it even then—it didn't cinch at the waist with a belt, it didn't have a floral print or lace around the sleeves. But still, she sneakily made her way to the front and paid with her saved-up pocket money while nobody was looking, shoving the dress into a crumpled ball in her purse before rejoining her family in the back.

"You said the green matched my eyes," June replied in a flat tone, walking out the door first so her mother couldn't see her face. If she did, she would certainly know June was lying, and then June wouldn't get to make her mother feel embarrassed for being insulting, even if it had been accidental.

You're an awful young woman, she thought to herself with a little smile. *Just awful.*

Mom's Buick was roomy and noisy. June didn't have to talk much on the drive to the supermarket and was grateful for the excuse to let silence fall between her and her mother. It wasn't that they didn't like each other; sure, Mom always had things to say about June's personal habits and traits, but there were also times that they were able to share perfectly pleasant evenings playing cards or sitting on the sofa while June read and Mom knitted.

At the same time, though, Mom would never support June in her thoughts and ambitions. June knew that now. In a way the discovery was freeing, if not a bit sad. Sometimes acceptance was a bad thing, but sometimes it was good, and it was for that reason that June pointedly ignored the hurt that lingered from the realization. It was simply for the best.

But if you ignore it, will it fester? June often wondered during quiet or dark hours. In the end, she always decided that she liked to believe she had more control than that.

"So the first thing that I want you to understand," Mom said after parking the car and leading June into the enormous, brightly lit supermarket, "is that as far as taking care of a family goes, falling into the trends of the time is the worst thing you could do to yourself or to them."

"What trends?" June asked, already bored.

"Drive-through hamburgers," Mom said with a frown, her brow furrowing as her eyes scanned over the produce section. "And shortcut foods. No good cake mix comes out of a *box*. And no good breakfast does either. Those sugary cereals are trash."

"Why?" June answered, trying not to sound whiny. "You know the entire point of that stuff is to save time, right? It gives mothers more time to do what they like instead of cooking for hours every day, or having heart palpitations over making multiple dishes at once!"

"That's exactly it," Mom said in distaste, pushing the cart over to the onions and gesturing for June to grab a few of them. "What in the world is worth letting your children eat out of greasy wrappers that are dripping with ketchup? There are better ways to cut corners. It's shameful. It's disgusting!"

Disgusting was not at all the word June would use to describe the smell that took over her senses whenever they drove past a drive-through restaurant. It wasn't even the hamburgers that called to June, it was those french fries. Hot and crispy-salty on the outside, soft and fluffy on the inside. She licked her lips at the thought.

"The smart thing to do," Mom continued, selecting some bananas, "is take advantage of all the wonderful machines instead of giving in to garbage foods. With a good dishwasher, a clothes washer and dryer, a deep freezer, and a vacuum cleaner, you can save a whole lot of time, not to mention effort. You can keep your household clean and put a hot and fresh dinner on the table every night, and look good doing it. Grab some apples, please."

June did as she was told, although when she wasn't as gentle as she could have been putting the produce into the cart, Mom made her empty it out and get all new ones that wouldn't have bruises on them by the time they got home.

"You don't even know how lucky you are to have all of this available to you," Mom went on as they finally left the produce aisle. "Any food you could imagine, right here at your fingertips. I don't need to remind you of what my parents had to feed us during the Depression."

"No," June agreed. "You've told Fred and me about it a hundred times over, Mom."

June knew that's why her mother hoarded cans and boxes of nonperishables, and jarred and canned her own tomatoes and jam every summer. After going through years of never having enough, it was like she was personally ensuring that it'd never happen again. They never ate it all, never came close, and even after giving away freebies to friends and family throughout holidays and the rest of the year, there

was still always enough food kept in the house to feed a
family of ten for months. Especially ever since Dad and
Robert's father first cemented their business deal—Mom
had arranged for men to wheel an enormous deep freezer
into the garage, filling it with meat and vegetables and fruit.

"Please grab that bag of rice," Mom instructed, pushing
the cart, which was getting fuller by the minute. "And we
need to get more eggs before we go."

"When we get home, I think I may write for a while,"
June said, already dying to leave. She felt like they'd been
there for days. "And then I'll come down when it's time
to make the meat loaf."

"No, June Hardie, you will not." Mom stopped wheeling
the shopping cart and narrowed her eyes at her daughter.
"You are not going to lose any more time learning how
to keep a house. You graduate high school in just a few
months, and you aren't even close to ready."

June said nothing but felt her ears grow hot. "Besides,"
Mom continued, satisfied at the lack of back talk, "the type
of writing you do won't get you anywhere. It's a complete
misuse of the brain God gave you."

June remembered how Robert had reacted after reading her story, so dismissive and condescending. She knew
in her gut that they were wrong. People loved stories, and
if June was especially interested in the kind that were unsettling and strange, she knew that other people must be,
too. But where were these people? How would she be able
to find them if she was played through her own life like a
puppet, her mother and father the ones pulling the strings?
Here she was, growing up in the supposed land of the free,
and freedom was what she didn't have.

Once again, June said a quick little prayer begging God

to let her win that writing-retreat scholarship, even though it'd been weeks by that point. Regardless, it genuinely felt like the distant opportunity was her one and only hope.

"You are so lucky to have a man like Robert." Mom put five cans of creamed corn into the cart, even though June knew for a fact they already had half a shelf full at home. "He's handsome, he comes from money, and even now that your father's business deal has been finalized, he still wants you. As your mother, I refuse to let you mess that up, June!"

"Okay," June emphasized, crossing her arms over her stomach. "I get it, Mom. How I'm a total and complete ragamuffin, how wonderful you are for putting up with me—"

"Don't get sassy," Mom said, her voice just the slightest bit raised. "Stop acting like a moping four-year-old, and actually pay attention to what I teach you today."

The ride home was silent, but not in a good way like the drive there had been. June found herself fantasizing about writing, making up potential sentences in her head. So many possibilities for the unfortunate heroine of *The Gift of the Stars*. Would June make it so that the aliens pulled out her veins, raveled them around some sort of cold, clean metal torture device? Would she have worms start birthing from the orbital sockets that had been freshly scraped? Only rarely did June consider letting her main character escape. She knew most people would prefer an ending that gave them hope, but June felt almost insulted by such a rule. Hope was not for everybody. Hope was not a constant.

"Can I ask what you're thinking about?" Mom spoke up as she pulled onto their street. "You look more serene than I've seen you all day."

"Just the dinner we're going to make," June lied. "Do

you mix ketchup into the raw meat or do you wait until the end?"

Mom paused for a moment, as if unsure if she was being mocked or not. "The end," she said flatly. "You can mix in some mustard and brown sugar to taste."

"Lovely," June said, and the car jerked as they pulled over the curb into the driveway. "Let me carry the groceries in."

"Good girl," Mom said, smiling a real smile now. "That's the way."

June imagined adding to her story while she carried bag after bag into the kitchen.

The aliens put her eyes back, but everything looked different. The creatures standing over her were still ugly, but they felt more familiar now. She didn't like it. She still felt sore, like there were magnets pulling from somewhere deep inside her skull, and when she tried to move her head, she realized she couldn't.

June began putting the groceries away, but only made it through a few minutes before her mother slapped her hand away and started doing it to her own specifications. It didn't bother June any, though: if Mom was going to be particular about it, at least she was doing it herself. June sat at the table, out of breath from all the hauling and fetching, more exercise than she preferred.

"Are you paying attention?" Mom asked, looking over her shoulder as she resorted cans. "It's important that you keep everything together like this, with the label facing out, so you can always grab what you need quickly and easily. Organization is your friend, June, and never a hassle."

June thought of the shelf in the garage, loaded with perfectly sorted glass jars that would likely never be opened. "Okay, Mom."

"Give it a try with the deep freezer," Mom said, pointing to the bags filled with meat. "There's a place in there for everything we just bought, so that there's never any confusion when you need something. Go ahead and take those bags to the freezer, and load it up for me."

Suppressing the sigh already rising in her throat, June stood and took the bags, dragging her feet as she made her way to the door leading to the garage. "I'm going to check afterward to make sure you did it right," Mom called after her, even though June already knew it. "Don't just pile everything up."

June rolled her eyes to herself but had to admit the state of the freezer was nothing short of impressive. There were separate piles for pork roasts, beef roasts, ground chuck, whole chickens, chicken breasts, chicken thighs, sausages, bacon. June unloaded three pork roasts, two pounds of ground chuck, and a whole chicken from their trip to the supermarket. Why did they need so much?

Maybe the aliens on the ship have a deep freezer full of human meat, she thought to herself brightly, smiling as she shut the lid. "Done, Mom!"

"Good timing," Mom said, stepping into the garage. June could see that she'd changed into her slippers. "So am I!"

Mom gave the freezer a quick check, nodding at everything and only reaching in to fix one thing, a ground chuck package that wasn't quite straight enough. "Great job."

"Thank you," June said. She made a beeline out of the garage, heading up to her room before Mom could stop her. She had to write that paragraph down as quickly as she could. It was all she could think about: something that was required in order for her to go on functioning unbothered.

"Where are you going?" Mom demanded as June hurried up the stairs. "I told you before there's much more to do than just the groceries."

"I need to change my dress," June yelled back without slowing. "I sweat through the underarms of this one."

She knew it was the perfect thing to say in order for Mom to let her go.

days past

WHEN JUNE WAS FINISHED ADDING TO HER story, she almost forgot to change her dress like she had said she would before going back downstairs. This one was much more her mother's speed: lavender cotton adorned with light green leaves and tiny yellow birds. When she came back down, Mom nodded in approval before setting her to dust the furniture in the living room. After that, they changed the curtains, shook out the rugs, vacuumed all of the carpeting, washed the kitchen floor, swept the porch, watered the garden, and did Fred's laundry.

June was folding undershirts of Fred's when he came in through the front door, stopping in the kitchen to grab three cookies from the elephant-shaped jar before sinking down into the armchair next to June's. "How goes it, sis?" he mumbled through a mouthful, crumbs tumbling down his chin and onto his chest. "Not often I see you doing housework."

"Mom's making me," June replied flatly, adding a pair of underwear to the pile beside the socks. "She's teaching me how to become a 'better young woman.'"

"Good," Fred said, and June squeezed the shirt she was folding to keep from throwing it in his face. "You need to get yourself in order if you want Robert to marry you."

He started looking for something to watch on the television; June protested when he passed *Space Patrol* in favor of *The Ed Sullivan Show*, but he acted like he didn't hear her.

"I don't want to marry Robert," she said after he sat back down. "I want to move away."

Fred cast a sideways look at her for just a moment. "You don't know anything about anything. You can't even take care of yourself living at home. Your bedroom is disgusting. You're not the independent type, June."

"Yes, I am." She crumpled the next shirt into a ball, seeing if he'd notice, but he didn't. "I'll show all of you."

"What you'll do is make Robert run away, once he learns what you're really like." Fred's voice had taken an unpleasant and sharp turn. "You'd better start paying attention to what you need to do."

Mom came in from the kitchen, out of breath from moving the chairs back to the table from when they had washed the floor earlier.

"We have about two and a half hours until your father gets here with Robert and Mr. Dennings," she said to June, dabbing her damp forehead with the back of her wrist. "Let's take a half hour to freshen up, and then I'll meet you in the kitchen to start on dinner."

Yes! June thought excitedly, already heading up to her

room. She shut the door behind her and sat at her desk, reading over what she'd written earlier and making a few tweaks. By this point, she felt very connected to her story, almost profoundly so. The heroine had gone through a lot, but June knew she'd have to go through much more.

Would June let her live? She hadn't decided yet. After everything was said and done, death would seem like a mercy to the poor woman. June felt like killing her off would be the expected ending, though; who could endure all that orbital scraping and terrifying experimentation without shutting down?

She can, June thought, and just like that she decided that her heroine would live. *Even if she's a completely different person than before the abduction, and even if she never returns to Earth, she will adapt. She will continue.*

Whether or not June's heroine would be able to accept her new fate was the question now, but already she could hear her mother calling for her from downstairs, so she'd have to figure it out later. With an exasperated huff, June neatened her stack of papers and left them on top of the rest of the manuscript.

She never had a chance against the aliens, June thought of her character as she went down the stairs with lively little steps. *There's not a single thing she could have done to anticipate the ship capturing her during her walk in the woods, no amount of strength or smarts she could have used to help her escape or fight back.*

And that was what scared June the most about her story, the thing that made her head light and her heart flutter when she imagined reading it from someone else's hand. She loved stories like that: the ones that made you realize how very created our ideas of safety and basic rights were.

Everyone alive should know the truth. It was ugly, but it was there.

And it was terrifying.

"What were you even doing up there?" her mother demanded once June entered the kitchen. Fred was still seated in the armchair in the living room, staring blankly at the television, a sweating bottle of beer in his hand and a bowl of potato chips in his lap, which June knew her mother had brought to him. "It doesn't look like you freshened up at all."

"I powdered my nose," June lied, using her fingers to shake out her tangled curls. "Waiting to redo my lipstick until the meat loaf's in the oven."

"Well, come on already," Mom said, already turning back toward the counter, where a variety of ingredients were scattered. "We need to get the Jell-O mold in the fridge to set if it's going to be ready in time for dessert."

And that's how June found herself using a heavy, long knife to cut up bits of apples and carrots and celery, while her mother went on and on about how important it was to make sure that dinner was well under way by the time your guests arrived, because there was nothing more inviting than a house fragrant with cooking and nothing more rude than making your starving guests sit around waiting for too long. (June could think of many things that were more rude.)

When she was almost finished cutting the last of the celery, June nicked her finger with the knife and gave a quiet little gasp that wasn't heard over the sound of Mom's voice. June watched as blood trickled into the little pieces of vegetable, spreading itself through the watery, green veins, soaking into every piece it touched. June sucked her finger and poured all of the celery, including the bloody pieces, into the gelatin mold that Mom had already filled with bright red liquid.

Red and red, June thought absentmindedly as she tossed the knife into the sink. She knew Mom hadn't seen her do it, and it was just a few drops of blood anyway, so who cared? June only pondered the nature of why she'd make such a decision for a moment before she was distracted by Mom's instruction to help start the meat loaf.

Mixing it with her bare hands was just as bad as June had imagined. She felt embarrassed to be relieved by the idea that her blood was secretly tainting it all, leaving tiny traces as she squished the soft gooey pink into itself along with the eggs and breadcrumbs: sickly revenge.

June thought about what Fred had said to her, while she was folding his laundry earlier, about Robert running away once he knew what she was really like. As much as she didn't want to be insulted by the idea, she couldn't help it. If Robert left her at this point, her parents would never let her hear the end of it and would lose any hope for her, if they even had any to begin with.

That'd sure make it easier to run away, she thought, trying to console herself. But again her brother's words came back to haunt her: *You can't even take care of yourself living at home.* Would June be able to thrive out on her own? As much as she wanted to say *yes*, a horrible, heavy shadow of doubt draped itself over her like a blanket.

Stupid Fred, June thought, squeezing the raw hamburger mixture like it was a heart she wanted to still. *Stupid life*.

"That is quite enough," Mom said, setting a loaf pan beside the bowl. "Transfer it into the pan. See how I've greased it with butter? Make sure it's spread evenly on the top."

June did as she was told, and then her mother wrapped the pan in plastic and set it in the refrigerator beside the gelatin mold. "We'll put it in the oven in about forty-five minutes," Mom remarked as she shut the fridge door. "That way it'll be ready about twenty minutes after they arrive. It's the perfect amount of time for some drinks and appetizers."

"What appetizers?" June moaned, not even caring that she was showing her displeasure. "We've been preparing for company all day, Mom. Do you really think they'll care if there isn't something to snack on while they drink their scotch?"

Mom looked over at June, disappointment painting her face, and already June regretted opening her big fat mouth. *Just deal with it*, she reprimanded herself and then apologized to her mother, blaming her mood on a headache. She was lucky enough to be excused anyway, although it didn't feel quite right as she dragged her feet through the living room to the stairs. She could feel Fred's glare burning into her back as she went up from where he still sat before the television.

In her bedroom, she stared at her face in the mirror without blinking. She looked at the dress her mother approved of, all the lavender and the tiny cheery birds. What Fred had said had gotten her thinking. Did Robert know her, or didn't he? She definitely subdued herself whenever they saw each other, or went for their boring drives and dates. She didn't really act differently. She just didn't act all: she simply sat and listened and nodded.

But that night when she'd shown him her story, he had read it, glimpsed behind that curtain to see the part of her that was as vulnerable as it was possible to get. He had seen her brain naked. He had seen her body naked. They had connected, even if he had ruined it in the end by opening his stupid, condescending mouth. She hated him. She wanted to be rid of him.

But she also didn't.

June didn't want to be someone who didn't understand herself. Her forward-thinking brain, her most prominent voice, stubbornly insisted that she was meant for something special, that she was an especially strong and independent human who had the ability to throw all the pressures and worries of the world into the wind in order to live freely and happily.

It should have been easy to kick Robert to the curb. It should have been easy to like the idea of chasing him away with her natural personality. What did she care? She had confirmed to herself many goddamn times that she did not, in fact, have any sort of real love for Robert.

Then what was this desire to be liked? To be wanted? To let her father and mother tell her how to run her life, tell her who she was, tell her who she should be? *You need to learn to be a better young woman*, Mom had said. June wished with all her heart that she could just understand *why* she wasn't good enough. She had a bright mind. She loved things with all her heart, and she let herself feel things. And she felt the need to do something great. But nobody understood that. Nobody!

It was unfair. Rage-inducingly so.

June took the pillow from her bed, went into the furthest corner of her large closet, knelt down on her knees, and screamed as loud and hard as she could, using the pillow to muffle the sound and make sure nobody heard. And when her breath had run out, she took a quivering but massive breath to fill her lungs and screamed again.

Minutes later, she returned to standing before the mirror. All traces of powder were gone from her face, and her mascara gathered in nasty smudges beneath her eyes, which were bloodshot and glazed. She took a cold washcloth she wet in her bathroom and wiped all of it off, taking care to remove every last trace, leaving her skin red and raw and stinging. She was about to turn and throw the washcloth into a pile of dirty clothes in the corner when she saw something on her face that she hadn't ever noticed before. June stepped up to the mirror and peered forward, her nose nearly touching the glass.

There, directly beneath the bottom lash lines of both eyes, were long, single strips of what appeared to be scar tissue. Using the tip of her pinkie finger, June touched the rough little lines, completely at a loss as to how they could have gotten there.

Suddenly, she remembered the part in her story where the heroine's eyeballs were removed, her orbital sockets scraped, her sanity cracked. For a brief second she could actually imagine it, see it, feel the cold metal table beneath her naked body, hear the creatures' tools scrape, scrape, scraping away.

June backed away from the mirror so violently it was left rattling against the wall. Panting, she scurried around, gathering powder and rouge and mascara and eyebrow pencil, a hair brush, the unopened bag of plastic curlers.

Time to get ready for dinner, she thought, breathless even though she hadn't spoken, ignoring the open closet door and the memory of what she'd just been doing in there. *Time to show them that they're wrong about me.*

the institution

AFTER JUNE FLED FROM THE DOCTOR'S OFFICE, she went straight back to her room, unable to face the recreation area after everything that had just happened. Something wasn't right in this hospital. The way Nurse Joya spoke for the doctor, the way the doctor peered at her silently like an insect in a jar, the way they'd both cackled as June ran out in fear.

Even worse was imagining what could possibly come next. Nurse Joya had said the *treatments* were going to start immediately. *It may take a few tries and a few different methods, but believe me, we are fully equipped to handle you.* June shuddered and hugged herself, her eyes burning as she reached the doorway to her room at last.

Eleanor was reading a book in bed, the cover tattered and stained.

"Do you see scars beneath my eyes?" June demanded,

shutting the door and rushing across the room to the mirror. Eleanor sat up quickly, letting the book fall forward onto her chest.

"What do you mean?"

"My eyes," June repeated, putting her face up to the mirror until her nose touched it. She ran her fingers along the skin beneath her eyes, studying the fine lines, unable to figure out what she was looking at. "Does it look like there are scars underneath them?"

She thought of how it'd felt to write the part in her book where the heroine's eyes were removed, and she flinched away from the mirror. *Scrape, scrape, scraaaape.*

Eleanor, fascinated, scrambled off the bed and came close to June. "Hold still," she commanded, and leaned in as though she was going to kiss June. Right before their lips might have touched, she paused, staring with narrowed eyes at the area beneath June's bottom lash line. "There are definitely two lines...but they look so thin, thin enough to just be wrinkles."

"Identical wrinkles on each side?" June whispered, and their eyes met. It was then that June saw exactly how she'd look to someone outside, completely paranoid and at home in a place like this. "What's happening to me, Eleanor?"

"Don't call me that," Eleanor whispered, her eyes wide but her gaze soft. She swallowed. "And I don't know. You're definitely alive, though."

"So are you," June mumbled, turning away from her roommate at last, looking back at the mirror. "But...maybe we won't be for long."

"I'm already dead."

The door to their room burst open, causing both girls to jump. Nurse Joya appeared, pushing a tall but compact metal tray on wheels, an array of tools and multicolored pills assembled over the top.

"Here you are," she said with a toothpaste-commercial smile. "You scurried off so quick there before, Junebug. You didn't give us any time to get your first treatment rolling."

June's hands went all tingly. Eleanor quietly returned to her bed and began reading again, or at least pretended to.

"What's the treatment?" June managed, remembering the sound of Nurse Joya's laughter mixed with the doctor's when she'd fled the office. The nurse's very presence paralyzed June with terror.

"Just some medicine," the nurse said, rubbing her cherry-red lips together as she picked up a large syringe. "Lucky for you, I was about to make my rounds anyway. Otherwise I might have been a little grouchy about you running off. Sit down."

June sat on her bed, trying to keep her breathing steady. *Don't fight her. Don't draw unnecessary attention to yourself.* The nurse was making rounds—that meant the tray contained things for multiple girls all through the hall. At first June had thought it was all for her. Nurse Joya finished preparing the syringe and came to stand beside June, pulling the tray along behind her. She wiped at the crook of June's arm with a cold, wet cotton ball, then took the syringe and sank the needle into June's vein. All the time this was happening, June was trying to resist allowing it, but found that all she could do was sit there.

The amount of liquid in the syringe was so little that June didn't understand how it could have any effect on her. She sucked in a tiny breath through her nose as the needle came out, feeling scared and vulnerable to what would come next. She couldn't stop thinking about the women she had seen staring into space when she had first arrived, and she hoped and prayed that whatever she'd just been given would have a different effect.

Another question rose within: How exactly would they determine that she was what they considered *better*? They hadn't done any real tests on her, had just talked to her for a few minutes and made her feel funny. If all they had to go on was her word, then...was it possible she could get herself out of here immediately?

But Mom and Dad aren't themselves, she thought, and that's when she realized that she was smiling a wide, wide smile. Apparently a little went a long way when it came to the medication in the syringe.

"There we are," Nurse Joya said, giving June's knee a little pat. "That should reset your brain nicely." She then turned toward Eleanor. "And you'll be receiving the same exact thing, my illusive little corpse-baby!"

June's smile melted into a frown as she watched the nurse clean Eleanor's arm and stick it with the same needle that she'd just used on June.

"You're not supposed to do that," June said without thinking, feeling her thoughts flow through her like never before. "You can't share a needle like that."

Nurse Joya met June's eye with a glare that was so intensely pointed that for a moment her eyes appeared to become nothing but gaping black holes dripping down her face. *It's the drugs*, June thought in panic, raising her trembling hands to her mouth to keep from screaming.

"You'll both be out of here in no time," the nurse said after a moment, the holes on her face growing larger, nearly reaching her mouth. "We'll get you feeling right as rain."

"Right as rain," Eleanor repeated from where she sat, looking at June as though she had something more to say.

Nurse Joya began to whistle and pushed the cart back toward the door. Once it was out in the hallway, she turned back to them. "Toodle-oo!" she exclaimed, closing the door to their room with a loud, resounding bang.

"What did she give us both the same thing for?" Eleanor demanded right away, bringing her knees to her chest, the book sprawled forgotten in the sheets. "I haven't even had an appointment in four days!"

"Hospitals don't do this," June said, noticing now that the pockmarks in the wall appeared to be breathing. "This isn't right, this can't be right, they don't work like that—"

"I think those *are* scars under your eyes," Eleanor said, staring hard at June. "What happened to you? What could have made scars that thin?"

Scraaaape.

"Nothing." June shook her head back and forth, not wanting to allow herself to get carried away. "Nothing has ever happened to my eyes."

"Something's happening," Eleanor whispered, looking at her hands. "To me."

From outside the room came the sound of people screaming. Not the usual outbursts by patients, but something bigger, more serious. It reminded June very much of the screams that came from the crowd at the circus when she was ten, when a man in a suit and wide-brimmed hat had started shooting a pistol at random into the crowd.

"What is that?" Eleanor demanded, and June was relieved to know that her roommate could hear it, too. "Is there a fire?"

Both girls rushed to the door, only to find that it was locked.

"Hey!" June screamed, losing her cool and jiggling the doorknob as if she could break it by sheer force of will. "Let us out!"

Dull thumps rose up amongst the screams—the sound of many slippered feet running full speed through the recreation room and hallway. June whimpered, and both girls stepped back.

All at once, the screams and footsteps fell silent. Eleanor began spinning in circles, her arms held out. "Nothing can happen to us while we're in here," she said in a funny voice, like she'd had a handful of scotches. "Whatever is happening out there, it's bad."

June listened hard, her forehead growing damp with sweat. She suddenly couldn't tell if she was hearing things on the other side of the door or not and was overwhelmed with the desire to lie in her bed, so she did so. She knew she had the right to be appalled, totally outraged at the behaviors of the hospital. *Someplace there is surely a medical board that would shut the whole place down if they knew.*

But what if…the things that replaced Mom and Dad had brought her here on purpose? What if they'd known it wasn't a real hospital? But June had always seen this place from a distance as a child, resting on top of the hill behind the main road like a great stone dollhouse bolted to the earth with ivy. It certainly wasn't new. But at the same time, she'd never known anybody, either personally or by proxy, who had come here to stay. Not that she knew of, at least.

Across the room, Eleanor's dreamy haze appeared to come to a sudden end when she started shrieking and slapping at herself, as if she were being attacked by an army of unseen ants. June willfully ignored her, afraid of being pulled into the hallucination secondhand somehow, letting the voice inside insist over and over again that she'd be okay.

Except that with every repetition of the phrase, the voice became deeper, more ragged, angry. *You'll be okay*, it growled, sounding like a monster hiding in a cave. *You'll be okay*, it roared, in between the sound of gnashing teeth.

It occurred to June that the voice was lying.

Think about happy things, a different voice suggested, one that sounded a lot more like herself. *Think about writing on a Saturday afternoon, gazing out the window from your bedroom, while a thunderstorm booms outside, all while Mom cooks up some fried chicken downstairs, and the smell is lovely...*

If June closed her eyes, she could almost take herself there. In the house, the room dim from the heavy dark clouds that blocked out the sun. Her story in front of her, somehow unfinished, even though she'd finished it the night before she was sent to the institution. She thought about how things had ended for her heroine, brutal and unspeakably horrifying but beautiful at the same time, peaceful in a strange way, just right.

Necessary.

"We're going to the drive-in," Eleanor said from somewhere nearby, and June kept her eyes closed. "We're going to see a movie about sisters who murder people and turn the meat into food."

"Shut up," June said unkindly, filled with rage that her tenuous good vibe was falling apart because of Eleanor's stupid, ugly comment. The air felt like it was squirming against June's face now, making it harder and harder to lie still, and when she couldn't stand it anymore, she sat up and opened her eyes. *Get me out of here!*

There, on the wall that Eleanor's bed was pushed against, was a strange little hole that hadn't been there before, something between a cave tunnel and a crawl space. *This is what it feels like to hallucinate*, June thought, completely fascinated. She crawled off the side of her bed and over to the hole in the wall like a warm, fleshy spider, her hair hanging down over her face.

June couldn't believe how real the tunnel looked—she could see that it sloped slightly downward for maybe twenty feet before taking a hard turn to the right. The space was lined with dreary gray stonework that looked damp and cold. She reached her hand inside the space, expecting the wall to stop her hand, and nearly screamed when her fingers brushed against the stone instead.

The air in the tunnel was significantly cooler than in the hospital room—how was that possible? Visual hallucinations were one thing, June knew, but the fact that she was able to reach *into* the tunnel wasn't something she could get her head around.

"Eleanor," June said, moving her hand around the moisture-laden air in the tunnel. "Come here. You need to see this."

"I can't move" came Eleanor's breathless reply. "I won't move. The ants won't let me. All I can hear is the baby crying. Please make it stop crying…"

June was about to tell Eleanor to snap out of it when she heard a peculiar sound coming from inside the tunnel—the sound of something wet, crunching and ripping, very faint, very far off. Without thinking about what it meant or what consequences might come of it, June crawled into the hole. She looked back only once, to make sure the opening didn't disappear once she was fully inside. But the hole leading to her hospital room was still there, the ugly white light shining awfully bright behind her.

If this is what drugs do, June thought, *then I hope to never have them again. What is that awful sound?*

Was she really still on her bed, tripping out, or was this actually happening? June knew there was no way it could be true, but at the same time, the tunnel felt so incredibly real. She could no longer hear anything but the sound of water dripping, and whatever was making the strange sound somewhere in the bowels of the space. If she was really just in bed, shouldn't she have been able to hear Eleanor still? It was almost as though June herself had made the tunnel come into existence.

June crawled and crawled, only getting nervous once she made the first turn and was no longer able to look behind her to see the opening. *What a trip this is!* she thought, challenging it as hard as she could, trying to do something that would finally dissolve the vision and bring her back to reality. But no matter how far she crawled, no matter how much she dwelled on every detail as intensely as she could, the tunnel only felt more real. The stones beneath her knees were smooth, but still they wore and marked the skin there as she went along. She could smell the dankness, hear the echoes of whatever was up ahead.

When I see what's making the sound, I'll snap out of it, she knew somehow. *Surely that will be too much for even my make-believe senses to bear.*

The noise was much louder now. She would be reaching the source soon. She felt wetness underneath her hands and saw that the stone had little pools of blood all over it. She studied the blood on her hand, bringing it close up to her face. She could smell it, like water that was tinged with pennies and dead mice.

June was afraid now. The sound was very wet, very loud. Crunching, ripping, tearing. *Nothing you see in here can hurt you*, June reminded herself. *You're back in your bed, drooling with rolling eyes, sleeping even. It's not real. It can't be.*

And so she went forward.

She made another turn, crawled for a bit more. Whatever was making the sound was just at the end of this stretch, shrouded in shadow. June was only able to make out a few things from so far away. There was a person crouching—she could tell that much. The person was moving in quick, frenzied shudders. They were wearing white, maybe. *Crunch. Rip. Snap.*

There was a rectangle of bright light coming from a spot on the ceiling of the tunnel, about halfway between June and the shuddering person at the end of it. June took a breath and moved forward, up to the small opening, and looked out, too curious not to.

Through a metal grate that was painted white, June realized that she was looking into the office where she'd seen the doctor and Nurse Joya earlier. She recognized the furniture, as well as the old man that sat silently behind the desk. He stared ahead at the wall across the room, unblinking, his expression slack, his hands folded neatly in front of him. There was nobody else in the room with him. He looked like a machine that had been turned off.

"The doctor," June whispered accidentally, still feeling high. While the man behind the desk didn't seem to hear her, the wet crunching sound at the end of the tunnel stopped abruptly. With her heart seizing in her chest, June slowly lowered her eyes away from the vent.

There, at the end of the tunnel, crouched the person, looking directly at her. It was Joya, her crisp white uniform dress hiked up obscenely over her thighs, her sneakers planted on opposite sides of the dimly lit tunnel. The nurse's hands were curled into claws. The holes in her face from before were still there, huge and black, stretching all the way down to her mouth. As June watched, something poked out of one of Nurse Joya's eye holes, some sort of weird, pointed appendage that curled forward like an elongated finger.

"June Hardie?" the Joya-thing asked, her voice just as perky and bright as it was when she looked like a human, although she did sound very caught off guard. The eyehole appendage shivered ever so slightly.

Just in front of the nurse lay the remains of a human. The head was torn off, the torso ripped open. An arm pointed upward at an unnatural angle. A pile of guts glistened in the dark. June remembered the sounds she'd been hearing and her stomach threatened to empty itself, one way or the other.

"How did you get in here?" Nurse Joya sounded completely shocked, utterly fascinated at the sight of June. June's knees trembled painfully against the stone floor of the tunnel. "How on *earth* did you manage such a thing?"

"I—I'm tripping," June stuttered, feeling as though she was going to faint. Never in her worst nightmares had she seen anything like this. "I'm tripping from the drugs you gave me."

"But I locked your door," Joya said, a strange clicking sound coming from somewhere in the darkness of her face. "Very curious indeed. What a brain you have, June Hardie. What an absolute marvel!"

June was very much trying to fight the hallucination. She thought it'd be easy to break, like a dream that you realize you're having early on, but it was unbreakable. The sights, the sounds, the smells—it was too real. She would have lain down exactly where she was if not for the blood on the ground. On instinct, June threw a quick glance upward, out the vent again.

The doctor was staring directly at her.

"Come here," Joya whispered, and now an appendage was coming out of her mouth, too. "Tell me how you did that nifty little trick."

June started crawling furiously backward, wincing at the pain in her knees and hands. The nurse crawled after her, slowly, as if to follow rather than to chase. June didn't care: all she wanted was out and away. She looked down at the ground instead of at Joya and didn't look up again.

It took just as long to get out as it had to get in. Since June was too afraid to look up, she didn't know if she was still being followed. There was a turn and then another one, and June was becoming clumsy in her exhaust and fear. Finally, *finally*, she noticed a change in the light; the opening must be near.

"What in the world?" came a voice from behind her. Eleanor!

You're almost there, June told herself, still able to smell the blood on her hands. *Just keep going…*

And then, just like that, she was back in the hospital room, tumbling backward away from the mouth of the tunnel, colliding with Eleanor, who yelped in pain.

June sat back up as quickly as she could, finally brave enough to look up into the tunnel again. Nurse Joya was still there, about ten feet away from the opening, totally still. But the appendages were gone, the holes in the face were gone. It was just her regular face, peering curiously at June. "Fascinating," June thought she heard her say, but already the hole in the wall had disappeared and become just a wall again.

the institution

JUNE AND ELEANOR SLEPT IN JUNE'S BED ALL the way through until the next morning. When June woke up, it took her a bit of time to remember whose arm was wrapped around her waist, whose soft middle was cradling her back, whose feet were pressed up against the bottom of hers. Tiny wisps of breath puffed on the skin behind June's ear.

She thought of her first night here, and of how Eleanor had refused to talk to June at all besides the occasional announcement that she was dead. It'd only been a very short time since then, but June felt like Eleanor was all she had now, the only person she knew. And she didn't even know her! Regardless, as long as June had Eleanor, she wouldn't be alone. June settled into the embrace, soaking it in, surprised at how much comfort it offered.

Then she remembered the tunnel and her body stiffened.

What in the world kind of drug could pull off something like that? She sat up quickly, waking Eleanor in the process, and stared at the place on the wall where the opening had been. What had they done after the trip had ended? June could vaguely remember them crying together, June about the monster she'd seen, Eleanor about the ants. At that point, June had felt how she might expect drugs to make her feel: loopy and heavy and strange. She might even have enjoyed it, if not for the terrible trip that had come before.

It dawned on June just how awful and strange it was that after being drugged up yesterday afternoon, the girls had been locked in here without being given food, water, or access to the toilet. Just one more thing that she was convinced would be looked down upon by a legitimate institution.

"What did she give us?" Eleanor mumbled, rubbing the area around her eyes with her fingertips. "What was that..."

"What do you remember?" June asked, pulling the blanket off herself. Her knees were bruised, badly, and crusted with dried blood. A little bit of skin had been scraped off and was now scabbing, but it looked like too much blood to have come from the scrape. "Oh, holy shit!"

"What?" Eleanor squirmed out of the bed and stood over June's knees, staring at them with her mouth slightly ajar. "How did you do that?"

"What was I doing while you were seeing the ants?" June stood up from the end of the bed and went over to Eleanor's. She checked the floor all around it, looking for blood from her knees but failing to find any. "Did you see me at all?"

"No," Eleanor said, and crossed her arms over her chest. "I looked for you after you'd gone quiet for a while. But you weren't there. I told myself you were under the bed or something. Because where else could you have gone?"

Without speaking, June pulled Eleanor's bed away from the wall, getting down on the floor to look for blood from her knees. There were handfuls of dust bunnies, but no blood, no disturbance to the thin layer of grit that covered the floor. She scooted the bed back and looked at Eleanor in bewilderment. "What happened to my knees?"

"You hurt them," Eleanor said. "In that hole you crawled backward out of."

"You saw the tunnel?" June took Eleanor by the shoulders. "Don't you dare lie to me about this, Elle, or I'll never be able to trust you again."

"It had to have been the drugs," Eleanor said, wriggling out of June's grip. "I like that you called me Elle."

"You never even wanted me to know your name," June reminded her, feeling absurd for following such a change of direction. "I would have thought a nickname would irritate you."

"Well, it doesn't."

"Did you see Joya in the tunnel, too?" June went back to the place at the wall, leaned over the bed and put her hand over the spot. "Did you see her chasing me?" *Following*, her mind corrected, which was chilling.

"Joya? No," Eleanor answered. "I was barely even able to see *you* before you ran your ass into my face and knocked me backward. I had finally gotten off the bed to look for you underneath, but…then I saw something in the wall. I looked in there, and I saw you, hurrying out."

"No," June said, and started pacing the room. "No, goddamn it! It was the drugs that did it. We got the same thing. It's totally possible."

"I've been medicated more times than I can count since I came here," Eleanor remarked quietly. "There's never been anything like *that*."

"Tell me something," June said, a painful lump forming in her throat. "How often do new people come into the hospital?"

"How often?" Eleanor repeated, then looked up and bit her lip in thought. "You mean, before you? That'd be, um, never."

Never? Not in the three whole years since Eleanor was placed here herself? That couldn't be possible, June knew. Then she remembered how all the other girls had treated her at the first breakfast, so curious and desperate, and her stomach did another flop.

The things that replaced Mom and Dad brought you here on purpose.

There came the sound of a shifting bolt, and then the door to their room was open. "Checks," a nurse who was not Joya said, the same loud nurse who'd woken them the day before. "Good morning, ladies. Glad to see you're ready to go. Meds in five."

She left the door open when she left. And just like that, they were free.

"I need to clean up," June mumbled as they hurried out, and Eleanor followed closely. After they'd both used the toilet, washed up, and changed into the fresh dresses and sweaters folded in piles on a shelf near the door, the girls came back for their daily blood-red capsules.

"What do these even do?" June asked after Eleanor had thrown hers back. "If they're supposed to help keep us calm, they sure as hell didn't work yesterday."

"They never tell us anything," Eleanor said, her voice

low, as they headed to breakfast. "These red ones are kind of new, though. Whenever the doctor talks to me about my condition, he always goes about it as if there's some singular thought that can make it all go away, just like that." She snapped her fingers. "I want him to be right, but I don't know. Nothing triggered it, that I can remember anyway. I just…woke up dead one day. I think. It was so long ago now, it's hard to even recall."

At the mention of the doctor, goosebumps spread over June's back. "The doctor talks to you? Not Joya?"

Eleanor raised a brow. "Well, yeah," she said, sounding self-conscious. "He's the *doctor*. Why would it be Joya?"

June said nothing.

"You seem awfully obsessed with that nurse," Eleanor said after a few minutes. The girls made their way through the back hall to get to the cafeteria. "First you asked me if I saw her while we were tripping, now you ask if she's treating me and not the doctor. Maybe you have a crush on her."

June felt her cheeks get warm. "That is not the case at all. I'm very suspicious of her, if you're really wondering."

"She's very pretty."

"Eleanor," June said in a tired voice. "Stop."

"Don't tell me you haven't noticed. I know you have."

Both girls went through the line, each collecting two hard-boiled eggs, a piece of toast, and a small mug of steaming hot tea. They had both missed dinner last night, what with being locked in their room and all, and June couldn't wait to devour every last morsel of what she considered to be a surprisingly high-quality breakfast. With everything she'd seen so far, it felt almost shocking that they weren't being served curdled milk and moldy fruit.

June and Eleanor made their way to the same table they'd

eaten at before, and June noticed right away that something was wrong with Lauren, the pretty girl who was obsessed with eyes. Her soft brunette waves were gone, replaced by thickly wrapped beige bandages. In some places, a pinkish clear fluid stained the fabric. Everybody else at the table was completely silent.

"No," Eleanor said, nearly dropping her tray onto the table. "Lauren, please tell me they didn't."

Lauren didn't say anything. She didn't move. Instead, she sat in a wheelchair with her back hunched, her lips parted just the slightest, her eyes staring through the table. Her sweater hung crookedly on her shoulders; her fingers were twitching. *Lobotomy!* June's mind screamed.

"Nurse Chelsea brought her over to us like this," Adie said without looking up from her plate. The other girls were a showcase of nerves: Jessica bit at her nails; Cassy turned her unpeeled egg over and over in her hand; Simpson twirled her hair around her finger agitatedly. Eleanor's devastated expression lasted a few moments before she sat down at the table. She took an egg from her tray and slammed it down against the cold metal of the table, pulling the pieces of shell off and throwing them onto the floor.

June sat by Eleanor, unable to resist sneaking a sideways peek at Lauren, whose lips were chapped raw. She remembered how lively Lauren had been not so long ago, with her bright eyes and sweet smile and her promise not to tell whatever she saw in June's future. Now, her chest moved in little heaves as she took quick, shallow breaths.

"How drugged is she?" June asked quietly, and all the girls looked at her.

"It doesn't matter." Adie's eyes were enormously sad. "Once they end up like this, they never come back. Just watch. In a few days, she'll be gone, and they'll tell us that she's been discharged."

"Discharged?" Anger flashed within June. "They think this is better than who she was before?"

None of it made sense. The way the place was run or the impossible drug trip where she'd seen a monster nurse in a tunnel that simply couldn't have been there but was. June ran her hands over her knees under the table, wincing at the sting.

"It's the worms," Simpson said, still twirling strands of hair as if she were trying to pull them out. "It's our brains. They want our brains."

June remembered what the nurse monster had said in the tunnel. *What a brain you have, June Hardie. What an absolute marvel!*

"Why do you say that?" June asked Simpson, taking a sip of her tea, wondering if there was poison in it. "Why do you think they want our brains?"

"Because they put a worm in mine," Simpson said. She turned to June, biting at her lips. "One night while I was sleeping, some nurses came in and held me down, and I felt something go into my ear. I can hear it eating every so often—I swear I can. I can hear it *crunching*. And just look at what they've done to Lauren! She isn't the first, and she won't be the last. Discharged, my ass."

Eleanor was already on her second egg. Cassy and Jessica had started in on their breakfasts at last, all while Lauren just sat there with her jagged breaths and glassy gaze. June's stomach growled, so she ate, delirious with fear and wonder at how different her life was now, compared to when she'd been living at home and dating Robert. The two realities seemed worlds apart, and thinking back to those times of grocery shopping and learning to make meat loaf and writing her story made something in her head feel buzzy.

Mom, Dad, Fred, Robert, Mr. Dennings. Did she miss them? Not exactly, but home seemed like heaven compared to this. The things she had considered problems back there paled in comparison to what was happening now.

But what *was* happening now? What had she ever done to deserve being locked up in such a place? Why had her parents changed like they had, who had done it to them, and, most importantly, why?

I'm going to die here, she knew in her gut. *Something is not right, and I am going to die. We all are.*

The other girls at the table knew it, too, June suspected, including Eleanor, maybe even especially Eleanor. They had already gone back to their usual strange chitchat, and it was as if Lauren was no longer there at all. June could sense the cords that had been severed, cords connecting each of the girls to their lost friend, never to be heard from again, even though she was sitting among them, technically alive.

She did catch Eleanor shooting a pained look back Lauren's way when they were all leaving, though, her face wistful, and it made June's heart ache. They'd all been there for years, those girls, and it was very clear that none of them fully remembered or yearned for whatever their lives had been like before they came to this place.

How long would it be until June forgot? As she scuffled in her slippers through the hallways and toward the recreation room with Eleanor, walking so closely to her that their hands kept bumping, she feared that it would be very soon indeed.

days past

THE SCHOOL WEEK HAD BEEN FILLED TO THE brim with mundane homework assignments and moments spent alone on the bleachers, so June was happy when it was Saturday at last.

After lots of pondering about what she thought of herself and what she wanted for herself, June decided that tonight was the night she would finally break things off with Robert. Her hesitation before had only been rooted in feelings of self-doubt, and she was proud of herself for being able to recognize that. Who cared about what Robert thought? He was boring, plain and simple, and if June stayed with him she feared her future would be much the same.

The business deal had been closed for months now, definitely long enough in her opinion to warrant a split without causing a complete ruckus from Mr. Dennings. Her own father would be a whole other story, she knew, but as long as the only person capable of actually breaking up the business didn't mind, then their family would be okay, and Dad could continue on his new and improved path. Business was booming. Both men were happy. The silly relationship between Robert and June didn't matter anymore.

That was why Dad would get over it eventually. He'd have to, right? She was his daughter, for goodness' sake.

She reviewed her appearance in the mirror, the night air fragrant and lovely as it whispered in through her open window. She wore a plain white blouse with a pink poodle skirt, which certainly made her *feel* like a dressed-up poodle, but she knew that Robert had always wanted to see her in one, and this would be his last chance. She swung each hip back and forth, causing the skirt to lift and swirl around her legs, rather liking the feeling.

Next she applied a thick layer of a vivid red lipstick that reminded her of the beautiful models dressed as nurses in advertisements for aspirin or what have you. *They ought to call this shade Nurse Betty Red*, she thought before carelessly tossing it back onto her dresser.

Ordinarily, June wouldn't have given a damn about what Robert thought of her outfit, but the truth was that even though she didn't love him, she didn't wish him ill will or any sort of pain over their breakup. She suspected that he took them pretty seriously as a couple, and he was probably going to be really upset when she broke the news to him.

So hopefully the poodle skirt could make it a bit easier, or maybe it'd be the little black scarf that June tied around her neck that would help soften the blow. The scarf she enjoyed. She could pretend she was wearing it to hide a scar from an imaginary decapitation incident, in which the aliens from her beloved story had to reattach her head through cauterization. If the scarf was removed, everybody would know her secret.

"June," Mom's voice rose up from downstairs, cheerful in a way that revealed that Robert was already here and inside. "Robert's here to pick you up for your date!"

What would Mom say when June returned home and told her about Robert? Her stomach felt uncomfortably heavy at the thought. There would be screaming, for sure, maybe an impassioned slap or two, definitely slews of personal insults against June. No matter how intense the reaction would be, June hoped with everything she had that, when all was said and done, Mom would agree to break the news to Dad. June would cry, beg, whatever it took. The idea of doing it herself made her stomach now feel watery.

"Coming!" she called brightly, ready to please the pants off of all of them in order to lay the groundwork for later, or so she hoped. She hopped down the stairs and shot them smiles, Mom and Robert and Dad, as they all stood there near the front door and looked up at her in amazement.

"June!" Mom exclaimed, her hand on her chest. "I have never seen you in a poodle skirt, honey. And that scarf!"

Everything will be okay, June knew once she heard that. *She's pleased with me now. That means it's possible she won't be mad for long.*

"You are a vision, Junebug," Dad agreed, swatting her on the back a few times as though he was trying to burp her. "You lovebirds have fun tonight."

"We will," she blurted, immediately regretting it. *Don't push it too far.*

And that's when she realized that she already had. What had she been thinking, dolling up like this? If she'd come down the stairs unbathed and unkempt and unwilling to make eye contact, at least maybe they could all start mentally preparing themselves for bad news. Still, she knew that being her messy, unlovable self in front of Robert would be like the ultimate betrayal to Dad—it'd humiliate him and paint the wrong kind of picture of his family—an unforgivable offense. So at least she was dodging *that* bullet.

"You look stunning," Robert remarked after the front door had closed behind them, and they made their way across the lawn to where his convertible was parked. "What shall we do tonight? I thought maybe we could grab some shakes and fries and take a drive."

"Can we bring them to the lookout point?" June asked, immediately feeling the need to clarify that there would be no making out involved. "I thought we could look at the stars and talk."

"Oh, that sounds lovely." Robert hopped off the curb in a cheerful little way that made a bud of dread bloom inside June. "I would love to."

June found herself trying to delay everything. She insisted they go inside instead of using the drive-through to order, and then waited until after their food was ready to announce she needed to use the ladies' room. She wiped off all of her lipstick and then reapplied it again. She powdered her nose. She fluffed out her curls.

"There you are," Robert said after she reappeared. "I was about to have one of the other ladies go in to check up on you."

"That's sweet," she answered, believing nothing of the sort. "I just wanted to freshen up a bit."

"No worries, darling," he said, and she hated him for being so goddamn proper, making it harder on her like this. "Let's get going already. There aren't any clouds in the sky tonight. It'll be perfect for stargazing."

June felt hot and sticky with sweat. She held the bag of soggy french fries on her lap as they drove to the outskirts of town, one milkshake in her hand and another in between her knees. Robert went on about his day at work, but she paid no attention, instead resting her head against the headrest and taking in the sight of the streets at night. She hummed a tune under her breath, low enough that Robert couldn't hear it. Everything would be all right.

When they arrived, she marveled at the sight of their town from above, all twinkly and small, while she ate the greasy fries and sipped the cold, chocolaty thickness of her shake. When she was done, she finished off the rest of Robert's fries, as well as his shake. He watched her, almost aghast at first, and she thought, *Good. Let him be disgusted by me.* But by the time she took the last noisy slurp from the white paper cup, he was smiling again.

"You're one of a kind, June, that's for sure." His grin turned wicked, and she knew for a fact that he was thinking about that night in her bedroom. She could almost go for that again, but only if she'd never see him again afterward, so it really wasn't an option.

"I've been thinking," she blurted, ready for this to end already. "About...us."

"So have I," he said, stopping her from continuing. "I think we're quite the pair. I could really see you as being an interesting wife." He looked at her body shyly, before forcing his gaze away. "And a very pretty one, at that."

Despite her situation, she couldn't help but feel a little triumphant over his words. *Hear that, Mom?* she thought. *He thinks I'm pretty. Not so homely after all, huh?*

"That's just the thing, darling," she said, closing her eyes painfully at her awkward use of the pet name. Jesus, she was nervous. "I have a hard time seeing us as spouses. I'm not sure why, I just…can't imagine it."

Please let it be this easy, she begged the stars, willing for Robert to nod knowingly and offer to drive her home.

Would he ever be violent with her? She wondered it in a completely random flash, and her heart fluttered nervously. She'd never considered that before now, but here she was, about to cancel his planned future with her, and they were all alone at the lookout point with nobody to hear her scream if things went poorly. *Don't be ridiculous*, she scolded herself. *You have no reason to fear Robert.*

"Don't be silly," he said, his smile still as carefree as ever. "Of course you can imagine it. We've talked about it so many times—don't you remember? You could imagine it then."

"Yes," she tried, suddenly sick from all the food. "But, you see, I really just can't anymore. I think I want to travel a little bit instead of live at home as a wife. And also, it's about my writing. It's not just a hobby, it's… I want to do it for a living. And I don't care how unlikely that is."

She felt herself going on and on, revealing too much, explaining things as though she were obligated to. When she finished, he just stared at her as if waiting for her to continue, but when she didn't, he set his hand heavily on her knee.

"Thank you for telling me how you really feel," he said with earnest. "It's clear to me now how much of a dreamer you are, June, and I think that must be one of the things I really love about you the most. It makes you special, do you see? It sets you apart."

She wasn't quite sure what he meant by that, or how to react. She opted to stay silent, already feeling like she'd said too much without cause.

"You said you want to travel," Robert went on. "Well, I would be happy to arrange little trips for us here and there. Anniversaries, birthdays, we could go to the next town over for a day or so. We'll travel *together*, do you see?"

She didn't see. Did he even know what travel was?

"And about your writing," he went on. "Well, I see no reason why you can't continue doing it however you like, assuming of course you find the time outside of your other things."

Things, another word for *duties*, June knew. It was miraculous how much he assumed that things would be a certain way between them. That *she'd* be a certain way. He spoke as though there were no other option. It was the same way her family talked, too. It made her feel so strange, like she was living in a snow globe, unaware that she was just a porcelain girl frozen in time.

"Listen," Robert said, taking her hand. "I can see you're thinking things over in your head, darling. There's nothing to worry about. There's no pressure for marriage. We'll wait until it's time, and for now let's just continue to enjoy each other. You do enjoy me, right?" She looked up to find his eyes boring into hers.

What could she say? *No?* He was too goddamn thick to understand it. He was a machine, built to entrap June, to keep her from her real destiny, whatever that may have been. She hadn't thought it would be possible for the roots to creep as deep as they had in such a short time. She had only agreed to date him because Dad had made her for the business deal. Things had gotten too out of hand, and he certainly wasn't going to make ripping herself away easy.

Because she would, she promised herself, right then and there. She would get away from Robert and this entire mess somehow.

"Yes," she said, her voice flat. "Of course I do. You're my sweetheart, Robert. I'm just not ready to become a wife and won't be for a long time."

"We will wait until you're ready," he assured her. "You have my word."

Good, she thought, relief making her chest swell. *I'll just simply never be ready. And then one day, I'll be gone.*

She looked out over the town, looked at the reaches of outer space twinkling very far above. June had always loved this spot, even as a little girl. She used to sneak out after bedtime and ride Fred's bicycle for a full hour to get here, and then spend entire nights lying awake on a blanket in the grass, gazing into the stars and the Milky Way as if there were someone there watching back. She thought about the weird blinking light in the distance that looked like it was attached to some sort of hovering aircraft; how she'd convinced herself that aliens were real; how she believed that if she came out to this spot enough times and waved to the strange light they'd take her up into space with them and help her fulfill her destiny.

Now all she could think about was how badly she wanted to go home and work on her story, forget all about Robert and fall back into her weird, personalized land of make-believe. Let Robert look down on her as much as he wanted to. She would find a way to break free before long anyway.

At the end of the night, Robert kissed her on the lips.

She could feel in the embrace that he was desperate to keep her. In the front hall, Mom and Dad greeted them and asked how the night had gone. Robert, his mouth embarrassingly smeared with lipstick, said that it had gone wonderfully, shook hands with Dad, and left. Mom followed June like a puppy as she went into the kitchen for a glass of milk and some cookies, going on and on about how great June looked and how nice it was that she was finally getting the feel for things by dating and "acting her age."

After June had finished the cookies, she told her parents she was going to bed, went into her bedroom, and wrote three full chapters for her story, all by hand, so as not to make noise with the typewriter. It took all night.

days past

A LETTER ARRIVED FOR JUNE A SHORT TIME
later. She'd made a habit of getting the mail every day,
which pleased her parents and allowed her to see everything that came in before anyone else. Even though months
had passed since she'd sent in her application, June couldn't
bring herself to give up hope, refused to accept the failure.
When she saw the envelope addressed to *J. Hardie* one warm
Saturday in late spring, she slipped it down the front of her
blouse smoothly and quickly, as though she'd anticipated
finding it in the pile of mail all along.

But she hadn't anticipated it, not even a little bit. And
now her answer was here, for better or for worse, and June
had to fight not to run back inside and up to her room,
instead strolling back up the driveway as if she hadn't a
care in the world. She made herself keep her easy pace as
she dropped the remaining mail off on the coffee table for

Dad, even refilling his drink and bowl of pretzels for good measure before quietly slipping upstairs.

Once the bedroom door was locked behind her, all bets were off. June nearly tore open her blouse in an effort to get the envelope out. There was a single page inside, which worried her, because surely if it was good news there'd be more information than what would fit on one sheet. Her hands trembled as she unfolded the letter.

Just a few nights prior, she'd told herself that if she didn't get into the program, it was a sign from the universe to keep on going down the path that she was already on and succumb to the idea of one day marrying Robert. The idea of having to swallow such a verdict here, today, *now*, made her throat constrict as if she was going to cry, or scream, or both. She would take back the stupid little deal she'd made with herself—no one piece of paper should have such a massive influence on how she was going to live her life.

Unless, of course, the piece of paper said what she wanted it to say. It had been put into the typewriter and thus produced crookedly.

The warmest of hellos to you, J. Hardie. Your unsettling prose and clear distaste for certain aspects of American culture caused your application to shine bright among the other entries we received. You have been awarded a full scholarship to our program that will begin this summer, on the first of July.

Please respond within two weeks so we can confirm your acceptance and have our secretary send you an information packet. This will include plans for your travel, as well as details about the retreat grounds. All expenses during your stay, including food, will be taken care of. We look forward

to shaking your hand and sharing perspectives over cigars in
the Common Room after dark.
Best regards,
Bill Lancaster

June let out a mad little giggle of disbelief. She'd really done it! She'd found a way to leave and go somewhere exciting, and write and write without needing a single goddamn dime. It'd worked out! She read the letter over and over again, always having a laugh at the line about *sharing perspectives over cigars in the Common Room after dark.* What a stale, old idiot that Bill Lancaster sounded like! And yet, she didn't care.

She didn't care that she had partly lied in her application, speaking as though from the perspective of a man. She'd dress like one if she had to while she was there. She could easily pull it off with her face and figure.

She also did not care that Mom and Dad and Fred and Robert were all going to go completely ape over this. The program was months long, and it didn't start until after graduation. There'd be nothing they could do about it once she was gone; she'd leave a vague note that would let them know she wasn't dead but not much more than that. They'd have all the time in the world to calm down about it.

June's chest swelled with elation at the knowledge that she wouldn't have to tell anyone about this, wouldn't have to ask permission and let someone else make the decision. She was soon to be a full-fledged adult, and honestly *this* was what she felt being a *better young woman* was: being someone who took chances in order to be happy. And just look at how it was turning out so far!

When Monday came, she sent in her reply, again waiting sneakily for the mailman to come so she could see her envelope off with her own two eyes. When he was gone, it felt even more official.

She had made her decision, and nothing could stop her now. June felt invincible.

In between school, and trips to the supermarket with Mom, and vacuuming underneath Fred's feet while he watched TV and helping prepare dinner for parties with Robert and Mr. Dennings, June kept her mind's eye on her book. She realized with an electrifying jolt of excitement that she'd be typing *THE END* while in a private cottage somewhere in upstate New York. She'd make sure to arrange it so that she finished very late at night, so that immediately afterward she could go outside and climb up onto the little roof and lie there to look at the stars and thank them for her story. She could get drunk up there, eat chocolates, embrace what it felt like to be herself.

Then, she could spend the rest of the retreat making edits and forging connections with anyone in attendance who might know how to pursue a publishing house in New York City and move on to the next stage of *trying, trying, trying…*

June thought maybe she ought to sit down and write out an outline for all the chapters that were left so she could lay the story out properly and make sure the pace would be satisfying to her readers. She'd already decided that the heroine would live, but still didn't know yet if the character would end up back on Earth or if she'd stay in outer space.

June went carefully through her book of star maps while she thought it out one rainy afternoon, tracing her fingers along the imaginary illustrated lines that made everything look so structured and purposeful in space. Was the infinite blackness a path to something better? Or was it a churning pit of cold, nightmarish chaos? When she was ready, she sat down in her chair and put a new page in the typewriter. Downstairs, she could smell chicken frying, which combined marvelously with the cool, rainy air coming through the window. This was what it was like to be content. June wrote:

Her new vision was nothing like her old sight. She knew her eyes were the same ones she'd had before, since they had never been completely detached from their roots while the creatures were poking around in her eye sockets, so she drew the conclusion that something very specific had been done to her brain.

At one point, the creatures undid the straps that were holding her down to the cold metal table. She sat up, shivering, not as self-conscious about being naked as she would have imagined she might be in such a spot. These things were nothing like her, and she doubted very much they cared about the details as much as men from Earth would. They looked at her, and she looked at them. She wondered what they could possibly be planning.

Clearly, it wasn't as simple as her being hunted and killed for sport. They had taken her with a specific purpose in mind, but what was it? What had they done to her brain? The more upset she got, the more nervous the creatures became. At one point, the girl locked eyes with one of them and just started begging. The creature made increasingly urgent sounds at her cries, almost as if it were in pain. The others swarmed over within a few moments. One of them sprayed a greasy mist into her face from a device on its arm, and she passed out instantly.

Suddenly, the door leading to June's bedroom burst open. June knew before even turning around that her brother had come in. She closed her eyes slowly and sighed, breathing her rage out through her nose.

"Mom asked me to find out if you wanted to learn how to make gravy using pan drippings and potato water."

No, June did not, not even a little bit. But in order to keep up with the image she'd been projecting since the poodle-skirt date with Robert, she had to act interested.

"Sure," she mumbled under her breath as she finished the sentence she was working on, then leaned back to read over what she'd written. It took her a few moments of peaceful silence before she realized that Fred was curiously reading over her shoulder. She worked her eyes to his face as nonchalantly as she could, so as to not let him realize that she was watching.

His lips moved slightly as he read, and she could tell that he at least found it interesting because he didn't pull away for quite a few seconds.

"That the story you've been working on for months?" he asked as she stood up from her desk. Outside, thunder sounded in slow and heavy rolls. She nodded and picked at her elbow.

"Yes," she said. "Why?"

He looked at her with an eyebrow raised for a good, long time. She stood still, taking in his ridiculous side-combed hair and brown slacks, a miniature version of Dad, including the crumbs on the shirt from snacking on the couch.

He'd always talked to her like she was an idiot, but he also had a history of rare, brief and bewildering moments that showed he could care, like when as a child her Halloween jack-o'-lantern lollipop had broken on the sidewalk, and he had instantly given her his. As they'd grown up, June could tell that it worried Fred how *unconventional*, to use his word, she was.

He wanted the same things for her that her parents and Robert did, which was just to ensure that she'd be safe. Happiness wasn't as important as safety. If she'd just shut up and go along with things as she was supposed to, she'd always be taken care of by others.

June felt no inner remorse knowing how she'd soon give the family one hell of a shake-up by disappearing for her writing retreat. Screw Fred and her parents and Robert!

"That is a very strange story," he said finally, his face completely void of anything that could be construed as warmth, turning back to the open door. "You're a very strange person."

June went to follow him but stopped at her mirror for just a brief moment, to look at the lines under her eyes again. They couldn't be scars, she told herself again. That was simply impossible, impossible, impossible. They were wrinkles, fattened with whatever disgusting natural oils and skin cells were permanently clogging them, two strange wrinkles of the exact same size.

They were very hard to detect at all unless you stared at them, anyway. June needed to stop thinking about them, remove that stress from herself completely.

So she went downstairs and listened with her hands folded neatly in front of her while she watched Mom pour out most of the grease from the chicken pan into a metal bowl, then used a whisk to stir some flour and potato water into the newly emptied pan. No salt or pepper, and when June politely suggested it, Mom scoffed.

"Simple is best, June," Mom said while the gravy thickened and bubbled. "This is how my grammy taught me to do it, and nobody's ever complained. The excitement's all in the chicken."

June smiled and nodded before being sent off to finish setting the table and getting everyone's drinks arranged. She made up the plates while Mom got Dad and Fred seated. June loaded the men's plates significantly more than hers and Mom's, just as she'd been taught. She so desperately wanted to give herself more mashed potatoes, just as much as Fred had on his plate, but knew Mom would raise a big stink about it if she tried. *That belly of yours doesn't need any more.* June could hear as if it were really being spoken.

After everyone had eaten and dishes were done and everyone was asleep, June woke up, got out of her bed, went downstairs, and headed into the kitchen. She took the bowl of leftover mashed potatoes that was covered in plastic wrap, sat on the floor, and ate it all with her fingers. She threw the bowl away in the trash can by the street. She crawled back up the stairs and into her bed.

The next morning, she didn't remember any of this. When Mom asked with irritation in her voice where the leftover potatoes had gone, June only shrugged.

the institution

"LET ME ASK YOU SOMETHING," NURSE JOYA said from where she stood behind the doctor. Her bright red lipstick was as bold as ever, a clean white cap still pinned impeccably around her perfect blond bun. "Do you think it's possible that the stresses of your everyday life have culminated in this manifestation? By making you believe that your parents have been replaced by impostors?"

June was once again sitting in the office with the yellow and brown triangle carpeting, on the white wooden chair facing the enormous desk. She'd been brought in a few hours after she'd finished breakfast with the girls, where Lauren had sat silently in her wheelchair, her head still covered in bandages postlobotomy.

When she had first been called back, June was afraid that the doctor and Joya would somehow know about the weird drug trip she'd had. Now, she nervously threw a glance over to the spot she thought was where she'd seen the doctor through the air vent.

In that location, there was a trash can pushed up against the wall, completely out of place and blocking her view. June did not remember seeing it the last time she was there, and she thought she'd been thorough as she looked over the room.

Don't be silly, she scolded herself. *Of course there isn't an air vent there. The trash can was there last time, and you missed it.*

"June." Nurse Joya was still waiting for an answer.

"Sorry," June said, looking away from the trash can at last. "Can you repeat the question?"

She wished so badly that the doctor would speak, for any amount of time. She didn't like Joya, and she also knew that he was the one who spoke whenever Eleanor was in here. Why would he not speak to her?

"Your life at home." Joya looked down at the chart in her hands, rubbing her lips together. "Was there anything going on in your life that was especially stressful before the incident that led you here? Anything that weighed on you or caused you distress?"

At least she was saying the sorts of things that June would have expected from a medical professional. It may have been the first thing about her stay so far that felt normal. She felt hope begin to unfold in her heart for just a second before remembering Lauren with her pus-stained bandages and her forever frown.

"Not anything that would amount to something this drastic," June answered after hesitating. "It was just the same old stuff."

No it wasn't. There *had* been some extra stress, loads of it actually, surrounding her graduation, and the writing program and everything that came after, especially the big party that took place the night before she was admitted. But was it enough to push her brain over the edge in such a visceral way? She doubted it.

On the other hand, here she was.

"Last time you mentioned that you knew your parents had been replaced because your mother had called you—" she turned a page "—*Nightingale*. You said that she wouldn't have called you that, especially after that previous night. So what happened that night? You got too nervous to talk about it last time."

Good morning, Nightingale.

"There was...a party." June desperately wanted to leave. She missed Eleanor in a strange and unexpected way, very much wished she were here right now. "It just didn't go very well, that's all. My parents were...very unhappy with me." *Because I hurt someone very badly.* She thought back to it, remembered the sounds of the glasses breaking and people shouting, her mother hysterical. Fred grabbing her roughly, lifting her from the floor. *Get up, June.* Move, *damn it!*

"Why?" Joya was getting impatient. "Tell me everything. Everything that happened that night. Everything leading up to it. *Everything you remember.*"

The urgency in her voice made June take pause. It was like Nurse Joya was looking for something important, more important than possible sources of stress—something personal to herself and not just to June. The paranoia bloomed in one unfurling motion.

June remembered the last time she was in here, how the nurse had essentially threatened her with various *methods* of *handling* her in order to find out what had happened that night. She remembered what the monster in the tunnel had said about her brain and what Simpson had said at breakfast about worms being implanted into brains. June looked again to the trash can shoved against the wall and shivered.

"I can see that you're not going to make this easy for us or yourself." The nurse snapped the chart shut, and the doctor gave a quick but sharp nod, causing the old skin on his neck to ripple. "We'll have to continue your treatment until we can get to the bottom of this and decide together when you're ready to go back home. All it'll take from you is honesty, June."

Nurse Joya led June back to the enormous door, while the doctor stayed seated behind the desk. June followed, relieved to be leaving the duo. The uncertainty and fear that were flooding her were overwhelming, making her feel as though she might faint at any minute. Was there an air vent behind that stupid trash can or not? Was there an underground tunnel snaking around below the institution or wasn't there? Did these people want their *brains*?

Impossible.

"The doctor hopes you can begin the process of accepting our help to fix yourself," the nurse said cheerfully, laying a heavy hand on June's shoulder. "If you help us, we can help you. That's all we want here, Nightingale."

June's spine tingled, and her mouth went dry. Joya was watching her very closely. Why would the nurse say such a thing, especially after June had just talked about what had happened when her mother used the word? It felt intentionally antagonistic. That wasn't how it should have been; she was certain of that.

Mumbling a hurried *Thank you*, June walked away as quickly as she could, already turning over Nurse Joya's words in her head, already building a plan from them. The next time she was brought into the office, she'd tell Joya everything that had happened that awful night, the night that still haunted her with confusion and upset. Then she'd lie through her teeth and confess that the incident with her parents must have indeed been a coping mechanism. And then she'd be free, discharged to the care of the parental intruders, but after that she could run away immediately. She could escape both options. She could get out of here before she ended up like Lauren.

Clearly, she wouldn't be able to go home, but June would have been happy to cross that bridge in lieu of this one.

"That didn't take long," Eleanor remarked as June approached her in the recreation room, on the couch where the other girls were lounging in various states as *Fantasia* played on the television set in black and white. "What'd you say to get out so soon?"

"Nothing," June said, sinking down next to Eleanor, leaning against her. Eleanor leaned back. "I didn't say anything. Next time I'm going to, though. Next time I'll tell them everything."

"It won't help," Eleanor whispered. "They never stop looking for the answer."

I'll just help them find it, then, June thought, and turned to see Eleanor looking at her. They stared into each other's eyes for a lingering moment before June asked, "Where's Lauren?"

The other girls all looked at her then. "They came and took her away pretty soon after you left," Adie said sullenly. "She's gone now."

Somewhere behind her, June heard the sound of squeaky wheels and a rattling tray. Her heart skipped a beat as she turned to see Nurse Joya pushing her little cart toward them, a serene grin on her brightly painted mouth. She felt Eleanor stiffen beside her and fully expected to be stuck with a monster needle any second; instead, the nurse kept pushing the cart past them and ended up parking it behind Simpson.

"Just a little something to relax, babycakes," Joya cooed, preparing the injection while the other girls watched in frozen horror. "You've been all up in a tizzy these last few days."

"No, I haven't," Simpson cried, but she didn't try to run away as the nurse cleaned her arm with a wipe. "I'm calm, Joya. Look at me. I'm just sitting here, watching *Fantasia* and minding my own goddamn business…"

"You know what I'm talking about," Joya insisted with a sudden edge to her voice and stuck the needle into Simpson's arm. "You've been saying some wicked things lately, haven't you, buttercup?"

June watched as Simpson slumped back against the couch, her breathing already long and deep. Joya noticed the other girls were watching her and shot them all a theatrical wink. "I've got to go get ready for more appointments with the doctor," she said as she began to wheel the cart away. "Eleanor, after I finish up with Miss Adie here, it'll be your turn, darlin'. Adie, please follow me."

"Okay," Eleanor said, and June could tell that she was nervous but trying to hide it. "It's been a while."

"Yes, it has," Joya replied over her shoulder. The sudden coldness in her voice was chilling. "We sure do have a lot to talk about. Adie, now please."

Adie stood up and walked after the nurse quietly, her hands curling into themselves.

Nobody moved or said a thing until she and Joya were

completely out of sight. After the click of the door to the office echoed down the hallway and into the rec room, the conversation level resumed its normal, constant buzz. "That goddamn bitch," Simpson slurred from where she was slumped on the couch. "I know just what she's doing."

Cassy and Jessica, who had been sitting right next to Adie, moved over to the couch with Eleanor and June, as if the other girl had been cursed by Adie's summons. *Sometimes you only get called back once in a blue moon*, Jessica had told June sometime during her first day there. *Sometimes you go every day.*

Simpson's eyes were red and wet and unblinking, and she wasn't talking anymore. June went over to her and took her hand: nothing. Complete dead weight. "Simpson," June said directly into her face. Again, nothing.

"Damn it." June turned back to face Eleanor and the other girls. "What was she going to say? About Joya?"

"Why are you so obsessed with Joya?" Eleanor asked, grabbing at the ends of her own sweater.

"Why are *you* going along with all of this like it's okay?" June shot back, her voice raised. "This isn't a real hospital—you said so yourself. Nobody here is a real doctor or nurse. Something is happening..."

The girls looked as though June had just spoken in tongues.

"What do you mean?" Cassy broke the silence. "Why wouldn't we do what they tell us? They're caring for us."

"What?" June felt the space behind her nose tingling. "What about everything you've talked about before? Have you ever heard of anywhere that treats patients like this? What would your parents say if they knew how things were in here? Your friends?"

"We are each other's friends and family," Eleanor answered, and the other girls nodded. "We've never had anyone else. We've never been anywhere else but here."

"No," June cried out, then realized that there were a few nurses behind the glass partition watching her. She knew she needed to calm down, or else she'd soon be drugged out like Simpson. She took a second to breathe, tried to look more at ease in her body language. "You guys had lives before you came here," she tried again. "You had to have."

Still, silence and stunned gazes.

"Eleanor." June sat down beside her roommate and took her hand. "You told me that you came here three years ago. After you died. You talked about your family. Cassy, what about all that stuff about the *Titanic*?"

Eleanor's face looked strained. "I... What in the world..."

"What's wrong?" June asked. Cassy and Jessica looked as confused as they did before. "Don't you guys remember? Don't you remember anything about your lives before this place?"

The girls' faces were all overcome with the same blank confusion. It made June feel sick, truly sick to her stomach. Why could she still remember her life? Because she'd only been here for a little while? Would she forget soon? As of now, she remembered everything. She mustn't let herself slip away, she knew, and decided that every morning and every night she would remember her old life, repeat everyone's names in her mind, as painful as it may have been.

"We were all born here," Cassy said, and June knew it was a lie. She'd be far more willing to believe the time travel story than this. "You're the only one who's ever been new."

It wasn't true.

"*You're* the weird one," Cassy went on, her eyes welling up despite her triumphant stare. "You're here because you think your parents were *replaced*." She giggled cruelly, and a single tear fell down her cheek. "How does that even make sense? You are *never* going to get out of here."

Beside her, Jessica started to rock back and forth slightly, her long hair falling forward and covering her face. Eleanor stared at June. Simpson didn't move, her mouth slacked open. June wondered what Adie was going through right this very second. What had happened to these girls in the short time that June had been here?

"Simpson mentioned that thing about the worms," she said aloud, trying desperately to understand something, anything. "Is that what Joya meant when she said that Simpson was saying wicked things?"

Was it possible Joya and the doctor needed to silence her for whatever reason? Was it possible Simpson had seen something?

One night while I was sleeping, some nurses came in and held me down and I felt something go into my ear, June remembered Simpson saying at breakfast that morning. *I can hear it eating every so often—I swear I can. I can hear it* crunching.

"Something feels funny," Eleanor said. "Whenever I try to think about what's outside these walls, I…" She appeared unable to speak.

"You had a family," June urged, tightening her grip on Eleanor's hand. "Remember them. Fight it! Whatever is doing this to you, fight it—"

"You're right," she says. "How did I die? And why?"

"You're not dead." June was finished playing along. "You're alive. Your name is Eleanor, you're seventeen years old just like me, and you're alive."

"I am dead," Eleanor said. She looked into June's eyes. "I don't know how I know it—I realize it sounds insane—I just... I *know* I'm dead."

"Because they told you that you were?"

"No." Eleanor's eyes went glassy like she was remembering something. "I...died before I came here. I remember that much. It happened, and then they brought me here. It was like the doctor had been expecting me or something. They acted like this was my new home from the start..."

"Tell me more," June urged. "What were your parents like?"

"My head hurts," Eleanor whimpered, lifting her free hand to her temple. "Please stop."

"Stop fucking with her," Jessica hissed from Eleanor's other side. "And shut your fat mouth unless you want them to find out what you're doing—"

"They'll punish you if they know," Cassy interrupted. "They'll punish all of us. Just look at Lauren and Simpson. Look what they did to them."

When Lauren was lobotomized, June remembered, the other girls had instantly cut all emotional ties to her. June had felt it happen in that moment during breakfast. And now they were ready to do the same thing to Simpson if it came down to it.

"But the worms Simpson mentioned..." June said weakly. "And all the things that are wrong with this place..."

"Stop it," Eleanor pleaded. "Please...my head. I think I need to lie down..."

"I'll go with you back to our room." June helped pull Eleanor to her feet, happy to get away from Cassy and Jessica. She cast one last pained glance Simpson's way, making a note to have a private conversation with her as soon as Simpson came around a bit more. It was possible that she knew things.

"They were mostly leaving us all alone until *you* came along," Cassy said bitterly after them, before they were too far away so she could keep her voice low and still be heard. "And now they just won't stop digging."

the institution

WHEN THEY WERE IN THEIR ROOM AND THE
door was closed behind them, the girls sat on June's bed. Eleanor drank the water she'd picked up from the nurses' station on the way, along with a few aspirin for her headache.

"Don't mind them," Eleanor said, still rubbing her temple gently. "They're just upset and scared. What happened
to Lauren was...awful. And sudden. They're trying to pretend it didn't happen. Things around here are getting worse
by the minute." She looked to June, her mouth pulled into
a thin line. "I have to admit Cassy wasn't wrong about
things changing when you arrived."

June swallowed. "But that doesn't make sense. What
would I have to do with any of it?"

"I don't know," Eleanor admitted. "It's not like you're
the one who planted the seed in Simpson's mind about the
brain worm. And who knows what Lauren said at her ap-

pointment that got her lobotomized. If that's even how they choose who gets it." She shook her head.

"Do you think the worm thing is real?" June couldn't believe she was asking this question, seriously considering it. *This is how things are now*, she realized in horror. *Your parents have been replaced, and you've been brought into some sort of hell house.*

"Of course not," Eleanor said, almost defensively. "I know we were all joking about that sort of stuff before, and things here are bad, but they're real. Brain worms are *not* real. And if they were, doctors would not be putting them into our brains." She paused, and her breath started to quicken. "It doesn't matter anyway. I'm dead." She touched a hand to her face as if checking herself for a fever. "But the good thing about it is that I get to live forever now, in this state. I can feel the truth of that in my bones, June— I will live forever."

Maybe you goddamn will, June thought. *I'd believe it at this point.*

June looked at Eleanor until she returned her gaze. "How do you feel about the idea of getting out of here someday?" June asked. "I mean it. Think about it. What if they let you out?"

Eleanor considered it. "I think," she said and gave June a little smile, and June felt her cheeks warm, "I think I'd like that."

"Okay, then," June said, grasping at this budding plan, believing it could happen someday. "Let's promise each other right now. Somehow, we'll both get out of here. And we can live in the world however we want, together."

"Okay," Eleanor said, her face lighting up slowly but surely. "It's a promise. We'll do it together."

"Together," June confirmed and smiled back. "Don't forget our promise. Don't get too used to this place like Cassy and Jessica have."

She realized that they were holding hands. June liked how Eleanor's fingers felt in hers, liked the way their palms rested against one another. She decided that she was glad to have been roomed with Eleanor, and not any of the other girls. She'd been scared of Eleanor at first, but now June was wondering if that had been on her.

Nothing in this world made sense anymore, but Eleanor had looked out for June from the beginning. June thought that maybe she was starting to fall in love with her. The realization gave her stomach a lovely little flip, an unfamiliar wave of emotion that June felt curious to explore.

The door opened, and Nurse Chelsea poked her head in to peer at the girls curiously. "Sharing secrets, are we?" she asked, and grabbed at the end of one of the golden braids that were resting over her shoulders. She was chewing on a piece of gum and looked as though she'd just stepped out of a Sears catalog, just like all the nurses June had seen.

Who were these women who worked for the doctor who never even spoke? Where did they come from? What lives did they live outside of here? Did they even *have* lives outside of here? They were all always around.

"Keep this door open unless a nurse closes it, please," Chelsea went on, smacking her gum impatiently. "This is your only warning."

The girls nodded, but the nurse continued to stare, even narrowed her eyes just the slightest. "Nurse Joya wants me to tell you that it's time for your appointment, Eleanor."

"Okay," Eleanor said with a weak smile. "I'm coming."

When the nurse didn't budge, Eleanor stood and nodded

at June before heading out the door. Then June was alone. Soon she heard the call for lunch and went alone to the cafeteria. She picked up a tray of food and looked around, spotting Cassy and Jessica at the usual table, Adie sitting with them. Cassy didn't look happy to see June, but Adie waved her over. Simpson was nowhere to be seen.

"Where's Simpson?" June asked casually, refusing to make eye contact with Cassy. "You're her roommate, aren't you, Adie?"

"I am," Adie confirmed through a bite of egg-salad sandwich. "I haven't seen her since my appointment, though. I was kind of wondering where she was, too. Maybe she's having her appointment now."

"Eleanor is," June said, and Adie's chewing slowed.

"You sure?" Adie asked, looking around the room for Simpson and failing to find her. "That's weird."

"She got up and left after you and Eleanor went back to your room," Cassy said, so quietly June had to lean in to hear her. June knew Cassy was afraid that they were being spied on or somehow monitored. It was what had set her off earlier. "Whatever she was on seemed to wear off. She said she wanted to take a shower."

"So quickly?" June asked, at least somewhat glad that the girl was talking to her without a tone. "She seemed pretty out of it before."

"It was weird," Jessica mumbled. "She seemed weird."

"We have to stop talking about this sort of stuff," Cassy said, her voice pinched tight with anxiety. June could see that she was about to cry. "Please. You're going to make them hurt us. Think about what happened with Lauren. Just stop."

It was wrong, the way these girls refused to question

how this place was run. It wasn't like hospitals murdered anyone; June had heard of things like lobotomies long before she came to this place. It was about the conditions of the institution: the unconventional medical practices, the needle sharing, the aggressive comments, and the overall feeling that something bigger was happening in the office with the expensive furniture and the odd carpeting.

"I'll check on Simpson, then," June said, ignoring her sandwich and standing to go. "So none of you have to involve yourselves. But if you really think it'll somehow make you more of a target than every single one of us already is—"

"I'll go with you." Adie stood, too, and Cassy looked like she was about to have a panic attack. "It's fine, Cass," Adie insisted, nudging her with her arm. "We're just going with each other to the bathroom. No big deal."

"You need to settle down," Jessica nearly hissed at Cassy under her breath. "You're gonna get yourself a doozy of an injection."

June went over to the tray carriage and waited for Adie to slide her used tray in, too. They walked together out of the cafeteria and back toward the main hall. The shower room was in the back, on the opposite end of the hallway from the doctor's office.

June could hear water running before she even stepped into the room, which was covered floor to wall with small white tiles. Not wanting her slippers to get wet, she took them off, and Adie did the same. The girls stepped carefully over the damp tiles. "Simp?" Adie called through the steam that hung thick in the room. "Are you in here? It's lunchtime."

Nothing. June was suddenly afraid for Eleanor, who'd

been out of her sight too long for comfort. *She'll live forever because she's already dead*, she told herself wildly, stepping deeper into the shower room.

An odor hit the girls at the same time: something immensely heavy and metallic. June knew Adie could smell it, too, because she pinched her nose as they went on. "Why is there so much steam in here?" Adie demanded, using her free hand to wave it away. "The showers don't even get very hot. It doesn't make sense."

June knew the smell nearly choking them was blood, no doubt about it. *Jesus Christ*, June thought, breathing through her mouth. *Please don't let her be sitting on the floor with her wrists slit.*

It was an awful thought, and she hated herself for having it. Simpson was probably fine, and if she wasn't she was most unlikely to be in here. It's not like they did the lobotomies in the shower. As they approached, the steam started to thin. Adie gasped and grabbed June's arm as a terrifying sight came into view: the floor before them was pooled, *flooded*, with blood. It was stark against the white tiles, running in torrents toward the drain in the center of the room.

Adie whimpered, and the girls stepped around the edge to avoid it flowing over their toes. June felt like she might be sick. The smell was overwhelming.

"We need to find someone who can help—" June began, and that's when Adie started to scream.

Simpson sat in the steam, her legs splayed, jutting from beneath her blue cotton housedress. The steam made it hard to determine what had happened, but it was very clear that Simpson was the source of all the blood. Her dress was soaked with it, her legs, her slippers. June squinted through the steam at Simpson's wrists but didn't see any cuts. The steam was too thick to make out much of anything above her waist, but based on the amount of blood and the terrifying stillness of Simpson's body, June would have bet anything that the girl was dead.

Adie sprinted away, still screaming, calling for help. June stood alone, her own legs like noodles. With her hands trembling and her heart pounding, she took a tentative step forward into the liquid, then another, then another, until she was standing at Simpson's side. She waved the steam out of the way, and that's when she screamed even louder than Adie had.

Simpson's face was gone. Her lips were gone, her nose was opened up, her eyeballs had withered away into nothing. Bright red meat, shockingly bright, stuck out over the front of the skull in thick, gummy clumps that wept fluids and blood. Her teeth were exposed, the pointed canines gleaming.

June didn't understand at first exactly what had happened, until she saw the opening of the pipe directly on the other side of Simpson, level with her face. The pipe hissed angrily every time condensation from the ceiling dripped onto it. June stopped screaming, held her hand out toward the pipe, and discovered that it was emanating immense heat, enough to burn without even touching it. Below the opening, a small wheeled valve handle dripped with bloody water.

Simpson's face had been steamed off.

June heard running footsteps in the distance, then the echo of a nurse shouting out her name. She backed away so fast that she nearly slipped and fell onto the tiles slicked thick with Simpson's blood. "Over here!" she cried out, and her voice cracked. "Please help!"

That's not an injury that can be helped.

June's vision went a little funny, and she dropped to one knee, afraid she might pass out or vomit or both. The lights overhead flickered as Nurse Chelsea and two other nurses rushed forward and grabbed at June with urgent hands.

"Joya will be here shortly," Chelsea assured her, squeezing June's arm and pulling her up so hard she cried out. "In the meantime, everyone is on emergency lockdown. Get to your room now, please."

June didn't need to be told twice. She fled, slipping through the shower room, then running past the hallway of doors that were all already closed except for hers. When she passed the room that Simpson and Adie shared, she could hear Adie's anguished screams from behind the door, a sound that made her heart feel like it was being squeezed. A nurse was waiting at her door, a big ring of keys in her hand. June stepped into the room, and the door was immediately closed and bolted.

When June turned toward her bed, she started at Eleanor's presence.

"What happened?" her roommate asked, propped against the wall and wrapping her sweater around herself. "I was in my appointment, and I heard screaming, and then Nurse Chelsea opened the office door, asking for Joya all frantically. They made me come straight here. They made me run."

June tried to find the right words, tried to figure out a way to help Eleanor understand without having to explain every detail, but she burst into tears instead.

the institution

"OH, MY GOD," ELEANOR SAID, AND WENT TO June. They wrapped their arms around each other, and June wept.

"Simpson's dead," she managed, and Eleanor went stiff in the embrace.

They slumped down on Eleanor's bed and talked through it. June told her all that had happened leading up to finding Simpson, but couldn't bring herself to describe exactly what she'd seen. She told Eleanor about all the steam, about the state of the floor, and about Simpson's blood-drenched dress and legs.

"I can't believe she'd kill herself," Eleanor said after they'd talked for a long time and shared stunned silence. "I knew she got upset from time to time about the brain worm, but why now, after all this time?"

"That sort of thing doesn't always make sense," June

said, thinking of Dad's brother, Lawrence, who had killed himself when he was nineteen years old. Dad never talked about it, but Mom had spilled the beans to June one evening while they were washing the dishes, before the business deal and the dishwasher and everything else that had changed their lives forever. "Brains get sick. People can't help it. It isn't fair."

As she said it, June wondered if suicide was really what this was. Was it possible? *Yes.* Was it also possible something else had happened to Simpson? Her gut said *yes*, as terrified as that thought made her feel.

What would become of them all? What was the point of all this? Did this place have any real interest in treating people properly or not? It was bewildering. Everything was so wrong, but everybody went on like it was the most normal thing in the world. It wasn't. And yet, there was nothing to do about it.

Or was there?

Nurse Joya had seemed pretty interested in the details of June's life leading up to the morning she'd come downstairs to the Mom-thing waiting for her. What if she just told Joya what she wanted to know and saw what happened? June could play along until she had nothing more to offer them, and then she'd leave. Once she escaped, she could go get Eleanor and they could find help, tell somebody about the atrocities that were happening within the walls of the place, get the other girls out, get them all real help.

But do I need real help? June wondered, a question that haunted her constantly. *Did Mom and Dad really get replaced? I feel like they did. But I'd feel the same way if I was ill, wouldn't I?* She asked herself if she believed that was possible and, if so, how. She remembered what she had said about aliens to Joya at her first appointment. It was always aliens with June. In her mind, in her story… She reached up and ran her fingers over what she was telling herself were wrinkles but she was secretly afraid were scars.

She loved to think about her story before she came here, loved to bask in the unexplainable bond with it that she felt like she'd built in her daydreams, a weird tale of the macabre. She'd always been a little obsessive, she knew deep down. And she'd always known she felt a little off.

But why?

She felt like there were no good options to explain any of it. More paranoia washed over her, made her feel sick, made her tremble and twitch a little bit. She felt unabashedly angry at her own body. It wasn't supposed to hurt her like this, fail her like this. And if it wasn't, if her body wasn't sick like people were telling her, what did that mean about the world she was living in, or the one she'd written about in her story?

It was all too terrifying to comprehend. June wished she could opt out, then remembered Simpson and recalled that she didn't know if Simpson had killed herself or was murdered. The trembling and twitching worsened.

"Do you remember our promise?" Eleanor whispered, breaking the long silence at last. She leaned slightly into June, absorbing some of her trembling energy, breathing long and deep until June did, too.

"I won't forget it," June answered. "But… I'm really scared, Eleanor."

"So am I," Eleanor admitted. "But I don't remember feeling any other way. At least now, you're here."

"Do you remember your family, now that I've prompted you about them?" June asked, scared to hear the response.

"Yes, I remember them" was the answer, and June breathed a sigh of relief. "But they feel more like a dream than anything else. I haven't seen them since I've been here, not even once. I feel like something happened to them. I don't think it's right, this place."

"It's not," June assured her. "That's where our promise comes in."

"Right."

They fell asleep in the silence that followed, limbs tangled, their chests rising and falling as the hours went on. When June awoke, Eleanor was gone and the door to the room was open.

Trying not to panic, June pulled her sweater on over her rumpled dress and wiggled her feet into her slippers. She stuck her head out of the room, and noted most of the other doors in the hallway were open, too. She looked in the other direction and saw that the recreation room was pretty bustling. She shuffled over and took a second to locate Eleanor on their usual couch, reading a book, while Jessica and Cassy watched television nearby.

"Where's Adie?" June asked and as she sat, she realized it was in the chair where she'd last seen Simpson alive. She remembered what Simpson's dead face had looked like in a cruelly realistic flashback, and pulled her legs up onto the seat so she could hug her knees.

"Medicated in her room," Jessica said, while Cassy pretended not to hear June.

June sincerely hoped Adie wasn't having some sort of terrible trip on top of seeing her roommate's demise. June dwelled on Simpson's missing face, then immediately recalled the Nurse Joya monster in the tunnels also, dismembering a body like she was shucking corn. June's eyes darted around the room to the nurses' station where, of the four nurses, two were looking straight at her.

Breathe, she told herself. *Don't give them reason to pay much thought to you. Sit still. Act casual.*

And she did, until it was time for dinner. June had hoped she'd somehow get called in for another appointment, but apparently she would have to wait.

Three weeks passed, and just when June was starting to wonder if they'd somehow read her mind already and weren't ever planning to call her back, she woke one morning to find Nurse Joya sitting at the foot of her bed.

"Early start today," she whispered, dramatically raising a finger over her lips while she gave a sharp little nod in the direction of Eleanor sleeping the next bed over. "Don't want to wake the dead girl, now, do we? Meet me at the nurses' station in two minutes for your meds, and then we'll walk down together."

June sat up and dressed, giving Eleanor a little shake before she left so that it wouldn't seem as though she disappeared. Staying aware of each other's whereabouts was the least they could do to help suppress their worries and the unbearable tension that had been building in the days since the events surrounding Lauren and Simpson. "Going to my appointment," she said when Eleanor's eyes opened. "Wish me luck."

"Good luck," Eleanor said sleepily, and turned over to face the wall.

After taking the blood-red capsule under Joya's watch, they went together to the office behind the giant door. It made June even more nervous that this was only her third visit since she'd arrived. That felt like forever ago. The other times, she'd been close to all but demanding the old doctor behind the desk speak to her, but now it was different. She would go along with whatever they wanted, in hopes of her unlikely release.

This time, the vent-obscuring trash can was gone. But one of the grand bookshelves had been moved from one end of the room to the other to cover the spot instead. *No way*, June thought, the pit in her stomach clenching. *No way!*

"Something wrong?" Joya asked from her usual weird place behind the doctor, her red lips turned down. "You look awfully interested in that bookshelf. Mind telling me why?"

June felt her face heat up. She looked to the nurse, who was regarding her with a startling intensity. It felt so much like she was challenging June about what she'd seen in the tunnels. But that couldn't be possible, she thought, even though it was one of June's darkest fears that it very much was indeed.

"I'm ready to talk about my life with you now," she blurted in reply, desperate for her plan to work. She forced herself to breathe slowly in order to appear as relaxed as possible.

"Oh?" Nurse Joya sounded surprised. The doctor gave a little grunt and leaned forward. June couldn't help but stare at him. She'd finally gotten *something* out of him. This really was what they were looking for. This was what would set her free!

"Yes," June said and cleared her throat. She looked to her lap. "I've been thinking about what you said, about the stresses of my life at home contributing to…what happened with my parents. Telling myself they weren't themselves."

"Do you still believe they were replaced?" Joya asked, pencil in hand, ready to record everything.

"No," June said, strongly. "I didn't want to go through with all the things they wanted from me. I wanted to do my own thing. I almost did, actually." She thought about the letter she'd received addressed to *J. Hardie* months prior. She thought about how she wouldn't finish her book in a retreat cottage in upstate New York after all. "But it didn't work out, and things kind of exploded in my family. All because of me." She was saying this because she thought it was what the nurse and doctor would want to hear, but it was a harder truth to face than she'd expected. "My parents thought I should have been a better young woman."

"But you didn't want to be."

The nurse couldn't have looked more genuinely interested in June's answers, to the point where June second-guessed her assessment of this place for a moment. Then she saw the newly moved bookshelf out of the corner of her eye, remembered Nurse Joya's intensity when she'd asked about it just now and remembered Simpson and the brain worms. *Get yourself out of here!*

"I did want to be," June lied. "I just wasn't very skillful at certain things, I suppose."

"Things like…" It was the doctor who spoke this time. Still as a statue, Joya glanced down at him.

June felt a flare of hope in her chest again and looked into the old man's eyes. Something about him wasn't quite right: his body's bone structure seemed disproportionate to the size of his head, his wrinkles folding so deeply into themselves that they looked fake. His voice was much perkier than she'd imagined, though, almost matching Joya's in tone.

Let me go! June thought with all her might, looking desperately into the doctor's eyes. She remembered the first time she'd been in here, how this man had washed over her body with his eyes. She leaned a little closer to the desk and licked her lips.

"Things like cooking fancy dinners," June answered, almost sweetly. "I love to bake but never got the hang of cooking things like a nice roasted chicken or a meat loaf. That was my mom's strength. She just wished I had that facility, too." She paused. "Maybe I just should have stopped struggling against the current and let her teach me, really pushed myself to try."

The doctor and Joya were quiet for an uncomfortable length of time. June once again was struck with the odd feeling that the two staffers were somehow communicating without speaking.

"That all sounds fine and dandy, June Hardie," the doctor finally said, his voice growing dark. "But what we'd really prefer to hear from you is what things you *were* good at. I read in your file that one of your hobbies was writing."

Book, book, my book, my book, I miss it, I miss my sweet book...

"Not really," June said, feigning confusion. "I liked to read for sure, maybe played around with a short story or two when there wasn't any more housework to do, but generally, not as much as I enjoyed baking or playing cards."

My book is done but it doesn't feel finished, oh I miss my story so much, the stars, the creatures, the girl, the gaping holes in her head, the way she made everyone on Earth scream after she returned...

"Interesting. I don't see *baking* in your file at all," Nurse Joya said, reviewing the folder in her hands. "Your parents seemed to have left it out, which is confusing. You'd think they'd remember to include it since you loved it so much."

June was still, her mind racing with potential ways to answer.

"It's almost like the people who filled out this file are not the same people who raised you," Nurse Joya suggested, and a mean little smile grew on the doctor's lips.

She's trying to trick you, thought June. "Of course it was the same people," June said. "I've been thinking about it, and it's just not logical that they were replaced. But there is one thing I remembered. I really didn't sleep at all the night before the incident." She found herself talking faster and faster. "That's probably why I lost my head for a little bit there. But I think I've got myself together, and I'm ready to go back to my parents and help them around the house and everything else."

It was so much more difficult than she'd anticipated, to appear genuine and calm when she couldn't stop thinking about Simpson's melted face and Lauren's fluid-stained bandages and the tunnel that had appeared in the wall.

"That'll be enough for today," Joya said suddenly, and the doctor gave a little nod, causing the loose skin on his neck to waggle around. "You sure had a lot to say, compared to your other appointments. I think we may be making some progress at last."

"I think so, too," June answered excitedly, working her hands together as she followed Joya out. She glanced at the doctor to offer him a goodbye wave, but he looked angry. He glared at June as she retreated, causing a chill to run down her back. "What are the next steps, now that we've gotten to this point?"

"Well," Joya said, opening the door and offering June

a wide, perfect smile. "Next steps will be up to our dear doctor, of course, but rest assured we will let you know. And next time when you come in—"

"Next time?" June couldn't help but interrupt. *No, no, no!*

"Yes," the nurse said, her smile fading into a hard frown. "Next time you'll tell us what happened the night before the incident that brought you here. The party you mentioned before."

Thinking about the party made June's throat close up, but she shook it off as best as she could, desperation driving her fully at this point.

"I could do that right now—" June tried, but Joya threw her hand up to stop her.

"No." Nurse Joya looked back at the doctor, then back at June. "We should probably wait until you're ready to tell the truth."

"The truth?"

"Yes," she said, looking smug. "Liar."

June's stomach felt heavy. "Excuse...excuse me?"

The nurse leaned close enough for June to smell the waxy perfume of her lipstick. "Liar," she whispered, then straightened up and began to shut the door. "Just like that poor little Simpson girl."

This time, she heard no muffled mocking tones behind the firmly closed door. There was only silence, which somehow felt much worse.

days past

BEFORE SHE KNEW IT, HIGH SCHOOL GRADU-
ation had snuck up on June, and she found herself shopping
for a dress at Sears with Mom. Ever since she'd gotten her
scholarship acceptance letter for the writing retreat in New
York, June's life at home had been significantly less difficult to handle. She continued to go on dates with Robert
and was relieved that he never brought up marriage during their hour-long walks in the park or while they were
watching movies at the drive-in. She even let him take her
dancing one night, something she had always wanted to try
but felt too clumsy to do outside of her bedroom.

There was something magical about living a life that she
knew she'd be leaving behind soon, June realized as she
bounced and swayed to the wonderful new rock-and-roll
music that had started playing at the clubs, laughing herself
silly while Robert beamed. She could enjoy it as something

separate from herself, a trivial thing with zero power over who she was and what she would do with herself next.

"Just look at these!" Mom clapped her hands together in delight as she looked down the row of fancy dresses. They were all cut almost exactly the same, only varied by pattern or color. "These are gorgeous, June! What do you think?"

June strolled right over to the rack and picked out a sleeveless dress, mint green with a lace trim. It had a snug bodice, and the full skirt was made of a swishier material than the usual, less giving crinolines.

"This one's lovely," June said, knowing her mother would love it.

"Oh, my word, that is beautiful!" Mom stepped forward to rub the skirt material between her fingers. "I've never seen you pick something like this before—it's amazing!"

June fantasized about the writing retreat almost every night. She had to make a true effort to stop herself from writing too much, because she didn't want to get too close to the end and then have it be easy and quick once she arrived in New York. She wanted to get to the real guts of the story while she was there: the payoff of it all, the reason she wanted to tell it in the first place. It was surprisingly difficult to refrain from sitting down to work on it, though; a few times, she found her forehead damp with sweat with the effort of having to find something else to do in between housework tasks.

"I think it's just swell," June said, smiling at her mom.

Schoolwork helped, too, but not as much as it used to. Since the end of the year was so close, all of the major assignments had been completed, all the tests had been taken and returned marked. June did neither well nor poorly on her finals: she did just okay, and she was glad she'd never have to feel like her worth was connected to these high-pressure outcomes again. Mom and Dad didn't care about grades at all, though, didn't think June would have much use for them the direction her life was going. June figured that as long as she had books, she'd be just fine.

"Well, go ahead and try it on!" Mom urged. "I can't wait to see it on you."

Every time June remembered that, one day soon, she'd be gone from all of this, away from Mom and Dad and Robert and Fred, her face couldn't help but light up. It put a bounce in her step, allowed her to refill Fred's potato-chip bowl without wanting to smash it into his skull, gave her the energy to diligently use her hair curlers before dates.

She let herself kiss and fool around with Robert more, now that she knew she was going to disappear. He was glad for it, and so was she: it was nice to be able to indulge with no strings attached, on her end, anyway, thanks to the diaphragm she'd stolen from the drugstore after her first time with Robert. She couldn't manage to care about his end.

June stepped out of the changing room, the dress swinging around her legs as she spun in a circle for Mom, who actually gasped and started clapping when June came out. "I just cannot believe my dumpy little girl has become such an upright young woman," she said. "These past weeks have been so rewarding to experience with you, June. What a change! I'm proud of you. You've grown up."

Dumpy. Homely. Lazy. Words that June didn't consciously process anymore because she was so used to hearing them from her mother's mouth.

Be a better young woman, June thought, scoffing. The girl who smiled, obeyed, picked mint-green dresses. That girl was only there to humor Mom, make her believe that she'd finally gotten the daughter that she'd always wanted, just before it would be made achingly clear to her, once and for all, that she was wrong.

The sound of her teeth grinding filled June's head, loud and grainy and violent. Her tongue got pinched in the chaos, and she tasted blood.

"Thank you, Mom," June said without skipping a beat, giving one final whirl. "So, can we get this one? First dress I tried on—what luck!"

"Of course," Mom said, rising from the cushioned store bench and straightening out her blouse. "I'll go ahead and let the nice woman up front know."

June went into the changing room, closed the door, and took the dress off, replacing it with the plain cotton housedress she'd worn there. She fluffed out her curls, re-applied her lipstick—and wondered what exactly the insides of her head would look like if somebody cracked it open. At the thought, June's breathing slowed. Her shoulders sank, her eyes widened enough to clearly show the color of her irises, and she found herself compelled to open her mouth wide and lean toward the mirror to peer into the darkness of her throat.

Suddenly, Mom was knocking on the door and asking in an unsure voice if June was all right, saying that she'd already paid for the dress and that they could leave. June straightened up, closed her mouth, rubbed her eyes and emerged. Mom said she had been knocking for close to twenty seconds without an answer.

At night, it was hard to keep still. June would stare at her typewriter from where she lay in bed, look at the shape of it in the dark silhouetted by the moonlight coming in through the window near the desk. She couldn't stop thinking about her story, seeing it in vivid scenes in her head whenever she was bored. She could not wait to work on it again, was desperate to. *Only nine more days*, she told herself every time it got especially hard to resist and she unwittingly started grinding her teeth again. *Eight days. Seven days. Six.*

She started getting stomachaches from the intensity of her feelings, and headaches, too. So many headaches.

Every night she dreamed about it, dreamed that she was in a spaceship with big windows and many creatures for crew, some of them humanoid, others not. As she drifted off to sleep the night before graduation, June imagined writing.

Day after day they hunched over her. They looked and they looked, and they communicated with one another, and she desperately wished she knew what they were saying. Because of what had happened after they let her free the last time, she was once again restrained with straps and metal clamps and invisible fields of pressure.

June would always cut herself off once she thought of a few sentences, the excitement making her heart pound. All this thinking had revealed to her the true nature of the creatures' motivations. She knew exactly how she wanted the story to end. She knew what would ultimately become of her heroine, who would soon be returned to Earth in order to fulfill her true destiny.

Just like her heroine, all through June's life there was this eternal, low buzz of knowing within herself that said she would live to become something truly great one day. The heroine didn't understand at first why the creatures had taken her away from Earth, how she could possibly end up so doomed and unlucky. She wasn't able to think beyond the circumstances, beyond the torture and the testing.

Once June arrived in New York, she could finally reveal to her heroine exactly why her suffering was so very relevant to the destiny she had always felt was hers. June knew it'd be a perfect and excellent ending.

On the morning of graduation, she rose before the sun was up and spent three hours secretly packing a suitcase for the retreat. Once done, she put it back in her closet in the place she always kept it, which she felt was the best hiding place possible—it wasn't as though it looked stuffed full. She would be leaving early the following morning.

June felt like she was walking on clouds for the rest of the day. She took a hot bath, ate the eggs and bacon and waffles that Mom had made for breakfast to celebrate her graduation, and then had ham sandwiches and potato salad for lunch. Every time Mom approached her with a mundane inquiry about anything that would be happening beyond today, June just smiled and nodded, agreeing to anything and everything, knowing she wouldn't actually be there to do it.

After lunch, she started getting ready for the ceremony, the fabric of her new dress pleasant against her skin. She powdered her face, groomed her eyebrows, put on mascara, applied lipstick. When she was finished, her parents oohed and aahed, while Fred scowled from the kitchen table, his arms crossed. June used to think that her brother hated how she was before, but from the looks of it, he wished she'd go back to irritating their parents so that he could be the golden child again.

Just you wait, June wished she could tell him as they rode in the car to the school football field. *It'll be you again after tomorrow morning.*

The ceremony began shortly, and once all the speeches were through, the principal began the roll call. June watched her classmates go up one row at a time, all the people she'd known for so many years but had never really grown close enough with to keep in touch after it was all over.

She found so many of them endearing now, especially through her new lens. She smiled along with them, waved back when someone waved to her. Maybe she'd go out with some of them after the ceremony, she thought. Maybe she could have an adventure before she took off, one last hurrah to propel her into the adulthood that was awaiting her at the bus stop tomorrow morning.

June looked to the audience and saw her family and Robert and Mr. Dennings there, which made her stomach sink. Why was Robert's father there? She didn't like his presence. It somehow felt different than business-related dinners and brandy at home. She'd been pushing herself to believe that the business her father and Mr. Dennings had created was completely safe from being destroyed by her departure tomorrow, that there were no tightly attached personal strings. After all, Robert was too much of a grown man with his own life for it to really have any lasting effect.

Right?

She had to admit, she realized as she watched Robert lift a hand to wave at her, lately the talk at the dinners had been less business-focused and more personal. Mr. Dennings had complained about his housekeeper, asked Dad's advice on which brand of aftershave to use, shared anecdotes about his dead wife, and all the adults would laugh and drink and exchange their own anecdotes. There was no way the business would fall apart just because she went on a writing retreat, right?

It doesn't matter, she told herself, waving back to Robert and shooting him a smile. *That shouldn't be for me to fret about. It's not my fault that Dad forced me to date Robert.*

Still, she could feel her feelings of invincibility deflate just the slightest bit. If the business were to somehow fall apart, it would be a massive shock to her parents and put them in a difficult spot financially.

Maybe the opposite will happen, though, June thought as her row was called to stand and make their way to line up beside the stage. *If they're such great friends, maybe Mr. Dennings would take pity on Dad, and Dad could take pity on Robert.*

"*Mary Anne Harbinson*," the principal called into the microphone, and the girl in front of June stepped onto the stage to the applause of many. She smiled, waved, held her pose as she took her fake diploma for the photographer's benefit. Then she stepped down from the platform, and it was June's turn.

"*June Ellen Hardie*," the principal enunciated.

June stepped onto the stage and walked across it with her head high, her new dress completely hidden beneath a graduation gown that flowed behind her as she went. She looked into the audience and saw her family cheering. Robert whistled. Mr. Dennings grinned and shot her a thumbs-up. June lifted a hand to them before accepting the rolled-up piece of paper bound with blue ribbon, posing for her picture and walking off. On the way back to her seat, more classmates whooped and waved than she had imagined would.

When she sat back down, she took a deep breath through

her nose, and told herself that everything would be okay. *You've always known, remember?* she told herself, an eerie amount of calm taking over her. *You've always known that you were meant for something great. You've always known that your life would be spectacular.*

This time tomorrow, June would be on a plane, soon to land in New York.

When the ceremony came to a close, everybody threw their hats into the air. June made a wish, threw hers as hard as she could, then watched as it flew high enough to get stuck on one of the cottonwood branches that loomed over the edge of the field. June smiled at the sight of the hat, then turned and strolled back toward the parking lot, through the sea of students hugging family members and each other.

"Hey, June!" A girl called Esther waved frantically from where she sat on top of the backseat of a beat-up white convertible. "Joanna Volpe is throwing a massive party at her parents' lake house! Wanna come along? We can give you a ride!"

Esther and June had always been friendly—they'd met in elementary school and had had several classes together though junior high and high school. A few other girls were piling into the car, and a few guys, too. June imagined drinking liquor at the party, dancing with all those other girls, maybe even convincing them all to jump into the lake naked with her. The memories would last a lifetime, as memories were supposed to. It'd be the perfect way to spend her last night in town.

She smiled at Esther and took a step toward the car, but stopped when someone grabbed her by the arm from behind.

"Where're you going?" Robert's voice was casual, but

his grip was strangely snug. "I've been trying to find you. Your mother made a cake and wants us all to go to your house to eat it."

June's head whirled with different ways she could say there was no way in hell that she'd be going back to her house to eat cake instead of Joanna's party at the lake house. She felt like the best option was just to leave, here and now, and just deal with getting yelled at by her parents when she came home. Then they'd send her off to bed, go to sleep themselves, and when they woke up, she'd be gone.

"Oh, Robert!" June said sweetly, looking into his eyes while she pulled her arm back. "My mother must have forgotten. I already told her before we came to the ceremony that I would be with my friends tonight to celebrate. I'm sure she'll remember if you just go remind her."

"Come on, June!" Esther cried out excitedly, reaching out with her hands, her fingers wiggling. "Let's go!"

June stepped toward the car, and then Robert's hand gripped her arm once again, this time even tighter. June winced and looked back at him in surprise; his face was still as relaxed as ever.

"I'll meet you there!" June called to Esther, and the boy behind the wheel of the convertible pulled out, all of the passengers launching into their high school's fight song.

"Robert," June said, turning toward him. "I'm sorry if you assumed we would be together tonight. It's just that I've already made plans!"

"Who would you rather spend a night like this with?" Robert's voice was flat but loud. "Your family and the people who love you the most, or some shameless punks you never seemed to care about until tonight?"

Who was he to talk about her life as if he actually understood it? He knew nothing. June noticed there were a few people looking at them, giggling behind their hands, whispering into each other's ears as they took in Robert and his suit and his hair that was slicked to the side.

"Let's talk about this someplace else," June said, dipping her head. She dragged him by her own arm to the side of the building. "I'll be going to the party tonight, and can celebrate with all of you tomorrow night. Aren't you and your father coming to dinner anyway, since it's Saturday?"

Without any warning, Robert shoved June up against the brick wall, her skull connecting hard enough to make her teeth click.

"June," he said with a light little chuckle, his eyes sparkling. "I appreciate your lust for life, but take it from me. It'd be a much better choice for you to come on home with me."

June's eyes stung. She was ashamed to realize that she was trembling. How dare a pitiful piece of shit like Robert take the upper hand with her? *Move away*, she begged herself. *Rip your arm out of his stupid little hand, and then punch him hard enough to break his nose.*

She couldn't, though. June didn't know if it was because she didn't want to cause a ruckus enough for someone to call the police, or if it was because despite the shove against the wall and the death grip he currently had on her arm, Robert appeared to be perfectly calm, *jolly* even. In the end, June supposed it was because she was scared.

"Okay," she said, forcing the corners of her mouth upward. As she spoke, she gently pulled her arm out of his grip. "Let's go, then."

June would forget about the party, forget about her vision of the perfect last night in town, follow along with everyone else's plans this one last time in order to keep the peace. If it wasn't for the packed suitcase and bus ticket waiting for her at home, June wondered if she'd be able to stand living through even one more day of this life. She didn't think she could. The realization chilled her.

Almost free.

Robert chatted all the way home as usual, and as usual June didn't listen to any of it, only remembered to nod or *mmm-hmm* every few seconds to keep him satisfied. The back of her head was sore from where it'd hit the brick wall, the wrinkles (*scars?*) beneath her eyes felt warm and unpleasant. At home, everyone was already waiting, happier than June could understand. It would seem that the occasion was more momentous to them than to June.

Still, she forced herself to go along with it, to eat a piece of the lemon buttercream cake that Mom had made, the top garnished with candied lemon peel and sliced almonds. She drank hot tea without sugar, but didn't blow on it before gulping it, so she burned her tongue and throat. But still, her face beamed.

"Oh, I know!" Mom cried out happily after four cocktails, her lips bright red from the maraschino cherries, her face flushed from the drink. "Let's play charades!"

"That sounds swell," June said, wishing she could stand and turn over the coffee table with a guttural scream, throw things in their faces, slap them and scream. "How should we choose the teams?"

The telephone started ringing from Mom and Dad's room, barely heard over the drunken whoops and laughs coming from Mr. Dennings. Dad barked at Fred to answer the telephone and clapped a hand on June's shoulder for the tenth time that night. "We should have the kids on one team and us more experienced folk on the other," he said, and Mom agreed.

June moved over to sit next to Robert, leaving a space for Fred on her other side. Robert set his hand on the small of her back, and she wondered if he could feel her recoil. If he did, he didn't move his hand away.

"I wonder who's calling?" Mom asked, impatient to begin. June sometimes suspected that her mother was able to feel more useful playing charades than doing most things in her life, based on how enthusiastic she was about the game. In fact, she had such a competitive spirit about it that June always hoped to end up on the opposite team.

"Fred, tell whoever it is that it's a family night and that you're busy!" Dad bellowed into the hallway leading to the dark bedroom. A few seconds later, Fred appeared, his eyes alive with excitement.

"Sit down already," Mom urged, pointing to the empty space beside June. "We're going to begin."

"But the phone call…" Fred said, and went to whisper something in Dad's ear. June watched her father's face fall from its drunken high as her brother spoke. After a moment, he put his hand up to stop Fred and stood, everyone watching curiously.

"So sorry, Stewart and Robert," he said, putting his drink down on the coffee table. "It looks like we're going to have to cut the night short."

June felt Robert's hand stiffen on her back.

"Is everything okay, Bill?" Robert's dad asked, looking concerned. "Can I help?"

Dad went to the front door and opened it. Robert rose beside June, taking his hand away at last, but she didn't even notice, since all she could think about was how Fred had looked at her when he'd first come out of the bedroom, and how Dad had refused to look at her after the initial stare when Fred had started whispering in his ear.

"Thanks, Stewart," Dad said, a pained smile on his face, "but everything's fine. Just a bit of a family issue to be discussed privately."

You've been caught somehow. He knows about New York.

She had been so careful! She'd intercepted not just the acceptance letter, but the additional information that had been mailed to her, even the bus ticket and flight itinerary that had come in a third letter. June hoped with all her heart that it was news of a relative's death instead, but then she realized that Fred's face wouldn't have been flush with excitement like it was. She thought about how irritated Fred had seemed whenever Mom or Dad had praised her in the past few weeks.

As soon as Robert and his father were gone, Dad shut the door, locked it, then picked his drink back up from the coffee table. After gulping down what was left, he stared at the glass in his hand for a moment, turning it slowly as if it were a kaleidoscope.

"Well, what on earth is it?" Mom demanded, clearly upset at the lost opportunity to play charades. "What was so important that it couldn't wait?"

"That was the bus station that called," Dad said, and the pit in June's stomach became a cannonball. "They wanted to let June know that her ride to the airport was going to be delayed by a half hour."

days past

WHAT FOLLOWED WAS A RUSH OF PURE AND total agony. June felt everyone's eyes on her, studying her quizzically. Maybe if she was very, very careful about how she handled this, it could still work somehow. Maybe if she convinced them to let her go…

"What do you mean *the airport*?" Mom asked, confused. "June's never even been on an airplane before."

June returned Fred's stare, narrowing her eyes in a way that she hoped told him how much she despised what he'd done. If he'd just kept his stupid mouth shut, if he'd tried to pull June aside privately and let her explain before telling their parents, if he'd taken *two goddamn seconds* to realize that letting her go would have meant giving himself all the space in the world to be the favorite child…

"I haven't," June said. *Careful, careful.* "But I'll be getting on one tomorrow."

"But to where?" Mom wailed at the same time that Dad yelled, "Over my dead body!"

The lines beneath June's eyes burned and burned. "I applied for a scholarship," she started. "For a—"

"College?" Dad roared, throwing his glass down, which landed with a heavy thud on the carpet. "You were going to disappear to college without thinking to talk to your Mom or me about it? I already told you, June, you don't need college. You have no use for it!"

"No, it wasn't—" June tried to correct, but was cut off again when Dad went on a rampage about honor and respect and the fact that June totally lacked either of those things (*"Either* of them!"). In her mind, there was a curious tingling feeling, like a hand made of bees had come down slowly to rest over the soft, pulsing tissues of her brain.

The very air in the house smelled different. She was suddenly aware of the stars in the sky on the other side of her ceiling. She just as suddenly realized that she wasn't going to be going to New York after all.

She would not be living in a retreat cottage, drinking and napping and going for walks, away from all the stupid little people in her stupid little life. She would not be finishing her book late one night, would not cry and dance and lie on her roof until the sun came up. She would not be meeting anyone who knew how to go about getting published.

"You were going to disappear?" Mom repeated clumsily, grasping to understand the concept. Just moments ago her drunken state had given her pep, but now it weighed her down, made her mouth hang open, made her face pitiful and ugly. "June Ellen Hardie."

"It would have been okay," June said and realized that

she had been crying for a long time, her cheeks cold and soaked. "I would have come back."

"How dare you?" Dad asked and went across the room with a sudden movement that made her jump. "Robert didn't know about your plans, did he? He would have lost you just like the rest of us."

Lost you, as if her presence in their lives was something that was even close to necessary, as if their minor disruption could ever compare to her enormous freedom and the potential that would come with it. They were just used to getting what they wanted, how they wanted it. To consider her feelings fully would be an empty and uncomfortable task.

"I think I should go to bed now," she felt herself say. "Could we please talk about this in the morning?"

"Give me that bus ticket." Dad's voice was deadly. "Now."

June walked halfway up the stairs, then looked over her shoulder and gave them all a glance. Mom looked like she was about to be sick in multiple ways. Dad looked like he was about to have a heart attack from rage. Fred looked stunned.

"Fuck you, Fred," June said, then went up the rest of the stairs.

She cut the sound of Mom's gasp and Dad's barking with her bedroom door. As soon as it closed, she paced her room madly, her hands on her head as she considered wildly what to do next. She could leave now, right now; she could take the bus ticket and sleep at the station until her ride came; she could hop the plane and leave no trail for them to follow.

Dad would know where to find you. He'd have police swarming that bus station well before yours even pulled up.

June went to the closet, opened it, and stared with the heaviest of hearts at the suitcase tucked carefully in its place. She lifted it out, laid it on her bed, thumbed the latches. Resting directly on top of her story, which was bound with oversize rubber bands and nestled among a packed array of clothes and shoes and candies, was the bus ticket that had been sent to her from the people at the writing retreat.

June laughed out loud then; she hadn't even gotten to tell her family that it wasn't college she was leaving them for, that it was her book. The difference would mean nothing to them. It was all the same.

June's door opened, and Dad came in. Without hesitation, he went to the bed and snatched the bus ticket up from the open suitcase, glaring at it before tearing it into pieces. Then he went for June's story, and it was then that something in her broke with a cold hard *snap.*

"Put that down!" she screamed and ripped it from his hands. She hugged it close to her, backed into the corner, sunk down into it. She was vaguely aware of her head hitting the wall as she thrashed about, sobbing, shrieking, totally out of control and a stranger to her own body. She would never grow up to be her own person. Just a shell, always on display, always expected to be better. Stuck.

Be a better young woman.

"June, Jesus!" Dad cried, and took her by the shoulders to shake her, the second time that night a man had caused her teeth to click. "Stop this! What's happening to you right now? I'm going to get your mother. Just shut the hell up, for God's sake. The neighbors are going to think we're murdering you!"

Then her mother was there, a cool hand patting June's bare foot. June did not remember taking her shoes and

stockings off, did not remember how she'd got from the corner of her room to the bathroom, vomiting into the toilet as the lights flickered overhead.

"What a time for the bulb to go out," Mom murmured, and June realized for the first time that she was completely silent. When had she stopped screaming?

"My story," June croaked, cringing at the flickering bulb, hating how even when she closed her eyes she could still see it. There were magnets in her head again.

"It's on your desk, June," Mom scolded. "No need to get hysterical again."

By the time June's breathing slowed, the lightbulb was no longer flickering. When she felt up to it, she sat up, her mother sitting silently beside her, appearing much more sober than earlier. "That," Mom said in all seriousness, "was not okay."

"I'm sorry—"

"You're not," Mom snapped, putting her finger over June's lips. "You're not sorry for applying to college under our noses. You're sorry that you got caught."

"It wasn't even college, Mom. It was a writing program."

Mom gave a shrill little laugh then. "Oh, it was a *writing program*, and that's supposed to—what?—make me forget that you've become a liar and a deceiver and someone with absolutely zero regard for anyone's feelings other than her own?"

June rested her head in her hands.

"And that *fit* you had," Mom went on. "You don't feel like answering for your own mess, so you resort to the most childish of reactions, screaming and thrashing. It was so selfish, June. You've always been selfish. Except..." She trailed off, and June's breath caught in her throat.

"Your recent change," Mom said, straightening up as if realizing something. "All the times you cooked and cleaned without complaining, all the help you've been offering, all of your sweet talk about Robert. None of that was real. You knew you were leaving. You've been planning this for weeks!"

She stood, stepping away from June in disgust. She looked down at her daughter, her arms crossed. "I don't even know who you are, June. I need to talk to your father about all of this. Your little outburst sure has put things on hold here. How convenient for you."

"Mom," June said. She struggled to keep her voice from breaking, and had to take a slow breath in through her nose before continuing. "You do know me. You just don't like me."

Mom turned and left June's bathroom. A few seconds later, June heard the door to her bedroom close.

After a few minutes passed, June stood and shambled out of her bathroom. The first thing she saw was that her manuscript was indeed sitting on her desk, disheveled as all hell. She went to it and let out a tiny cry as she gathered the papers into her hands, straightening them out as best as she could. She noticed a smear of dried blood on the title page—had she been cut without remembering? She inspected her arms and hands without result, only for her fingertips to discover a streak of something dried and crusted over below her nose.

She must have had a nosebleed at some point, June realized as she looked into the vanity mirror and saw that the dried crust was red. She almost looked dead, with all the blackness of her mascara staining the skin around her eyes, and her lipstick smeared. Her perfectly set curls had been torn into a wild, dark mess.

The dress that had fit wonderfully earlier in the evening now felt tight in all the wrong places, an unforgiving meat casing of pastel green and chiffon. June peeled it off and put on a nightgown that her mother had always compared to a potato sack. She washed her face in the bathroom.

"I'll still finish it," she whispered to herself after she was done, holding the stack of papers to her chest again as she rocked side to side. "I'll still write the end."

For a moment June considered changing the ending, keeping the heroine away from Earth forever, making her suffer unspeakably before killing her in a long and undignified way. She waited and waited for her parents to come back into her room, but they never did, and at three in the morning June stupidly realized she was the only one awake in the house. Finally, she unpacked her suitcase and turned off the lights.

No, she decided as she drifted off to sleep at last. She remembered abruptly that she had graduated high school just hours ago. *She'll go back to Earth like I originally planned. She still has to fulfill her destiny. Even if she wanted to escape it, she couldn't. It's fate.*

And oh, what a marvelous bloodbath that fate would turn out to be! Her heroine would certainly have earned it by then.

The next morning, June awoke to both parents standing in her room, studying her like an insect under a magnifying glass. Her stomach sank.

"It's nearly noon," Mom said, unimpressed. Gone was the disheveled drunkenness her mother had radiated last night, replaced with a polished bun, and clean sweater, dress, and slippers. "You've had long enough to sleep."

"We've had a chance to talk about all the choices you made," Dad started, and June's stomach sank even further than it already had. "Needless to say, you are going to be grounded for a very long time."

"I'm already grounded," June mumbled. "I always have been, haven't I?"

Without warning, her mother reached forward and slapped her on the face. "You will *quit it* with that sass," Mom sputtered, her face red. She looked simultaneously embarrassed. June was glad.

"There are no words to even begin to describe how much of a disappointment you've become to us," Dad said, and turned away from June to stare out the window. "I will never be able to forget your betrayal of this family."

Did it all have to be so dramatic? Was anyone surprised, *really* surprised, that the oddball child with a penchant for everything out of the ordinary would attempt to, say, live her goddamn life? From the looks on their faces, yes, they were surprised. Apparently June had done a really fantastic job at pretending. She had a flashback to the night with the poodle skirt, the night she had tried to break up with Robert and failed, and wanted to vomit again.

"I want you to consider what Stewart Dennings would have done had you disappeared this morning as planned," Dad said, but instead June considered where she'd be at this exact moment had she made it. She'd surely be waiting at the airport by now, sipping an ice water while she nervously tapped her foot, scared to death at the prospect of her first flight but out-of-her-mind excited to board.

"I'll tell you what he would have done," Dad went on

after it was clear June didn't plan on answering. "He would have assumed that all of our kindness thus far was to sucker him into going into business. He would have thought that your dating Robert was all a big ploy."

It was, June yearned to say, but didn't fancy the idea of another slap on the face from Mom. *That's exactly what it was, and you know it.*

How he could sit here like this and talk down to her as if his hands were clean astounded June. She steeled herself not to let them get the best of her, not to let them make her cry because she knew the moment she started to tear up, she'd be accused of trying to manipulate. As if they knew when she was manipulating and when she wasn't.

June changed her mind, then, about what she said to Mom the night before. Maybe neither of her parents really knew her at all. Was that her fault? Theirs?

"You could have ruined our entire lives," Dad said. Mom was crying now. June wished she'd just shut up already. "You're going to spend a whole lot of time in here thinking about what you've done. Figure out how to turn it all around and get it together, June. This is the last time I will allow something major like this to go by without consequence."

June remembered her fit the night before, how she'd lost control, lost time. The flickering light that had given her a headache. Mom calling her selfish and hysterical. *Without consequence*, she repeated slowly in her brain. *Bullshit.*

She wouldn't meet their eyes and, after a few moments, Mom and Dad left. Mom lingered for just a moment before closing the door behind her. "You're going to stay in here until you come around," she said sadly. June thought about when they'd made the meat loaf together and felt a stab of regret. "You have a bathroom, and I'll bring you lunch and dinner. No visitors. There'll be nothing to do but think about what you've done."

And then the door was closed, and June was alone. But she wasn't really, because there in the corner of her bedroom was her desk, and on top of her desk was her typewriter. Wiping her eyes with a little whimper, June got out of bed and went to it.

Now, maybe, she thought to herself as she inserted the most recent page back into the typewriter carriage, *maybe having to exist in a single room forever won't be too awful of a thing.*

the institution

"WHAT DID YOU SAY?" JUNE ASKED NURSE JOYA, who had popped her head in after lunch to relay a message to June.

"I said," the nurse answered, her eyes glittering in excitement, "that there's someone here to visit you. Let's go."

A visitor? June had never heard of any of the other girls getting visitors. She was desperate to know what Eleanor would think of the whole thing, but Eleanor was in the bathroom washing up. June wondered if Nurse Joya had deliberately waited until she knew June was alone.

"A few visitors, actually." Joya led the way through one of the never-ending hallways that spider-legged out from the recreation room. "But we're still unsure whether it's a good idea to let you see your parents first. We'll start off with Robert, your husband."

"He's not my husband," June said through gritted teeth. "And my parents are here? With Robert?"

"That's what I said!" Joya's voice was too bright not to be either sarcastic or phony. "It said on your admission sheet that you were married to him."

June was too shocked to bother answering or correcting Joya. It had been difficult for her to even remember that they were real people these past few weeks—it was just like Eleanor had described, like a dream. She just couldn't believe that Robert and her parents were actually *here*, after weeks of what June had assumed was a hospital-imposed ban on all forms of communication from the outside world.

In fact, what if this *visitor* business was just a trick to lure her away from the main part of the building where everyone else was? Eleanor must have been beside herself by now, to return to their room only to find June missing without a trace. It was against the rules of their pact. She'd know that June had been taken. She'd be worried sick.

June wondered if Cassy had been right all along, that June's insistence on finding out what had been happening at that cursed place, even if only to gather just enough information to protect herself and Eleanor and the rest of them, was going to be her death sentence in the end. She thought of all the times nurses would stare at her wherever and whenever she was trying to convince her new friends to wake up and smell the coffee.

Maybe she'd done this to herself: death at last, after everything that she'd been through, after not growing up to do something great after all. She'd been so *sure* there was a relevant purpose for her in store, a destiny that now couldn't be further away from becoming reality.

My story, my story, I miss my story...

They walked past many doors. *More rooms?* June thought, astounded. Were there patients in them that she'd never seen before in the other part of the hospital? Nurse Joya finally stopped in front of a door that was a different shade of gray than the others.

"Here we are," she announced, swinging the door open. June flinched, ready for anything, from the doctor to a surgical table to a monster with appendages coming out of the holes in its face.

But it was only Robert after all.

He sat behind a simple table in the middle of the bare room, his hair combed and gelled to the side like it always was. He wore his work suit and was fidgeting with the edge of the sleeve. When he saw June, his eyes lit up as if they were meeting at an ice cream shop or on a park bench. He stood and went to her, drawing her into a hug, holding her close. She could smell that he still wore the same aftershave.

"Wow!" he exclaimed under his breath. "You sure have lost a good bit of weight! You look wonderful, darling."

June was absolutely goddamn speechless.

"What—what are you doing here?" was all she could manage to stammer after he pulled away. It was really him, really Robert from the outside world, from her old life, standing there in front of her. June felt like she was in some sort of science fiction simulation. Why would the hospital allow them to speak when June could expose them?

She looked back at Nurse Joya, who was watching with a thin grin. "You two have a good time catching up," she said before closing the door. To their right, June saw an unusually large mirror built into the wall. She knew, instantly, that there were people behind it watching them both, listening in. It didn't matter. She had to try, for herself and for Eleanor. This might be the only chance June would get during her time here—one last opportunity to rise up and meet her destiny like she'd always believed she would.

"Robert," June whispered after she'd sat down on the opposite side of the table. She didn't know why he'd even come to see her after they'd last seen each other at that party, the night before her admission. She figured that she'd never see or hear from him again after everything that had happened. "There is something horribly wrong with this place."

"I know it's nothing like living at home," Robert reassured her, reaching across the table to pat her hand. "But we've been happy to hear that you've made a little progress."

Progress.

"I've only seen the doctor three times," she emphasized under her breath, keeping strong eye contact with Robert, willing him not to look away. "The way they treat us in here, it's like we're animals. It's not a legitimate hospital, Robert. It can't be."

"Of course it is," Robert said. "I know it's been rough. You've been through…a lot, June. It was hard for me to understand at first, but what happened that night wasn't your fault."

The party had taken place only three weeks or so after graduation, after the night June's parents found out about the scholarship and she'd thrown a fit over Dad trying to grab her story from her suitcase. June had thought by then that her situation couldn't ever possibly get any worse than it already was. But then it had.

And everybody saw it happen.

"Please," June said, closing her eyes to try and stifle the

memories that were now front and center. "We can talk about what happened later, and I do think we should, but please, please listen to me. Girls are *dying*."

"I know you've had some challenges," Robert said sullenly. "I heard that another patient who you were close with committed suicide. Awful, just awful. You poor thing. Promise me you'll never end up that way."

The room felt warmer than it had when she first came in. June wished she had left her sweater in her room.

"Listen," he kept on. "There's something specific that I came here to tell you. Something to hold on to while you heal."

"What could you possibly tell me that will do any sort of good?" June said.

He regarded her in an almost amused way, like she was a puppy who wanted a bone, or an adorable child throwing an unconvincing tantrum. *Silly girl*, his affectionate gaze said. *Stupid girl*.

"I'm going to wait for you, June," he said, raising his voice in just the slightest. "Despite it all, everything that's happened... I still love you, and I don't blame you for anything. I know you must still love me, too. We belong together, June. We need each other..."

"Robert!" she cried, exasperated. "Please."

"And when you get out of here," he continued, hurriedly, like he'd rehearsed this in his head and was desperate to get it all out, "I'll be waiting for you."

"I'm not *going* to get out of here, Robert." The lump in her throat was making it hard to talk. "That's what I keep trying to tell you, what you fail to understand. This isn't the sort of place that helps people! They're never going to let me out if you don't do something. Have me forcibly

217

removed, have my parents sign me out—surely they can do that, can't they?"

Get me out of here, get me out of here, get me out of here…

"Oh, but…" Robert looked like he didn't know what to say. "Um, they wouldn't want to do that. Sign you out, I mean. You're…not quite better yet. They told us about your progress, though, and that's great. It really is."

"Better," June repeated then exhaled, incredulous. "What does that even *mean*, you idiot? Did you hear me say that in all these weeks I've only seen a doctor three goddamn times?"

"Your hysteria…" Robert knit his eyebrows together, and his mouth thinned. "It's taken over you, completely. Your parents admitted that you had some sort of fit leading up to the party, some sort of breakdown over wanting to leave town for a writing retreat. We think it all may have been building up for quite some time, maybe even before that."

June thought of the period she'd been locked up in her room after her parents discovered her plan. She thought of how bad she'd felt, how bad she'd acted. *It was natural to be so upset,* she told herself for the millionth time. *Nobody would have been able to handle such a situation with grace and dignity.*

"I don't blame you for what happened," he said again. "Even though you must think everyone does…"

"Of course they do," June shot back, rising a little bit but keeping her hands on the table. "I heard them all say it. I heard you say it, too."

June became hyperaware of the big two-way mirror. She realized with discomfort that she and Robert were talking about the very subject that Nurse Joya had seemed so desperate to know about during the sessions. June had tried to deny it before, but there *had* been something about what happened at the party that was a sign of something bigger.

What a brain you have, June Hardie, the monster in the tunnel had said to her. *What an absolute marvel!*

Was it possible that the hospital had set this visit up in order to get whatever it was they were looking for? Further, and a chill went up June's back at the thought, what would they do once they had the information? Once they had no more use for her?

She thought of Lauren. And Simpson.

"Listen," June said to Robert, changing her tune. "I'm really happy to hear that you'll wait for me. I'm glad you reached out and arranged this visit in order to tell me that."

"Well." Robert gave out a spiritless little chuckle. "It wasn't me that arranged it, but I'm happy that the medical personnel did."

I knew it. "Shit," June whispered.

"They just thought you might like to hear that you could come back to us one day, June," Robert said, oblivious as always. "You could come back to your family and me if you beat this thing—"

The door behind June opened, and Nurse Joya stuck her head in. "Time's up," she said sweetly. "We need to move this along if you're going to see your parents, too."

At one point in her life, June had wanted nothing more than to get away from Robert Dennings. And yet, when the nurse (*she's not a nurse*) with the perfect blond bun and the red lips was ushering him out of the room, June wanted nothing more than to go with him.

"Robert," she cried out, breathless, *"help me!"*

He gave her one last wink. "We'll be together again soon, darling. Don't you worry."

The door closed behind them and June was left alone in the room. She looked at her reflection in the mirror, saw how sweaty her face was, how wild her eyes. Trembling, she sat back down at the table and folded her hands over themselves in her lap. The emptiness weighed on her as she anticipated seeing her parents. What if it still wasn't them? What if it was still the things from the kitchen that morning? No, that couldn't be possible. She had to get out of here—she had to get out right away!

What if the things in the kitchen that morning were them all along? What if you made a mistake?

The more June thought about it, the more frantic she became, and the more she pushed herself to think her way around it until it made some sort of sense. She certainly had been going through a lot at the time. Robert's words came back to haunt her: *Your hysteria... It's taken over you, completely.* She'd never thought of herself as depressed, just miserable, which really on paper made it sound like she should have known. But even in her worst of times, she'd had things to keep her going, to give her joy and hope for better times. The stars. Her dreams.

Her story.

She had to stop herself from crying. Her parents were coming to see her. Maybe, within an hour, everything would be fine. Maybe she'd be out, maybe she'd be finding ways to get Eleanor out, and Adie and Cassy and Jessica. Had Simpson really died here? Had Lauren really been discharged? Nothing felt real anymore.

The door opened again, and June's heart caught in her throat. Nurse Joya stood to the side, propping the door open, grinning as June's mother and father stepped into the room. Mom was wearing a white dress with a green belt that June had never seen before, and Dad was wearing slacks and a polo shirt. Neither of them made eye contact with June as they scuffled to their chairs and sat. Mom looked at Dad, nervously, and he gave her knee an assuring squeeze. The nurse backed out of the room and closed the door without a word.

Then they both looked straight at June.

"Hello," Mom said, and June felt like something was off right away.

You could just be having a reaction of some kind, she reminded herself. *There's no way your parents could have somehow been taken away and replaced with something else.*

"Hello," June said, willing her lips not to quiver. "I miss you. Please take me home."

"June," Dad said softly, so softly it could not have really been Dad. Dad never spoke softly; he only barked or yelled or stayed silent. "You know we can't do that yet, honey."

"Why not?" June's eyes welled, stinging. "I understand everything that I did wrong. How I made things hard for you two, how I was a difficult daughter, how I ruined everything. I can't wait to make it up to you. Please, I can't wait to be home and cook for you and help take care of your errands and—"

"But honey," Mom said, her mouth bright with an orangey lipstick that June detested. "You're not well yet. The doctor told us all about it."

"The doctor doesn't know anything." June cast a side glance at the mirror, almost hoped the jerk was listening. "In all the time I've been here, I've only seen him three times."

"Oh, June," Dad said, disappointment lacing his still-gentle voice. "You don't have to lie to us anymore."

"Lie?"

"You've always lied," Mom explained, emoting with her hands. "You've always lied about yourself to us, about who you are and what you like. You lied about what you were going to be doing after graduation—well, you tried to anyway. You lied about feeling better. You lied about everything." She cleared her throat, cast a sideways glance at the mirror on the wall. This was when June noticed that her eyes were blue instead of green. Her mother had green eyes. This woman had blue.

"How are we to know who the real you is?" the Mom-thing went on. "Has *any* of it been authentic, dear?"

"You've always struggled," Dad said. "You've never been happy."

Her real parents had never believed that June's mood was anything significant. They had always glossed over everything, even her breakdown the night of graduation. Any upset she'd ever had was something to be controlled and reeled in and crushed, *period*. These things were no more her parents than Robert was her husband.

"Get me out of here," June whispered. "Get me out of this hospital, and I'll do whatever it is that you want."

"What we *want*, honey," the thing in the white dress said, "is to help you get better, no matter what it takes. When you're supposed to leave this place, you will."

"And Robert will be ready for you," the thing in the slacks and polo shirt added with a gentle smile. "Just keep doing well, Junebug."

It took everything in June not to scream. She nodded, fidgeting with her hands under the table. "You know," she said, licking her lips. "I don't think I feel very well. I'm very tired."

"Don't you want to know how everything is going at home?" Mom-thing demanded, a little shrilly. "You don't seem happy to see us at all. They said you'd be happy to see us."

"I am," June lied, and a tear fell down her face. She wiped it away as quickly as she could but knew they had seen it.

The door reopened then, and Nurse Joya popped her head in with that maddening grin.

"Time's up."

the institution

INSTEAD OF LEADING JUNE BACK TO HER ROOM after her parents were gone, Nurse Joya announced to June as they retraced the newly discovered hallway that her next appointment would take place immediately.

"You seem to be very caught up on how little you've seen the doctor," Joya remarked as they went through the recreation room. June saw Eleanor sitting in her usual spot with the others. When their eyes met, Eleanor looked like she could burst into tears of relief. Adie, Jessica, and Cassy all followed her gaze but didn't betray any noticeable reactions at the sight of June. "So we went ahead and bumped you right up the schedule."

June mouthed *I'm okay* to Eleanor and followed the nurse, even though she didn't feel very okay. Her parents still weren't her parents. Robert didn't seem to understand or notice anything. Nobody was going to help her get out of here—she'd have to do it all by herself somehow. She'd have to convince them. *She'd have to.*

"We're going to try something a little different today," Joya remarked as they neared the massive wooden door. "I think you'll like it."

June found that her knees were weak. What if they were going to lobotomize her? Her breath quickened as the door was opened to reveal the strangely patterned carpet and heavy furniture and wrinkled old man sitting behind the desk. The white wooden chair was in its place. Joya motioned for June to sit.

"So, today," the nurse said excitedly, perching on the side of the desk, causing the skirt of her dress to ride up above her thighs, as the doctor stared ahead, expressionless. "We're going to play a little game of sorts. It's called the Talking Cure."

June waited silently for instructions. The idea of playing anything with these two was enough to make her chest tighten. She no longer knew how she could approach saying the right thing to get out: she felt too scared that they were never going to release her, and would cut into her brain enough to mess her up for good once she spilled whatever it was they were after.

What if they're after nothing except wellness? a strange voice suggested in June's head. *What if the vision in the tunnel was truly just a drug trip? Or*—the voice got stranger, severely suggestive—*what if you're so unwell that you've been lying to yourself about everything that's happened here, as well as everything that happened in the days before you arrived? What if this entire nightmare has been a horror show of your own making? What if none of it is real and you're too far gone to ever be saved?*

June almost shook her head to get the voice to shut

up. She didn't recognize it; it wasn't like her usual internal voice. She didn't like it at all. It made her stomach feel funny, and her mind, too.

"I'm going to say a word," Joya said, and the doctor gave a faint smile. "And when I do, I need you to say whatever comes to your mind, immediately. Don't hesitate, don't think too much about it. Don't be embarrassed. We're not here to judge you, sweet pea, so please let us help you as much as we can by being honest."

"Okay," June tried to say, but her voice cracked. The vulnerability and paranoia felt like they were pulling tiny threads from June's body one at time, each causing her to fall apart just a little bit more. With this feeling came the knowledge that, at one point, a single one of those threads would become one thread too many, and would leave her split wide open and fallen to pieces on the floor.

"All right, sugar," Joya said, and looked down to the chart for just a moment. Her voice was gentle, like Dad's had been. "The first word is: *June*."

"Hardie," she said immediately. *Good job*, she told herself. *"Fred."*

"Brother," June said, again feeling like she'd given a correct answer, even though she knew there was no such thing in a game such as this.

"Eleanor."

"Love," June said, and she felt herself go red.

"Don't be embarrassed," Joya insisted. "That was good. We're just warming up here."

The doctor watched it all in silence.

"Home," Joya said.

"Not here."

"You've got that right." The nurse scribbled something on the chart. "Let's do that one again. *Home*."

"House."

"Again. *Home*."

"Upstairs."

"Again. *Home*."

"Stars."

More scribbling. The doctor leaned over to peek at Joya's notes, then nodded in approval.

"We'll move on from that one now," Nurse Joya said after she was finished. "The next word is *writing*."

June hesitated. "Fun," she settled on.

"No pauses," Joya said firmly. *"Writing."*

"Typewriter."

"Writing."

"Me."

"Writing."

"Necessary."

"Why do you feel as though it is necessary?" the doctor cut in, and Joya nodded and looked to June for an answer. "Do you feel like you have to do it? Even if it's against your own will?"

June thought about the period after her parents had grounded her to her room after graduation. She remembered how the typewriter had been her only friend, how she'd been almost manic in her love for it. She thought about how many hours she went straight without sleeping, just to write. She thought about how it used to make her cry at times.

"No," June said quietly, realizing fully that she was outing herself for having tried to lie about writing during her last appointment. She had to do what she could, she realized now. If she was lobotomized for telling the truth, maybe that's the way her life was supposed to turn out. "It just made me feel whole."

"But was it a feeling beyond you?" he pressed, looking deeply concerned. "Did you feel like there was an outside force pulling you to it?"

Yes.

"No," June said, and the nurse cleared her throat.

"The next word," she cut in, "is *God*."

"Bible."

"God," Joya said again, more harshly.

"Fake."

"God," the nurse insisted, as if June was knowingly holding something back.

"Spaceship," June blurted, bewildered at her own answer. "I'm sorry. I have no idea why I said that."

But it seemed to be the answer that interested Joya the most.

"Have you ever seen a spaceship?" the doctor interrupted again, curious. Very curious indeed.

"No," June said slowly, unsure as to whether he truly expected her to say she had. "I've written about one."

Don't tell them, don't tell them, don't tell them...

"In your story," Nurse Joya prompted, nodding eagerly. "The story you were working on when you applied for the scholarship to the writing retreat. The one you finished the night before you came here."

"Yes," June admitted, feeling like she had committed a great crime against herself. There was nothing left just for her now. She felt like a snake that had shed its skin too soon.

"What was the main character's name?" Joya said. "In your story."

"She…" June paused, thought back to the image of words appearing on white paper, the *tap-tap-tap* of each letter as her fingers hit the keys. "She didn't have one."

"She did, though," the nurse said, so matter-of-factly it chilled June's blood. Had this woman somehow gotten access to her story?

"No, she didn't," June insisted, speaking much more steadily than she had for the rest of the session. "I think I would know. I'm the one who wrote her."

Her heroine *hadn't* had a name. It was a choice June made before she even started. She thought it'd help keep things strange. And mysterious.

"She did," Joya said, her voice suddenly on edge. "I want you to say it. Out loud."

June had no idea what to say or do. What were they playing at? Were they purposefully confusing her? "I… She didn't have one!" June insisted angrily, and suddenly the trials of the day caught up with her and she swayed in her chair, light-headed. Had she really been talking to Robert only an hour ago? It didn't seem possible.

"That'll be enough for today," Joya said, and the doctor silently moved his lips along as she talked.

"What is this place?" June blurted out, over it all. Let them kill her on the spot if they needed to: she couldn't take any more. "What do you want from me? From the other girls? Was that you eating the person in the tunnel under the hospital? *Was that you with the holes in your face?*"

The nurse calmly stood from the desk, set the closed chart down, and smoothed her skirt down. "You've been seeing monsters in tunnels, have you?" she asked, *mocking*, bending down so her face was at June's level. "I wonder what that's all about."

"Let me out of here!" June screamed in her face. "Either let me out of here or kill me!"

She expected them to hold her down in the chair, call for Nurse Chelsea to bring a dose of something heavy. She was ready for it, willing for it to happen maybe, desperate to turn the lights out in her head and succumb to the peace and quiet.

"You poor thing," Joya said, making a pitying *tsk-tsk* sound with her tongue and standing up to go to the door. "It's been too much for you today, hasn't it?"

June sat in the chair, breathing hard.

"I think you should take the rest of the day to relax," the doctor suggested. "We can keep working on you another day."

Keep working on me?

"Please return to your room," Joya said, opening the door and waiting for June to leave.

So June left.

From the hallway leading to their room, she saw Eleanor, but June didn't feel up to facing the other girls right now. She didn't want them to ask what had happened, didn't want to end up screaming and raving and jumping through the window. Eleanor's eyes met June's, and then June went into their room and collapsed on the bed.

After a moment she heard footsteps approaching. The softness of the steps told her it was Eleanor in her slippers. She didn't move or open her eyes, even when Eleanor slid into bed next to her. June felt an arm snake around her side, a hand gently cradle hers. "I was so scared that they got you," Eleanor whispered, and June could hear she was crying. "I was so scared they did something to your brain."

Maybe they have, June thought to herself, still unmoving.

Her mind raced with theories and images and memories. *Maybe they should.* She let herself squeeze Eleanor's hand just the slightest, and then she let herself fall asleep.

When she woke up, Eleanor was still there. It was dark, which told June that they'd slept through dinner and through lights-out. It was so quiet that she could hear the nurse opening and closing doors for checks, somewhere very far down the hallway. There were probably ten or so minutes before their own door would open and shut with alarming intensity.

How long had June been running on disrupted sleep? Longer than she could remember. She almost felt like she was getting a little more now that she was at the institution, which was saying something considering how many checks there were each night, and how each and every one of them woke June up. The other girls had sworn that she'd get used to them, that she'd learn to sleep right through them, but that time had not yet come, and June doubted that it ever would. Still, before June had come to the hospital, she'd been getting even less rest.

"Are you awake?" Eleanor whispered.

"Yes."

"Are you all right?"

June breathed in deeply through her nose, let her feet rest against the top of Eleanor's. "I don't know."

"I've been thinking about something," Eleanor said. "I've been afraid to bring it up because it's...weird. And very possibly untrue."

"And what's that?" June seriously doubted that there could be anything more weird or untrue than their current situation.

"I had a really weird dream," Eleanor said. "After Simpson died."

June couldn't help but feel just a little bit disappointed; dreams could make lasting impressions on people, but they didn't really mean anything, did they? And June had been hoping for something to work with, anything. But she wanted for Eleanor to feel heard, so she listened.

"Oh?" June said, encouraging her to go on.

"It didn't feel like any dream I've ever had in my life," Eleanor whispered. "I stopped having dreams after I died."

June didn't know what to say. Eleanor's deadness seemed to weave in and out of relevance in a confusing and inconsistent manner. There was something not quite right about it, aside from the obvious. She suddenly remembered that Simpson had claimed to be able to speak with the dead.

"But then one night I woke up and Simpson was in our room," Eleanor went on. "You couldn't hear her. Her face was…" She didn't say anything, and June's heart skipped a beat. She thought of when she had seen Simpson's face, melted off and left red and glistening from the steam burn. But she'd never told Eleanor those details. "Her face was missing. I could see her teeth."

"What did she say?" June asked, very interested now.

"She smiled at me." Eleanor gave a weak little laugh as if she still couldn't believe it. "She said, 'I was right about them,' and she knelt down on the floor. She said that they'd found out she knew too much because of the worm in her brain. That the worm made her kill herself, against her will, but that it allowed her to visit me in the land of the dead. She pointed to a space on the wall over there…"

Eleanor sat up in bed, pointed directly to the spot where the tunnel had been during June's drug trip. "She said,

'They're looking for something. If we're here, it's because we might have it or know how to find it. And they will do whatever they can to find it first.'"

"Did she say what it was?" June asked, deeply unsettled. She had yelled in Joya's face about the tunnel before. At the time she'd felt like she had nothing to lose, but now she remembered, lying here with Eleanor in the dark, that she still did.

"No." Eleanor lay back down, crossing her hands over her chest. June turned onto her side to get a better look at her. "Just that whatever it is has the power to destroy this place."

This place, destroyed. What a wonderful vision indeed.

"There was another thing," Eleanor continued as June turned this over in her head. "She wanted me to thank you for her."

"For what?" June was almost reproved by the message. She had done nothing for Simpson. She could have done so much more.

"For not being as afraid of the truth as everyone else is. For being strong. She seemed to believe that you were going to be the first one to find the lost thing, whatever it is. She said to tell you not to let them get it, no matter what happens, or else the consequences will be more dire than any of us can comprehend."

"That is a very specific dream," June said, not knowing what else to say.

Was it real? Was it not? June couldn't know either way. On one hand, it made a sick sort of sense. On the other hand, who knew what Eleanor's brain was capable of coming up with in reaction to the death of a beloved friend?

No, June thought. *Be honest with yourself—you completely believe Eleanor right now.*

"That wasn't the end of it." Eleanor squeezed her eyes shut. "Simpson showed me a book."

"A book?"

"She said she'd stolen it from the library. That there was a library here at the hospital somewhere, but that nobody knew about it except for the staff."

June thought of the hallway she'd gone down to see Robert and her parents earlier. Was she ever going to tell Eleanor about that? She thought maybe, especially after hearing all of this, that it wasn't exactly safe to. She could tell Eleanor all about it once they escaped from this place.

The opening and closing of doors for checks were much closer now. It'd be any minute when a nurse stuck her head in.

"It was a book about illnesses of the brain." She rolled off her back, so they were facing each other on their sides. "Simpson pointed out two things. One, that there is such a thing as other people who are convinced they're dead."

"Really?" June's eyes widened. "So you're saying you understand better what's happened to you? That you're actually alive?"

Eleanor's eyes darkened. "No," she said. "But after reading all about the disease, I realized that it didn't describe me really, except for the dead thing. There are other characteristics that most all other patients shared that I don't. Big ones."

"Eleanor," June said softly, becoming overwhelmed. "You read all of that during a dream?"

"Listen to me," she urged, and June was sad to see that Eleanor's eyes were wet. She must have known how it all sounded. "After I was done, Simpson showed me a page all about people who believe their loved ones have been replaced by exact duplicates. But I'm not so sure they were quite like you either. I think…whatever's happened to us isn't as simple as a medical diagnosis."

The door to their room was suddenly thrown open. A nurse stuck her head in, mumbled, "Checks," then slammed it again. June had expected her to scold them for being in the same bed like she'd done before, but this time it was like the nurse had barely taken time to look or care. At any rate, they'd be free from interruption for a while.

"What do you think the dream was trying to tell you?" June asked after Eleanor didn't go on.

"I've been thinking," she answered finally. "What if it really was Simpson? I can't explain it, June. I know it just as much as I know I'll get to live forever because I'm dead. She came back to try and help. Whatever they're looking for…do you have any idea what it could be?"

"No," June said honestly. "I have no idea."

"Simpson said that once you find it, you'll know without any doubt." Eleanor gave a soft laugh. "To hear that you might be the one who's supposed to save this place, well…it doesn't surprise me, I guess."

June didn't like it. She didn't know what the thing was, she didn't know how she was supposed to find it, and she had no faith in herself to find it before Nurse Joya did. All she and the doctor had seemed to truly want from June was information about the party, and about her writing. Was it possible the thing they were looking for had something to do with either of those?

"Don't frown," Eleanor said, wiping a tear off June's face with her finger. "I feel so much better now that I've finally told you about the dream. You were supposed to hear it. I know that now. One last trick from Simpson."

"I don't understand," June whispered.

"I don't either," Eleanor admitted, "but I do know that you and I were meant to meet each other. Ever since you came, things have been different here. It's less cloudy, less uniform. I actually notice when days pass. I remember to think about the outside world. It's like you're the only thing that counteracts this place…"

June kissed her then. She hadn't meant to, not necessarily, but it'd been something she'd been thinking about for a while, and she couldn't stop herself any longer. Eleanor kissed her right back, and the girls found themselves nearly clawing at each other in their newfound excitement. Unable to find fulfillment with every rushed touch, they slowed down.

Eleanor's mouth opened, and June tasted the inside. She ran her hand up Eleanor's thigh, then under her dress, then up the side of her ribs and over her breast. Eleanor shivered in pleasure. They kissed luxuriously, June's hand staying where it was, her thumb rubbing over Eleanor's nipple with gentle rhythm, and soon Eleanor reached down and hitched June's leg up and over herself. They leaned into each other as they sucked and bit at each other's lips and tongues.

June couldn't help but think of the time she'd opened herself to Robert in her bedroom, what felt like lifetimes ago, and all the times they'd fooled around after that. The intimacy then had felt wonderful, just like this did, but she felt the difference almost right away in that Eleanor was somebody she cared about more than she could ever care about Robert.

If only Eleanor had been the son of Stewart Dennings, things might have turned out very different.

She felt Eleanor's hands work their way down, slipping through the top of June's panties, and June lifted her leg even more to accommodate. She felt Eleanor's fingers slip inside of her and moaned.

"Do the same to me," Eleanor whispered eagerly as she moved her fingers in and over June. And so June did. The girls worked their hands over each other, whimpering through their kisses, and June felt like she was going to melt from the ecstasy of it. Eleanor abruptly stopped kissing June's mouth and moved down her neck and chest and stomach before pulling her fingers out of June and putting her mouth there instead. June pulled her legs apart even further, lay back, and grabbed at the sheets on her bed as she writhed.

Everything bad about the world disappeared then. She peered down for just a moment, but the sight of Eleanor was almost too much to bear. June arched her back, craned her neck, and cried out as her mind exploded into stars— her favorite thing in the world: stars. She swam in them, relished the feeling of falling freely through them, not a prisoner, not a patient, just her and Eleanor in deep space.

When it was over, both girls were panting. Eleanor moved back up the bed and plopped down beside June, her bangs sticking to her sweaty forehead. "I love you," Eleanor whispered, "June the Heroine." They fell back asleep smiling.

They woke in the morning to the news that Adie was dead.

days past

JUNE QUICKLY BECAME VERY ACCUSTOMED to living solely in her bedroom and had no idea why her parents had thought it could ever be more punishing than being forced to be around them all day every day. When the sun rose each morning, June was always already awake and there to see it, sitting at her window seat and hugging her legs to her chest as she observed the birth of each new day.

She'd sit in that same position for hours, a gargoyle watching over her street, listening to morning sounds come from downstairs as everybody got up and moving. Soon, Dad would appear, walking to his car below June's window, briefcase in his hand. He never looked up though, not once.

At about seven thirty every morning, there would come a sharp knock on the bedroom door, and when June opened it there would be a tray of breakfast on the floor. She purposefully waited a minute or two before answering the knock, to ensure that she wouldn't come face-to-face with her mother. When June was finished eating, she'd set the dirty dishes just outside the door again, just as Mom had told her to.

For the first time in her life, June made an effort to keep her bedroom tidy, which surprised her a bit. She figured it was because she was cleaning it for her own benefit and not to simply meet Mom's suffocating standards. She spent her first few days in confinement straightening up and re-arranging all of the furniture, except for her desk, which she kept facing the window.

Things felt normal enough at first, but then whenever she tried to take a break from all the moving and organiz-ing, June found that her heart would race in deeply unset-tled anticipation until she went back to work.

When it was done and everything had a new place, June looked over the room, pleased, and realized that she'd been preparing a very important space: the space where she'd finally finish the story she'd been working so hard on for the past months. But she couldn't write during the day. It didn't feel right. The days were for preparing the area, and looking out the window, and writing in the diary she kept inside her left snow boot in the closet. Her handwrit-ing was very neat.

Day four of total isolation and so far it's going swell. If I have to stay home from New York after all, at least I don't have to look at any of their stupid faces. I have decided to re-claim this space as my own. I'm playing a little game where I pretend that this is my apartment, that I live in a big city somewhere, like Chicago or San Francisco or Manhattan. It's actually quite fun. Sometimes I can go for hours and hours without remembering the truth. I didn't know how I was going to live through this last night, for instance. But now I think maybe I'll be all right.

The nights were for the story. Even if she was tired from cleaning or reading or diary writing or simply doing nothing all day, June found that she wasn't able to go sleep when she wanted, even if she'd just spent four hours straight working on the story. Her typewriter would call out for her in the dark, demanding that she come place her fingers on its keys once again. So she worked into the night without any concern for whether the machine was loud enough to wake up her family. Based on the fact that nobody ever came knocking and demanding silence, it must not have been an issue like she'd previously assumed.

Only once during her time locked away, and for a brief moment, did she wonder why her parents hadn't taken away her typewriter, and her story, too, if they'd really wanted to ruin her. Maybe it was because, deep down, they knew what would happen to June if they did.

After going many days without seeing or hearing from the creatures, the girl woke up one morning back on the operating table, surrounded by six of them, only two of which were humanoid. They were communicating and gesturing around her face, which was held in place by a heavy metal vice that made her skull feel like it was about to be crushed.

June felt her eyes burn as she typed and realized she hadn't blinked in far too long. It hurt when she finally did.

She wanted to scream, her throat felt pinched and dry, and that was when she realized there was something long and metal embedded in the front of her neck, pinning her down, making it excruciatingly painful to try to move even in the slightest degree.

June wished that someone would have mercy and let her get herself some coffee. Going without it was causing headaches more awful than she would have thought possible from caffeine withdrawal. She licked her parched lips as she went on, not pausing between sentences, just letting it flow out of her like vomit on to the page.

Then she noticed that the creature closest to her, the one with long fingers that looked and moved like fleshy spaghetti noodles, was holding a shining metal tool that looked like a pointed spoon. The moment she saw it, the creature leaned over her and plunged it into the side of her eye socket.

The silence was almost as bad as the pain. Despite feeling it all, the girl was unable to scream, or thrash, or protect herself. One by one, her eyeballs were removed, again being set to rest on her cheeks as the roots were still intact. Then came the feeling, and the sound, of the other tools being used to poke around inside. Scrape. Scrape. Scraaaaaape. She was forced to lie there, still as a statue, her nose filling with the smell of warm sea water and formaldehyde as she heard the other creatures moving excitedly around her.

How many times are they going to do this to me? she wondered in her agony, wishing with all her heart that she was dead. *And why? Why? Why?*

Every night, June wrote until she was unable to lift her hands without wincing. The typewriter mechanisms were heavy and demanding, and no matter how quickly or how accurately she typed, it felt like her story was running further and further ahead without her. *Wait for me!* she'd think as her wrists screamed in pain, plunking out her last few words like an engine sputtering dead.

Even afterward, sleep didn't come. She'd lie there obsessing about what would come next on the page. "I need her to go through the procedure again," June whispered to herself, finally coming to terms with the fact that she was missing yet another night's sleep, crawling to the window seat to perch like the neighborhood gargoyle and watch the morning come to be.

Before her shower, June stood naked in front of the mirror and inspected every last inch of herself with careful and thorough eyes. She discovered a series of long red scratches on her arms and neck, nothing deep, but they were certainly noticeable. The thing was, she didn't remember scratching at herself, not while she was writing or lying awake in bed or sitting at the window. It was very peculiar indeed.

The days went on, and June's sleep-deprived condition worsened. She began to wonder how going without human contact for days would affect her. Whenever she tried to picture her family, the images her mind produced were elongated, melted portraits with gaping eyes and wide mouths, too exaggerated to be real. She dug through her closet for old photos to remind herself of their true appearances and came across an older album that she'd unearthed while cleaning. Before, she'd had no interest in looking through it, reliving her formative years. Now, in her nearly drunken state of exhaustion, it was suddenly very interesting to her.

The pictures inside the album felt like they couldn't possibly be real, even though logically June knew that she was indeed the chubby little girl in all the photos. She looked in amazement at herself licking an ice cream cone, or sitting with her feet dangling off the side of a piano bench, or standing beside Fred in matching holiday outfits that were as ridiculous as they were festive.

June realized as she was flipping through the pages that she'd been fixating on her own face. She was studying the photos to search for lines beneath her eyes. If they were there and she could see the proof before her eyes, it would mean there was no way the lines were wrinkles, unless she'd had wrinkles at age five. *As if wrinkles of that size at age seventeen are any more normal.*

Either way, the photos were too old to show any real level of detail. She could hardly tell what color her eyes were in the photos, let alone see something as subtle as the lines beneath her eyes.

What would it mean if they weren't wrinkles? she asked herself as she snapped the album shut and went over to her bed, turning off the light. Pondering the answer was far too much for her to bear, so instead she cleared her mind by once again falling into her game of pretending that the bedroom was really a studio apartment somewhere far away. She pretended it was the sound of distant sirens and people yelling joyfully in the street below that kept her awake, her eyes burning, her wrists aching terribly. Her head hurt.

She'd have her heroine go through one more procedure, gruesome enough that she would be praying and begging for death. Then, once all of her humanity was stripped away, June would have the creatures return the girl to Earth, to the exact spot where they'd abducted her, on the hill in the woods that overlooked the town. The heroine would look down upon the glittering lights of the homes below, her mouth slacked open, her eyes disbelieving what they were seeing—they'd returned her, they'd really returned her. She would take a deep breath, inhale the night air, feel the soft earth beneath her bare feet.

And then, she'd walk back to her old life, soon to become her new life. *And then,* June thought as a blissful smile crossed her face, sleep coming for her at last, at last, at last, *then she will finally be able to fulfill her true destiny.*

Finally, June slept. She dreamed that she was little again, like in the photos she'd pored over, her hair all short curls, her socks with frills. She dreamed that she was running through the woods behind her backyard, breathing heavily, running either *from* something or *for* something. Suddenly, she was up high, surrounded by pines, standing in the spot where she and Robert had parked the night of her failed breakup attempt.

June looked down, and she wasn't wearing a fancy dress with frilly socks anymore, she was wearing pajamas, the very same ones she used to wear obsessively when she was ten years old. She was also barefoot, and her feet hurt from being scraped open from running around outside. There came an overwhelming feeling that she should be looking for something. She looked to the sky to find it.

There, in the distance but not as far away as a high-flying airplane, hovered a strange, glowing orb. June's chest swelled at the sight of it, with both fear and the unmeasurable urge to reach out and touch it. She waved at it, and instantly the light started blinking, as if waving back. *They see me!* she thought with raw excitement. *My friends!*

But then there was a sound from somewhere in the woods beside her, a sound of wet crunching and ripping and tearing, a sound that reminded June an awful lot of somebody shucking corn. She looked toward the sound, squinting to see better, and was able to make out some sort of enormous animal in the bushes nearby, shuddering and jolting as it ripped apart whatever was in front of it.

June didn't know what the huge animal in the woods was exactly, but it was too big to be a bear, and she had no idea what sort of animal around here would be bigger than a bear. She knew that if it saw her, it'd rip her to pieces, too. Helpless and nearly paralyzed with terror, June looked quietly back to the blinking light, reaching her hands toward it. *Please save me!* she begged it in her mind, desperate not to get killed by the big animal. *Please take me away from here and help me to never be afraid for myself again.*

The crunching sound stopped, as if the thing could hear June's thoughts. She tore her eyes away from the blinking light only to see the creature making its way toward her, slowly, as if on the prowl. When it stepped into the moonlight, she saw that it was not an animal at all.

It was a monster.

June opened her eyes. She was on her back in bed, and the room was flooded with daylight. She'd slept through the night, at last, although now there was a pressing, guilty panic that she hadn't written anything. She'd try this afternoon, perhaps, rather than waiting until night. The only deadline was her own, but at the same time, it was important to meet it. June had the feeling that as soon as she finished her book, her *real* story could begin, the story of whatever it was in this life that she was meant to do.

She didn't know why she felt so sure that something big was coming, but she did, as much as she felt sure that she'd find a way to escape this place someday, to somewhere better and more productive.

June opened the bedroom door, and the plate of food that was waiting for her looked as though it'd been there for at least a few hours. She ate it eagerly anyway, the cold sausages, the cold toast. When she was finished, she went to her closet to retrieve her diary from the left snow boot.

I had a nightmare last night, she wrote after filling in the date. *It felt more real than almost any dream I've ever had. My heart still races at the thought of it.* Thoughtful, she bit at the end of her pen, before adding in a shaky hand, *Thank goodness monsters aren't real.*

She closed the diary and rehid it, refusing to add what she suspected to be the truth: that, even though monsters weren't real, deep down in the depths of her most powerful instincts, she felt like the entire point of the dream was to let her know that yes, in fact, they were.

days past

ON THE NINTH DAY OF HER CONFINEMENT, Dad came into June's bedroom without knocking and sat on the bed, which June had just made. She saw him look around, taking in the newly arranged furniture, and dared to wonder if he would compliment her on her cleanliness.

"It smells in here," he said, his lip curling, and June went to open the window. "Like something metallic, some sort of chemical."

June resisted the urge to put her nose to her underarm. "I don't smell anything," she said.

"You wouldn't. You're in here all the time," Dad said, then seemed to remember what he was doing in his disappointing daughter's room. "Listen, there's something we need to go over. And before I even start, don't be interrupting me with your crying or your eye rolling. Believe me when I say that I've had enough of that shit from you,

June. I have had enough, and I will not stand for it any longer. All of that from before, it ends now. You are here, and you have a duty to become a responsible young woman like your mother and I taught you to be."

June said nothing.

"Well?" Dad barked. "Is that understood, little lady?"

"What is it you were going to tell me?" June answered, her insides devoid of any emotion. With all the dreams she'd been having the last few nights, she hardly even understood that this was reality. How could she get so much sleep at night lately but wake up feeling even more exhausted? She didn't understand it. June was scared by how the world felt—nothing felt how it was supposed to.

"Robert took me out for a drink after work the other day," Dad started, and June's fingers curled into her palms, the deadness inside warming painfully to life. "He was decent enough to ask me for my blessing, to ask for your hand in marriage."

June stared, unblinking. "Marriage," she repeated without meaning to. Robert, that little prick. He'd promised June not to bring that up again until she was ready. How could he think she'd go for this?

"What did you say?" June asked, fearing the answer.

Dad looked at her as if she were dim. "I told him that you had confided in me that you were waiting for him to ask," he said, and rage filled her like hot air. "What could you ever hope to have in a husband that Robert doesn't have? He's got a good job, June. He'll take care of you and your children. And of course Stewart—"

"I don't care at all what Stewart thinks," June yelled, surprised at herself. "I don't want to marry Robert!"

Dad rose and stood over her and crossed his arms. "You

listen to me very carefully," he said. "You have shown us that you have absolutely no right to make your own decisions. You need to learn that your mom and I want what's best for you."

"You want what's best for *you*!" June interjected, and the pulsing vein on his neck made her lower her voice. "You want what's best for the business."

"I want what's best for everybody," Dad said, and paced back and forth in front of June. "I thought all this time alone in here would help you come around. Maybe you need some more."

"Please," she said, a little too drily. "Let me live in here forever if you're not going to let me do anything worthwhile with my life."

"How dare you imply that starting a family isn't worthwhile?" Dad cried out. "How would your mother feel if she heard you talk so poorly of her life? You wouldn't be around in the first place to whine and complain if we hadn't decided to make you, to bring you into our family."

"Maybe you shouldn't have," she said, and while Dad didn't slap her, he did stop pacing and, with a dangerous silence, reached forward to grab her chin and tilt it up so she was looking at him in the face.

"You're going to do this," Dad said. "You've lost the privilege of making your own choices. You'll thank me when you're older and happy as a clam with your husband and children, in a nice big house that has all the modern appliances a housewife could ever want. Hell, June! You'll probably even be able to afford for someone else to keep the place clean for you, since we all know how limited your skills are in that area."

June thought she should cry and scream, but she was

horrified at how still she was on the inside once again. It scared her. She wondered if she'd died sometime during her grounding and just didn't know it yet.

"Now," Dad went on, satisfied at the silence. "There's to be an engagement party for you and Robert."

"What?" June couldn't believe it. "How is that possible? I haven't even said *yes* yet! He hasn't even asked me face-to-face!"

"He will in the next few days," Dad said. "Robert is very eager to see you. He's under the impression that you've been fighting off a nasty stomach flu all this time. Is your head right enough to come out, June, or does the flu need to come back for another wave?"

"You can't make me," she whispered. "As soon as I'm eighteen, I can leave and never come back."

"Never mind the fact that you don't have a penny to your name that would allow such a thing," Dad said. "If you don't do this, I'll destroy that typewriter of yours. You'll never get another one. And I'll burn that story you're so keen on."

That got her, and he knew it. Her entire demeanor changed then: she went from emotionally dead and disbelieving to truly understanding. This was her life. Tears made her eyes feel heavy. The lines beneath them burned. From where she sat, she could see her story stacked clumsily on the desk.

"I can't stress enough how important it is that Stewart and Robert never suspect you're unhappy in any way," Dad went on, and June couldn't believe his nerve. "If there is one thing on this earth that Stewart refuses to take quietly, it's being duped. He has the power to take everything away from this family."

June realized for the first time that she didn't even know the details about what Dad's and Stewart's business was, or how it worked, or why. It'd never been discussed in front of her and Mom. She had no way to know if her father was exaggerating or underplaying Stewart's supposed ruthless side. She couldn't personally imagine him getting upset enough for it to make any real difference if she were to break up with Robert. He never seemed like the type to blow his top.

But then June remembered how Robert had shoved her into the brick wall at the school after graduation, caused her teeth to click together and the back of her head to hurt. How, before that moment, she'd thought herself silly for ever thinking he could be a threat.

"Don't you love me, Dad?" June asked, earnestly. She reached forward, took his big clenched fist and wrapped her hands around it. "Don't you care at all if I'm happy? I'm your daughter!"

Dad's face relaxed, and he sat down beside June on the bed. "Ah, Junebug," he said, still with too much of an edge to be considered gently. "Of course I do. That's why I have to do this for you, even if you don't understand it. I'm making sure you'll be happy, honey. You've always been so dramatic, your mother always says that, but I never really understood what she meant until recently. You love to act as though it's the end of the world for you, when really it's just the beginning."

"I love to act…" she repeated, her voice cracking, barely above a whisper. "You have no idea what happiness even is, Dad. And especially not for me."

He became rigid, pulled his hand back and stood. "You'll thank me one day," he said, walking out without another word and leaving June to her new room and her story and her open door. She was officially free from the isolation. *Nine days*, June thought in wonder. *It feels like it's been closer to a hundred.*

"June," Mom called from downstairs, as if none of this had even happened. "Your date will be here at seven tonight. Make sure to have a bath, and roll your hair first, dear!"

June ran a bath and sat in it for four hours. She spent the time thinking, allowing herself to sink into the tub as if she were a part of it. The only thing that moved were her eyes, following the bubbles as they rolled across the surface of the water before eventually thinning out and disappearing. She breathed out hard, hoping to expel some of the poison she felt inside. When she became light-headed from it, she still felt like she was rotting from the inside out.

She didn't roll her hair into curlers when she came out. She didn't put on any lipstick. She didn't smile at Mom and Dad when she came down the stairs, didn't make eye contact with Fred in fear that she'd kill him with her bare hands. This was all his fault, really, if you looked at it a certain way. June decided that it was much more Fred's fault than her own. Yes, that was better.

Robert looked shocked at June's appearance only momentarily when he arrived. "That flu really took it out of you, huh, kiddo?" he said with disgusting concern, taking it upon himself to push a lock of hair back from her forehead with his finger. "We can just do something low-key tonight, get a few bottles of ginger ale, and maybe rent a rowboat at the park."

June saw Mom's eyes sparkle as she slipped Dad a knowing look, and June realized that Robert would be proposing to her tonight, on a rowboat where she wouldn't be able to go anywhere. She looked at Dad, who seemed to be waiting to give her a quick little wink as he set his hand on her back, leading her to the door where Robert stood with his hand extended.

"Have a great time tonight, kids," Dad said. "Well, I guess I shouldn't call you kids anymore, not with this girl fresh out of high school and ready for next steps!"

June looked back over her shoulder at her father, and the sight of her face caused his to falter just in the slightest.

"Is everything all right?" Robert asked once they were in the car. "You seem...off."

June looked over at Robert, an unnaturally wide smile awakening on her face. "What could be wrong?" she said, her voice high.

He smiled back, a little nervously if June was seeing things right. It gave her pleasure to see him in discomfort. She spent the rest of the drive imagining being his wife. She could mix trace amounts of laxatives into his morning coffee, she could rub some cooking oil onto the edge of any stairs in their house. She could use a needle to poke holes through the soles of his shoes so his feet would get wet every time it rained. She could pretend that cooking was her entire pride and joy, and then purposefully make things that were bland and off, rotten ingredients eaten with a smile.

If she had to be a wife, June told herself, feeling at least a touch of comfort at last, that was exactly the kind she would be. She would stop brushing her teeth. She would eat with her mouth open. She would drink in the daytime and pass gas in restaurants and let their dirty stupid children wander into the street to play. At these thoughts, June smiled a little, and Robert instantly put his hand on her knee.

"We're here," he said, and June realized that the car was parked.

They were just down the street from the park, and they could buy the ginger ales at the drugstore on the way. June held Robert's hand and said nothing, letting him pull her around this way and that, having no reaction to anything he said. But of course he took no notice, just kept talking and talking about things that made June want to die from boredom. She picked a cherry cola instead of a ginger ale, but Robert gently took it from her hand and put it back.

"That'll upset your stomach," he said with a little laugh. "The ginger will help—it really will."

Her fingers itched to break the bottle over his head and then cut his throat with it, or her own. Either would be satisfying.

"Thank you," she said sweetly, her unnatural smile beginning to make her face ache. "You are just the smartest man alive, Robert. The greatest to ever live. How did I ever become so lucky as to have you as mine?"

He laughed it off, but June could see that flicker of discomfort that she was hoping for. She let it wash over her heart, a grim and beautiful pleasure, and she let herself become hungry for more.

Later, once they were in the middle of the pond and the soda bottles were empty, Robert asked June if she would marry him. "Your dad already said it's okay," he finished with, as if that would somehow blow away everything they'd said about it in the past. June wondered if he knew that her parents were already planning the engagement party. She wondered if he had anything to do with it.

June gave a cold and quick nod, grabbing the ring out of his hands and putting it on herself. It was so much lighter than she could have imagined. If she were to strike somebody with her fist, though, it'd cut the skin right open. Then she crossed her arms over herself in the cold, sniffed, and mentioned that her stomach was beginning to hurt again.

"I think I just remembered," she said as he pulled the rowboat up to the pond's dock. "I'm allergic to ginger."

"What a thing to forget!" Robert exclaimed, wrapping his arm around her as if she needed help making it to the car. "You should lie down right away, darling."

Darling. She despised the word more than any other she could think of.

When they got back home, June's parents were waiting there with Stewart. They threw confetti and popped champagne and started discussing the details for the upcoming engagement party. It sounded like they were going to be putting a great deal of money into it, inviting a whole lot of people from the business, since Robert worked for his father. Every time June tried to imagine what it might feel like to have a party that fancy thrown in her honor, there was a funny magnetic pull in her head that made it feel like there was a needle lodged in her brain.

After the celebrating was over and Stewart and Robert went home and Mom and Dad had gone to bed drunk, June retreated to her room and dug her diary out of its hiding place.

Tonight I was pledged to become Mrs. Robert Dennings, she wrote in her loveliest handwriting. *There will be a grand party.*

She started crying then, feeling like she couldn't even begin to explain how she really felt about it all, not unless she wanted to fill the rest of her diary and kill her already-weak wrists, which were still recovering from her typing binges. So instead, she let herself cry and finished the entry with just a single line before throwing the damn book back into the snow boot and getting into bed with all her clothes on.

I've been murdered. This is what it feels like to be dead.

the institution

JESSICA AND CASSY TOLD JUNE AND ELEANOR that Adie had supposedly died of a blood clot in the brain.

"A blood clot?" June was skeptical. She couldn't help but remember how hurried the nurse who was doing checks had been. It had to have been something. "Did any of you see her?"

"No," Jessica said quietly as the girls stood together in front of the nurses' station, waiting for their morning capsules. "Nurse Chelsea told us when she woke us up. But she's not here, is she?"

"Shh," Cassy hissed, turning her body away from the group and toward the front of the station, her sweater wrapped around herself as she shifted her weight from one foot to the other. "All of you, shut up! I mean it."

When June's name was called, she stepped forward to find two blood-red capsules waiting for her in the tiny plastic cup instead of one. "The doctor is going to double your dosage from here on out," the beaming nurse behind the protective layer of fake glass said. "Please take them right here, so I can see."

June hesitated. She didn't even know what these things were doing to her in the first place; as far as she could tell there was no noticeable reaction. Still, the idea of taking two capsules made her uneasy.

"Down the hatch, Junebug," the nurse chirped. "Open your mouth, and lift your tongue afterward so I can see."

June fought the urge to turn around and look at Eleanor, and instead poured the pills into her mouth and swallowed them with the water the nurse had provided. Once they were down, she did as the nurse told her, then moved on. By breakfast, June felt fuzzy. This was more along the lines of how she'd expected the pills to make her feel the first time she took them. She wasn't talking much, which Eleanor noticed.

"Are you weirded out about last night?" Eleanor whispered after they'd settled onto the couch in the rec room to watch the black-and-white television in the corner. "I'm sorry if I did anything wrong."

June still couldn't believe what'd happened with Eleanor. The images that flashed through her head when she thought about it were enough to make her body warm. She wondered if it would happen again. She hoped it would.

"It's not you," June assured her. "I promise. Last night was wonderful. It's just this extra pill, it's making me feel strange."

"I wonder why they gave you that," Eleanor said, biting her nails. "I don't like that. Sometimes they change up people's medication before…"

June waited for her to finish. She noticed that on the next couch over, Jessica was frowning and Cassy was shooting her a sideways glance, her brows knit together as if worried. Right away, she became afraid.

"Before what?" she demanded, but it only seemed to upset Eleanor.

"Just stop talking about it," Eleanor insisted, turning away from June, apparently no longer in the mood to talk. "There's nothing we can do but wait. Have you been looking for...that thing?"

June remembered Eleanor's dream about Simpson, how she'd said that Nurse Joya and the doctor and the rest of the staff were looking for something. That June would be the one to find it first. That when June found it, she'd have to make sure they *didn't* find it. But how was she supposed to know where to even begin looking? Furthermore, June didn't have the confidence that she'd be able to successfully hide anything that she did find. Nurse Joya had a way of knowing things.

"It's only been a few hours since we woke up," June said, a little defensively. "It's not like I know what to do, or where to look, or how to look. And honestly, it was just a dream anyway, wasn't it?"

As soon as she said it, June felt guilty. She knew that Eleanor didn't believe it was just a dream and, truth be told, June didn't either. But the sudden pressure that came with the knowledge that Eleanor was expecting June to save them all was immense. She suddenly felt a little itchy, sweaty. She tried to sit up straighter, tell Eleanor that she was sorry, but she was having a hard time opening her mouth. Eleanor was too busy giving June the silent treatment to notice.

I'll try to find whatever it is, June yearned to say but couldn't no matter hard she tried. *I'll find it and get us out of here. Just, please, look at me again.*

She didn't have to wait long. Eleanor did turn back and notice June's softened state, but it wasn't because she'd chosen to look back—her attention was drawn by the sound of squeaking wheels from somewhere behind June. The instant June heard the sound and saw Eleanor's expression, she knew that it was Nurse Joya coming for them. What if they tried to take Eleanor away? June wouldn't be able to fight.

She put all her strength into sitting up. It worked okay enough, but something was still wrong.

"What's the matter?" Eleanor asked, finally realizing what was happening. "Oh, my god, June, your eyes! Can you even hear me right now?"

"Sss," June slurred, an effort for *yes.*

"Hello, ladies." Nurse Joya's voice was extremely close. June realized that the nurse must have been stopped right behind her. "I'm here to collect June for her appointment today."

Good luck getting me up, June thought, and then there was a set of hands underneath each armpit, and with a swift motion June was lifted to her feet, by who she now realized were two additional nurses that had come with Joya. When they turned June around, she was able to see that it wasn't the medication cart that Nurse Joya had been pushing, but a wheelchair.

"Wait," Eleanor said, and June could hear the pure panic in her voice. "Wait, please…"

"Something wrong, dear?" Joya said with an edge. "We really must get going if we're to make June's appointment."

June heard Cassy say, "Sit down, Eleanor," and before

she knew it she'd been lowered into the wheelchair. She was able to keep herself upright, but not much else. The wheelchair began to move, the breeze blowing June's hair out of her face. She could hear Eleanor start to say something else before what sounded like one of the nurses cutting her off.

"June!" was the last of Eleanor's voice that she heard, and then all she could see was the big wooden door to the doctor's office getting closer and closer.

"It's a special day for you, June Hardie," Nurse Joya whispered in her ear. "A special day indeed."

When the door was opened for them, June noticed right away that something was different with the office. There was a white stretcher beside the doctor's desk, and he was standing beside it. June realized that she'd never seen him standing before. He was exceptionally short, almost shockingly so, dressed from head to toe in what appeared to be full surgical garb.

This is it, June thought, although the effect of the medication was allowing her to remain surprisingly calm. *This is when I die.*

"Let me ask you something," the doctor said, stepping forward. "Have you ever heard of electroshock therapy?"

She couldn't answer. In fact, June was vaguely aware that she wasn't able to think beyond the immediate. Trying to concentrate on anything that came before this was wildly difficult. It felt like a literal block had been placed in her head.

The nurses were already in the process of transferring June from the wheelchair to the stretcher. Her head was laid to rest facing the back wall. She noticed that the vent-obscuring bookshelf was now gone, exposing the wall.

There was an air vent there. The same one June had peered through while she was crawling through the tunnel that was pooled with blood.

"I have another question for you," the doctor said when June didn't answer, looking down to peer into June's face. "Who is Robert Dennings?"

Robert Dennings. Dennings. The name was familiar to June, but she couldn't quite place it. Robert? Someone she knew...when, exactly? When she tried to push herself to remember, a sharp pain bloomed somewhere deep inside her brain.

"Your face says all I need to know," the doctor said, satisfied. "And where did you live before you came here?"

The feeling of having no idea was tremendously terrifying. Again came the awful pain whenever June stretched to remember the truth.

Before I was here...I was...at a school?

In a house?

In outer space?

There was a place she could picture somewhat before the pain, a place that was metal and cold and smelled like formaldehyde. Outside, there were stars. Inside, there were creatures.

No, she thought. *That place wasn't real; that's from your story...*

Whose story?

"Patient appears to be confused and disoriented," Nurse Joya spoke into a large tape recorder that was running on the desk. "Increased dosage was successful."

Yes, June remembered now, without pain. She'd taken an extra red capsule this morning. Eleanor had been worried. She had been right to be worried. June would never get to see her again and tell her so. She was about to let Eleanor, Jessica, and Cassy down, and have Simpson's, Lauren's, and Adie's deaths remain in vain. She would die before finding whatever was supposedly hidden in this place.

It was in that moment June got her first idea of where to look for the thing Eleanor had dreamed about. If she somehow lived through whatever was happening, she'd try as hard as she could to get herself back into that tunnel.

"The air vent," June heard herself slur as Joya went behind the desk and put her hands on the wall. What on earth was she doing?

But the wall appeared to rattle at the nurse's touch, and then all of a sudden it was sliding sideways into itself, a large secret door that led to what looked like a laboratory of some sort. They wheeled June in and parked her at the near end of the room. There was a thick plastic sheet separating another side of the room, and it looked like there was another stretcher with someone lying motionless on it on the other side.

"What we're going to be doing today is essentially force a seizure on your brain to try and shake loose whatever nastiness has clogged its way through," Nurse Joya said. She was now wearing a crisp white mask that covered her nose and mouth, and bright blue gloves that made grotesque snapping sounds as she adjusted them. "I won't lie to you either, sugar. It's going to hurt."

"No," June tried to say, but already the doctor was binding her to the table with heavy straps. The nurse squirted something thick and oily from a tube onto her rubber-protected fingers and rubbed it on June's temples.

With every second that passed, June started feeling less fuzzy and more awake. She was able to remember her story now and felt like she was the girl on the spaceship getting cut into and experimented on. She suddenly felt sorry— very sorry—that she'd put her heroine through so much.

But she needed it, June thought. *She needed it to fulfill her destiny.*

June had always suspected that something great would become of her. Maybe finding the missing thing before Nurse Joya did was her destiny. Maybe she'd just failed it, and they had already found whatever it was.

"I can tell by your face that you think you're about to die," Nurse Joya said, placing a hard, thin bar in between June's teeth and strapping two metal plates against either side of her head. "But I promise you, you won't. We need you, silly girl."

There it was. The admission that they weren't trying to treat anybody at all, they just needed them to find whatever it was they were looking for. June remembered Robert and her parents with such a startling intensity that she jumped, as if she had already been jolted. Before she was in the hospital, she had lived at home with her parents. Robert had proposed. The engagement party had happened, and everything had been ruined beyond recognition.

And now she was here.

"You know what to do once it's through, Joya," the doctor said, his wrinkles very prominent in the lighting. "I think this may be it."

"I do, too," the nurse murmured as she fidgeted with whatever device was behind June's head, the one attached to the wires and metal plates. "There's something especially unusual about this one."

If they wanted to keep her alive, why were they speaking openly about her like this? *They know that you know.*

"All right," Nurse Joya whispered deliciously, out of sight, the smile evident in the sound of her voice alone. "Let's see what we've got here."

And then came a strange *wheeee* sound that got louder and louder, and just when June thought, *This isn't so bad*, there came a great crackling jolt that caused every muscle in her body to harden and seize. It hurt to an unfair degree. She could feel the straps holding her down too tightly as she convulsed, pressing into her bones, threatening to snap them.

She thought she heard someone gurgling, before she realized she was hearing herself.

Everything went white, then blue, high heat, dry heat, a head screaming in pain. The sound of the machine whirred sharply in June's ears, made them feel like they were bleeding.

Finally, finally, it ended. June could have sworn her eyes were open, but everything was black. She could smell something unpleasant, like burning hair. She didn't dare move a muscle, in case they weren't finished with her yet. She didn't know how she was even able to survive such a thing.

"Monitor readings are impressive," June heard the doctor murmur.

"Can you see what she's thinking?" Nurse Joya demanded. "Any signs that she's ready to talk?"

Someone was crying, far away. "Drat," the doctor said. "The other one's awake. I don't think we're going to find anything with her, to be honest. The language she hears can't be decoded in any way that we've found. It's another lost cause. Might as well do away with her."

June could hear Nurse Joya and the doctor step away,

then came the sound of the heavy plastic sheet wrinkling as it was moved.

"Please don't," a voice pleaded, and June recognized it immediately as belonging to Adie.

This was when June's vision came back, or she was simply able to open her eyes for real, she wasn't sure which. Her mouth was still gagged with the bar, and she could see outlines through the thick plastic sheet, Joya and the doctor standing at each end of the other stretcher. June recognized Adie's head of short, dark hair though the heavily blurred plastic. She was alive!

Then she remembered what the doctor had said before they stepped over there. *Might as well do away with her.*

"Adie," June called out clumsily through the bar, but wasn't heard over her friend's shrieks. She sounded terrified, but June couldn't hear any sort of machine running, and at first it appeared as though Joya and the doctor were standing still.

Through the plastic, June was able to make out that something was happening to them. The mass making up the doctor's head was expanding to an impossible form, as though it was a giant, fleshy, wrinkled flower that was opening up like a four-parted mouth. The gaping end of it lowered down over Adie's feet, and then June could hear a nasty crunching noise.

Her heart raced as Adie continued to scream. Nurse Joya's form was changing, too—it had grown slightly and was hunched over. Long appendages extended out from her face, shredding into Adie like a parcel on Christmas morning. Soon Adie's screams came to a bubbling stop and were replaced by loud, long slurping sounds. The two monsters shuddered, and their forms resolved to resemble humans once again. June was suddenly grateful that the plastic had made it so hard to see clearly.

Monsters. They're monsters!

When they returned to her side of the room, June closed her eyes and held still. "Her eyes are closed now," the doctor noted right away. "Do you think she came to during any of that?"

"Impossible," Joya said brusquely, and June felt her straps being roughly undone. "Nobody ever remembers anything with the voltage level we use. I am very eager for her to wake up, though, so we can see if it worked. Should only be a few more minutes."

If what worked? June thought, her pulse racing. *Whatever it is, it apparently didn't work with Adie.*

The bar was yanked from her mouth, and right away June's head felt like it was filled with wasps. She moaned as they wheeled her back out, then felt them lift her back into the wheelchair. They wheeled June out of the laboratory and back into the office.

"Her hair got scorched pretty good," Joya said, parking June beside the doctor's desk and retrieving something from a cabinet in it. "The skin opened, too, but that's to be expected."

June felt her head being wrapped with some sort of gauze. She must have looked an absolute fright. What would Eleanor think when she saw her? There was no way she would continue to love June, especially when she eventually realized that June wasn't capable of finding anything that would help them escape this place. They'd been so silly, getting close like that.

The Simpson in Eleanor's vision had been wrong about June. She had to have been.

"Wake up, Nightingale," Nurse Joya said, very closely, her voice deeper and more stern than it'd ever been. *Monster.* "Wake up, and tell us exactly what you did at that goddamn engagement party."

June opened her eyes. The nurse looked like a human. There were no holes in her face, but June feared that they'd appear any second, and then the terrible limbs would reach through them to rip June into pieces. She tried to make what had happened at the engagement party come back to her, but it didn't work because it wasn't a real thing to begin with; it had been a terrible coincidence was all.

The smile on the nurse's face faded fast. Minutes of silence passed as she stared at June, unblinking, expectant.

"It didn't work," Nurse Joya finally said under her breath to the doctor, and she got up. June vaguely registered the sharp sting of the injection needle in her arm. "She's still hiding what she knows."

What do I know?

When it was done, Nurse Joya grabbed the wheelchair handles and started pushing June incautiously. June half expected to be discarded by the monsters like Adie had been, but then she realized she was being wheeled to the office's exit, not back to the awful laboratory behind the secret door in the wall. "We'll just have to keep trying with some more...invasive procedures," the nurse said, clearly let down by whatever hadn't happened.

More invasive than this? June couldn't comprehend anything worse than what she had just been through, or what Adie had just been through. *Poor, poor Adie.*

"We won't let them win," Nurse Joya went on, and the doctor let out a gruff sound of agreement. "Those disgusting things think they can come to our home, wipe us out like bacteria. They don't even want to live here. They just want us dead. We don't have much longer to find where they've hidden the key."

Who are they? June wished she could ask, but already whatever she'd been injected with was drawing her into a deep sleep. She fought it only for a moment before giving in to the darkness.

days past

THE EVENING OF JUNE'S ENGAGEMENT PARTY, her mother came into her room with a new dress. June had spent the week doing every little thing she could think of that would appease her parents enough to leave her alone and, combined with the engagement, you'd think that her family had forgotten all about the significance of the incident on graduation night. Nobody wanted to remember the phone call, or the bus ticket, or June's wails in the night. Nobody asked her if she was all right or if she needed anything. Nobody acknowledged that she'd spent nine straight days in solitude.

As always, they were only able to tell June what they expected of her.

"I picked up your new dress," Mom said, as though she and June had chosen the dress together, which was not the case at all. "I need you to wear it with your stockings and yellow pumps. Rolled hair. Pink lipstick, not red—red would clash too badly with all the yellow."

The dress looked similar to June's graduation dress but was butter yellow instead of mint green. There was a thin white leather belt and a pair of tiny white gloves that didn't fit June's hands, which was good considering that June would have rather eaten a pair of lacy gloves than wear them.

"Thank you." June made a point of speaking to them only when absolutely necessary, although when it came to her brother she made a point of not speaking at all.

She may have been rolling her parents along, but June couldn't bring herself to acknowledge Fred's existence. Fred, the withering, spineless-fish boy who didn't even have it in him to take a leaf from Dad's book, instead trying desperately to re-create them on his own. But the final product was even worse, a poor imitation of a poor original. He spoke in a voice that was purposely loud and overbearing, and he took pride in telling Mom or June to get him another drink rather than asking them, while he sat there watching television. A real Little Man.

June hated him for what he had done to her. She would never forget that stupid little look of excitement in his eyes after he came back from answering the phone call from the bus station.

"And remember," Mom said, running her hands over the fabric of the dress's skirt to smooth it. "Good posture, be gracious, smile. This will be one of the most magical nights of your life."

"Can't wait."

Mom patted June's knee and got up, leaving the room without another word. June could tell that she was counting down the days until June was out of the house and out of her hair. Clearly, she'd come to the conclusion that there wasn't any way to fix her daughter or make her a better young woman. They could only cover up what they believed were her shortcomings, move her along, pretend she didn't disappoint them so immensely.

When the time came to make their way to the party, June took a moment to stare at herself in the mirror, clean and polished and dressed in all yellow. Her plans for her own future had gone from being necessary to being non-existent. Her book was only a writing session or two away from being complete, but she no longer felt hopeful that anything would come of it. She had purposely put off finishing it, since she'd always believed that something magnificent would happen to her shortly after she did.

Nothing magnificent was going to happen to June in this life. To face the fact that she'd been wrong about her story was more than she could bear, and she hid the feelings even from herself, stuffed roughly into the darkest corners of her mind.

She sat beside Fred in the car on the way to the party, and he kept trying to talk to her about this and that. He asked if she had invited her longtime best friend Sarah to the wedding, so he could try and date her for the third or fourth time. If June had been speaking to Fred, she would have told him that Sarah had stopped coming over two years ago because he gave her the heebie-jeebies with all his staring and his persistence. She had been disgusted with him, just as June was. June wondered how Fred would feel about *that*.

While June ignored Fred, Mom and Dad chatted about who had RSVP'd to the party and who hadn't, who would drink too much, who would leave their dropped napkins on the floor. First would be the cocktail hour. Dinner was to be served at seven thirty sharp, with dessert and dancing and more cocktails to follow. June wondered if they'd let her drink even though she was underage; it was her goddamn party after all. She decided that if they denied her alcohol, she'd sneak it.

The venue was a place on the edge of town, with a big wooden dance floor and walls made of glass that gave view to the lush lawn that was lined with colorful flowers and decorated with white stringed lights. When June's family arrived, the parking lot was decently packed, and people already lingered on the lawn with cocktails in hand.

"Make sure to say hello to everyone," Mom said under her breath while she gave a dainty wave of her frilly gloved fingers to a group of women June didn't recognize. "They're all here for you, darling, so show them how grateful you are."

June didn't see Robert anywhere, and she was glad. As long as he wasn't present she could pretend that this party was for her alone, a going-away party. In a way, she supposed, it was.

"Wonderful to see you," June said through a wide smile to a perfect stranger. "Robert and I are so pleased you could come."

A man wearing all black approached the group, a tray of drinks balanced on his upturned hand. "Gin and tonics, anyone?" he asked. Everyone in the group reached for one of the sparkling highballs topped with a slice of lime.

June took one, too, without hesitation, and made eye contact with Mom as she took a long, grateful sip. Mom looked away quickly but said nothing, instead busying herself by chatting with party guests. Another tray came by, this one loaded with pieces of deep-fried coconut shrimp. June hadn't been eating well, not since graduation, but she took at least three samples from each tray, keeping her mouth filled with food so it wouldn't have to speak words.

As well as the coconut shrimp, there were crab cakes, deviled eggs, and little paper cones filled with french fries. June dripped ketchup on the front of her dress, and her mother glared as though she wanted to commit murder.

Maybe tonight wouldn't be so bad. Just as long as June could block out the voices in her head that were crying and screaming for her to finish her story. She had known that stopping would be difficult. It had almost felt at times like she was working on it whether she wanted to or not, with all the late nights and early mornings and endless typing and endless thinking.

Still, when she'd realized the end of the story was near, she'd forced herself to stop. She thought the break would be good for her, would allow her to get some sleep and eat something proper and work on her life a bit before coming back to do the ending justice. But what had happened instead was frightening.

June had started sleeping even *less*, obsessing over how exactly she'd word certain sentences when the time came, how she'd bring the heroine face-to-face with her unexpected destiny. She'd dwell on scenes she'd already written, picture what the creatures looked like. She started seeing the creatures standing all around the perimeter of her room at night, hiding in the shadows, their metal tools glistening and clinking in the moonlight.

Finish it, she felt like they were whispering directly into her brain. *Finish it now. See what will come next. See what will happen to you once it's done.*

She resisted the impossible. She wasn't ready to face what would happen once she finished. She wasn't ready to face the nothingness, the empty ache of being lonesome and a failure. So she ignored the creatures that came into her room night after night, lurking in the dark, begging her to return to the typewriter. She started fearing it more than she feared them. They never hurt her. Sometimes they only stared.

But the typewriter *beckoned*.

Now, standing in the beautifully lit garden of the venue, she could see staff hustling to prepare the tables inside for dinner. All of the tables had candles, floral centerpieces, and lavish tablecloths. Gold, ivory, cream. How Mom must have delighted in all of these little details! June didn't want to imagine what the wedding itself would be like.

If the wedding ever came to be, that was. June had done a lot of thinking in her hours of lying awake. Never was she able to visualize the ceremony and what it would be like to actually live with Robert. She wondered if it would be possible to do something else. Maybe run away. Maybe kill herself. The shame of even considering such a thing was awful, unbearably heavy.

Rest. What June really needed was rest. She'd been using the eye drops from the medicine cabinet to whiten her violently red eyes. She looked fine enough, but it was only a matter of time before she shut down, and in the back of her mind, June knew she would. The gin wasn't helping that either, but it was helping with a whole lot of other things, so in the end June kept sipping from her glass.

"Boo!" came a deep voice at the same time that a pair of

arms wrapped around June from behind. She screamed, really *screamed*, and dropped her drink to shatter on the cobblestones. Everybody at the party looked over in shock, to the awkward sight of Robert stepping away from June, his face twisted in confusion.

"It was only me," he exclaimed, his hands up as though surrendering to police. "I didn't mean to scare you, darling!"

"Robert," June sputtered. "I'm so sorry. I didn't hear you coming…" She looked around at everybody, and spotted her parents standing with Stewart Dennings, staring in absolute horror. "I'm so sorry," June said louder, giving a silly little wave of her hand before turning back to Robert. "You're late."

"You're kidding, right?" Robert gave a little laugh, but June was able to read right through it: it was empty and irritated and supremely unamused. "You were the one who was late. I've been here since six."

Six o'clock was when June had been digging for eye drops, Mom bellowing up the stairs that it was time to go *now, now, now!*

"Oh" was all she could say. Her head felt light. "Sorry, I don't feel so well."

"I can see," he said, his mouth pulled into a line as he looked at her sweaty face and the ketchup stain on the front of her dress. "You know, darling, there's really no pressure here tonight at all. I feel as though you expect too much from yourself. You must learn to relax. Would you like me to get you another drink?"

What world was this?

She accepted the drink and let herself be guided inside, where dinner was being served. June and Robert sat at a large round table with Stewart, Mom, Dad, Fred, Stewart's brother Jack and Jack's wife, Barbara. A bowl of gelatinous orange soup with crushed cashews on top was already waiting at her place, with Robert's family digging in. June dipped her spoon into the soup but couldn't stomach the notion of actually eating it; suddenly all the appetizers she'd stuffed down sat heavily and made her feel sick.

Once all the tables were filled, Mom stood with a microphone on the empty dance floor and thanked everybody for coming. "We hope you'll all be able to make the wedding next winter," she closed with, and that's how June found out that she was to be married in the winter. At least she'd be old enough to run away without the police coming for her by then.

You won't be able to go that long without finishing the story, an eerie little voice whispered inside. June could hear the smile in the voice. *You have to finish it. Tonight. Do it tonight. Do it now.*

Her hands trembled as she pretended to gather another spoonful of the off-putting soup. She would not finish the story tonight. Perhaps she would never finish it at all. She could try to revisit it once she was away from here and somewhere safe. But who would take in a person like herself? She had no work experience, no money saved. How did she expect to find somewhere to live?

Likely, she thought as she thanked the waiter who came to take the soup bowls away, she'd simply end up cutting her wrists in a steaming bath.

It was a relief to her how quickly the courses passed. There was salad, fish in some sort of white sauce, roasted potatoes. There were tiny chocolate cakes which expelled thick, sticky syrup when cut into. June didn't eat any of it, only drank her new cocktail while she looked over the rest of the table, all of them shoveling food in as though it would be their last meal for a week.

June was most relieved when the dancing began. They'd have a real band at the wedding, Dad assured her, but for now they just turned a record player up beside the microphone while everyone shimmied and shook. June went into the bathroom, locked herself in a stall, and leaned against the cool, calming wall of metal, enjoying the silence.

It didn't feel like anything, just like she'd shut her eyes and taken a deep breath. But before she could understand what was happening, there was a loud banging on the other side of the stall door. She hadn't even noted hearing anyone come into the bathroom.

"June!" It was Mom. "We've been looking for you everywhere! You've been in here almost all night, goddamn it! Come out here, and listen to Stewart's speech."

Stunned, June straightened up and stumbled out of the stall. Apparently the alcohol was affecting her more than she'd thought. "Sorry," she mumbled as she followed Mom out, but Mom gave no sign that she'd heard.

Everyone was at their tables and stared as her mother walked her back to her seat. June tried to remember to smile but felt like she probably looked rather clownish. Whenever she made eye contact with someone, they instantly looked uncomfortable. What was she doing wrong?

"There's our June," Stewart said into the microphone from where he stood near the record player. "We were beginning to think you got cold feet."

Laughter rang through the venue, and June shifted in her seat. "I'll save those for the wedding," she called out in an attempted joke, trying to sound easygoing and silly but instead coming across as unhinged and borderline hysterical. Nobody laughed, and Mom looked like she was about to transform into a werewolf and eat June alive. Robert put his hand on June's knee under the table, heavily.

"Right," Stewart said, then continued a little louder. "The Hardies and I wanted to let you-all know just how pleased we are that you've come to celebrate Robert and June with us. It was fireworks when these kids came together a year ago, and it became clear pretty quickly that they were destined to be together."

Destiny. This idiot knew nothing of the meaning of the word. But then again, June thought, perhaps she didn't either.

There came a round of light polite applause. "Furthermore," Stewart said, "I wanted to surprise the kids tonight with something big."

An excited murmur grew in the room; if a high roller like Stewart Dennings said it was big, that really meant it was huge.

"I just signed the contract on a brand-new house for my son and the future Mrs. Dennings!" he announced in a theatrical voice, at which the crowd gasped and clapped and whooped. June's face went cold. "Robert will be moving in next week, and there he'll wait for winter to come so his new bride can join him."

June stood without meaning to. She realized that doing so caused a lot of people to look at her, expectantly, scanning her for her reaction to such a grand gift. She pulled a smile so wide it felt like it would cause her face to tear. Robert stood and pulled her into an embrace.

"Surprise!" he said in her ear. "You'll just love it. Wait

until you see it: there's even a room you can use to write until the baby comes."

So it wasn't a surprise to *the kids* after all. It was only a surprise to June. Robert had known about the engagement, the wedding, and now the house and apparently a fucking *baby*, all before she did. It wasn't right. The fairy lights that decorated the lawn outside shorted out, causing everything outside the window walls to disappear into pure darkness. The speaker that was amplifying Stewart's microphone gave off a faint buzzing sound.

"There's so much to say about June," Stewart went on, gesturing to his future daughter-in-law. "She came into our lives so shortly after Robert's mother passed away. It's hard to say who needed the other more."

I needed you and Robert in my life like I needed a brain tumor. A frightening calm took over June, and she put her hand over her heart and rested her head on Robert's shoulder. She was doing a better job pretending now: she could tell by the way her parents beamed at her, how the guests looked on in admiration.

"She was one of the most interesting women Robert had ever met or dated," Stewart remarked, his words slightly slurred by alcohol, and the crowd laughed. "When I asked him what she did in her free time, he told me that she liked to write stories about aliens from outer space."

June's heart skipped a beat. She lifted her head off Robert's shoulder.

"And while I don't think you'll ever be able to make a dime writing about aliens from outer space," Stewart went on, getting another laugh from the crowd, "you're lucky enough that you won't have to worry about that. Robert will take care of you forever, dear June, and you're a very lucky woman indeed."

People were still laughing about the alien story. Some whispered behind their hands at each other while keeping their eyes on June. June stepped away from Robert, her face undoing itself in anguish, as she went up to Stewart, her fists balled. She could vaguely hear herself growling—*growling!*—as if she were an angry tiger on the loose.

"How dare you mock me?" she yelled, her voice strained, and at the same time she began to cry. The entire venue fell dead silent. She heard a chair scraping and then saw her mother rushing over. "I never asked for this! I never asked for a stupid house or a stupid husband!"

Gasps from the crowd.

"June…" Stewart said, his eyes wide in shock, taking a step back. "I'm sorry, honey. I didn't mean to—"

"Why don't you just—" June bellowed, about to continue with *drop dead*, but at that exact same moment, Stewart Dennings's face relaxed into a blank expression, and he collapsed to the floor. A light flickered overhead, as did the string lights outside.

"What happened?" Mom cried out as she reached June, squeezing her arms hard enough to open the skin. "Somebody call an ambulance!"

"Father!" Robert was there now, too, dropping to his knees at Stewart's side. June stared at his gray face, his unblinking eyes, already in full understanding that he was dead. She dropped to her knees.

June had killed Stewart Dennings. Nobody seemed to notice this detail. In fact, people seemed to *finally* be looking through June as though she were invisible, which was all she'd wanted since arriving at this cursed party. People were yelling among the crowd, asking if there were any doctors present. There were. They whaled on Stewart's chest with their fists, taking turns, causing Mom to cry out in anguish with every blow.

And then Fred was there, grabbing June roughly, lifting her off the floor. "Get up, June," he growled. "*Move*, damn it!"

"Come on, Stewart!" Dad was yelling into the dead man's face. "We're not done here yet, Stewart! Wake up and snap out of it!"

"Dad!" Robert cried, holding Stewart's hand. "I need you, Dad! Please, don't leave me like Mom did. Don't you dare leave me, Dad…"

June stood and watched all of this, awestruck. Was she in a waking nightmare? Did that really just happen? "I'm sorry," she whispered, but nobody heard her.

The ambulance came. They told Robert that Stewart was dead, and they took his body away. The police came, too, to address the disturbance that someone had called in. When June shakily told them the truth of what had happened, they took her by the shoulders and looked at her sympathetically and told her that it wasn't her fault, that it had been a massive heart attack out of her control, maybe even an aneurysm.

June knew better, though. She knew without a shadow of a doubt that, somehow, it had absolutely been her fault. She had caused it.

Workers from the venue had been wordlessly clearing dirty plates and glasses and breaking down the tables. Most people left when the ambulance did, Stewart's body under a white sheet in the back of the vehicle. Robert sobbed from where he sat on the floor. June rigidly made her way to his side. She let her fingertips rest on the top of his head.

"You did that," he nearly spat, shaking off her touch. "I don't know how, but you did."

Across the room, June saw a blond woman with red lipstick lead her parents into a different room in the back, whispering in Mom's ear as though she had something important to share. They slipped away, but June was too shaken to think twice on it and didn't remember the woman later.

When Mom and Dad had returned from the room, they were a little more stiff than before. They walked to June, told her to get in the car. She complied and cried the entire way home. She expected her parents to yell at her, disown her, tell her they were sending her away forever, which might not have been such a bad thing. But instead they were uncharacteristically silent, with Fred looking blankly out the window as the car pulled into their driveway.

"Go to bed," Dad said to June after they walked in, in a voice that was calmer than June had heard him use in years. His business was ruined with Stewart gone, she knew. Robert wouldn't be able to fill his shoes by a long shot, at least not for a very long time. Maybe that had broken Dad somehow. Maybe he'd murder her in her sleep tonight. She'd be ready. She wouldn't fight it.

June went upstairs and closed the door behind her. She collapsed into bed without taking off her ketchup-stained yellow dress, didn't even peel off the awful stockings that burned against her damp skin like a rash. She turned the light out, and there the creatures were, waiting for her. June didn't give them the chance to whisper to her this time. She stared at them for only a moment before standing, turning on the light, and sitting down at her typewriter.

She finished her story in one long, furious sitting, all the madness that had gathered either releasing or multiplying, she couldn't tell, and her eyes burned ever so. The sun was just coming up as she typed *THE END* and then sat, in disbelief, at the finished page before her.

It was done.

She took a shower and put on clean clothes. She had no idea what awaited her downstairs, couldn't imagine the harshness of the words that were surely going to be thrown her way. It didn't matter what would happen to her now: the story was finished at last. And June had ruined everything— the business, the future of her family, her relationship with Robert. She'd face the music because that was what she deserved. After combing her wet hair straight back and giving herself an encouraging look in the mirror, June went downstairs for breakfast, ready for anything.

"Good morning, Nightingale," the Mom-thing said to her in greeting, and that was when June had begun to scream.

the institution

WHEN JUNE WOKE UP, SHE WAS IN HER ROOM. It was night, and Eleanor was missing. She sat up with a jolt and a gasp, her hand flying to the side of her head to feel the gauze that was still wrapped around it. Her mind clawed through what had happened, each second becoming significantly heavier than the one that preceded it. The secret laboratory behind the doctor's main office, the whirring machine and the metal plates on her head and the bar between her teeth. The plastic sheet hanging from the ceiling.

Adie.

"Oh, my god," June moaned, and barely made it to the wastebasket before she vomited. Her head ached desperately. Nurse Joya and the doctor were monsters. Real monsters. The vision in the tunnel had been completely real.

But *how* had June gotten into the tunnel? She stared now

at the space on the wall, went over to it again, ran her hand over it. Solid. The monster nurse inside had seemed fascinated and surprised at June's presence. Hadn't it been the drugs that she'd injected into June that had made that possible? If so, why didn't the nurse understand that?

But the drugs hadn't had the same effect on Eleanor, and in addition, the red pill that everybody took daily to make them forget their lives before the hospital had needed to be doubled to have any effect on June. Even then, it had worn off long before the nurse and doctor had planned. Why was she more immune to the treatments than other patients?

All this time, Nurse Joya had obsessed over the story of how Stewart Dennings died, dropping dead the second June yelled at him. Obsessed with her mind, trying to dig her way through it. *What a brain you have, June Hardie. What an absolute marvel!*

June touched the gauze again. If she'd really been the one to cause Stewart's death, just as she'd known in her bones the moment it happened, did that mean that she could have also forced the tunnel to appear? With…her mind?

She stared at the place on the wall, tried to imagine the tunnel vividly enough that it would appear for real. Again, and again, and again. The wall stayed solid. June shook her head as though trying to rattle loose her building paranoia.

Where was Eleanor?

June knew, without a doubt, that something awful had happened to her. But she was supposed to live forever! She'd said so! June felt that her face was wet with tears. She paced the room, making a plan—something had to be done, and it had to be done now. If there was even a chance she could find Eleanor, she had to be brave enough to try.

June remembered Simpson's ghost and what Eleanor had

relayed from her. *She seemed to believe that you were going to be the first one to find the lost thing, whatever it is.* June had been frustrated at Eleanor for pushing her to start looking right away, and now she regretted it more than anything. She had, as she always had in her life before the hospital, let fear get in the way. *She said to tell you not to let them get it, no matter what happens, or else the consequences will be more dire than any of us can comprehend.*

Now a new fear arose, a worse fear. The fear that it was too late.

But how will I know? June wondered. *Simpson said that once I find it, I'll know without any doubt.*

It wasn't until now that June thought that maybe the reason Eleanor was able to receive a message from Simpson beyond the grave was because she was *dead* herself. Goosebumps flourished over June's back and belly and arms, remembering what else had been said of the vision: *whatever's happened to us isn't as simple as a medical diagnosis.*

It was as if this were all planned somehow, set into place by some mysterious force. Destiny? June's heart skipped a beat at the thought. If it was fate, if the gut feelings she used to get were more than wishes and were in fact intuition, then that would mean everything would be okay in the end. That was how June always knew it'd have to turn out. That was the only part she'd ever felt sure of.

She remembered Eleanor's soft laugh from that night, the night they had become intimate. *To hear that you might be the one who's supposed to save this place,* Eleanor had said, her breath warm on June's face, *well…it doesn't surprise me, I guess.*

"I'm coming, Elle," June whispered, standing now to

face the closed door leading out to the hallway. If the door was unlocked, it was meant to be. "Please wait for me."

The door was unlocked, and she stuck her head out. The hallway was dark, the only sounds the cries and grunts and howls coming from the rooms of the other patients, that harmony of despair that had haunted June so much on her first night here, but now sounded as natural as crickets or wind in the trees. The nurse in charge of bed checks wasn't anywhere in her sight line, which meant June had managed to wake up within the delicate time frame that fell between the constant patrols.

Destiny was working in her favor already. Suddenly, June felt stronger and more capable than she ever had. Something was protecting her. She didn't know what, but she knew it was there. She had to find whatever the monsters were looking for, and she had to find it now, along with Eleanor.

It was her fate.

June stepped softly but quickly across the hallway and enormous recreation room, the nurses' station emitting a dull glow in the darkness. June went along the edge of the far wall like a shadow, never taking her eyes from the glass of the station, behind which four nurses sat chatting and blowing bubbles with their gum and smoking cigarettes, their uniforms so pristine, styled hair, red lips, *fake, fake, fake.* June wondered if they were monsters, too, and guessed that they probably were.

Either way, they didn't see her cross the room.

June searched through the forbidden hallway that Nurse Joya had taken her through on the day that Robert and her parent-things had come to visit, recalling on the way her surprise at all the rooms she'd never seen before. She peeked through the windows of each and every door as she made her way through. Most of the rooms were shrouded in solid blackness, and June had to convince herself that anything worth seeing would be illuminated to her by fate.

Just as she was starting to doubt herself, she found a different type of door and peered through the dark rectangular window in the center. It was a library, the bookshelves lit with tiny lamps mounted on the ends. Simpson had taken Eleanor to a library in the vision. To see it with her own eyes made June miss Eleanor even more. *I'm coming.*

The door to the library was locked, so she moved on. At the end of the hallway there was a sharp turn to the right, and when she turned the corner, June saw two rooms with the lights on. The first was near the end of the hallway, the door open, the light flooding into the hallway like a blinding white warning. The next room also had a light on, but the door was closed, the space at the bottom aglow.

What if the monsters were in that first room, ready to kill her on sight? June had to trust herself. She had to remember that something was protecting her, that she was special, that she was the one who would stop the dire consequences threatened by this place and the monsters inside it.

She walked slowly up to the room, listening as hard as she could for any signs that she should stop and back away. But there was nothing, only the low croon of a jazz tune playing from a radio or a record player. The melody was deeply calming. June was drawn to it, which led her to believe that she was very much supposed to look in this room for whatever the special thing was.

Her breath caught in her chest, June turned the corner into the room, the light harsh enough to make her squint for the first few moments. There was a hospital bed against the back wall, the sheets and pillow splattered with yellow and red. It stank deeply, creating an extremely incongruent combination with the music that had just been calling to June. Her instincts were now urging her to run.

In the center of the room, Eleanor sat in a wheelchair, her mouth open, her hands splayed open on her lap. Her hair was gone, crudely shaved, or at least what June could see of it. Around her head was gauze similar to June's, but June knew right away something was different than with what had been done to her.

Blood seeped through the bandages, dripping down the sides of Eleanor's face, onto her shoulders and chest. Eleanor breathed heavily, and her eyes were open, but she didn't see June, didn't see anything. June let out a strangled whimper and went to her, lifted the sides of her bandages to peek underneath at an incredible black gap in Eleanor's skull, cut in a perfect circle that wept fluids.

Lobotomy.

"No," June whispered, moving to look into Eleanor's eyes again, but to no avail. "No, it's not supposed to happen this way, Elle! Look at me, know me! Sit up! Move!"

Nothing. It wasn't a temporary state brought on by drugs, this much was obvious. Eleanor looked like Lauren had but even worse. They had cut into her brain, the fucking sons of bitches! They'd disconnected her from the now. June thought of the last time she'd seen Eleanor, how she'd hurt Eleanor's feelings by saying to her that the dream of Simpson had been "just a dream" after all. How panicked Eleanor had sounded when she yelled June's name, as June was being wheeled away by Nurse Joya.

"That can't be the last time we saw each other," June pleaded, forgetting to stay quiet, forgetting what the hell she was doing in this room in the first place, forgetting all of the strength and drive that had flooded her here earlier like some sort of adrenaline rush. She wept over her lover's body, alive but not alive, alive but dead. Eleanor, the dead girl who'd scared the wits out of June during her first night at the hospital.

June had failed her.

"I'm so sorry," she cried into Eleanor's ear, only vaguely aware that there had been the sound of footsteps behind her and that the footfalls had come to a stop.

"What a shame," Nurse Joya's voice said, and June looked at her, still holding Eleanor's hand. "She didn't have what we were looking for. Didn't even have anything that could help us find it."

"I've already found it," June lied, clumsy in her voice, pitched high with panic and fear. She was desperately clinging to the idea of her destiny. "I know where it is, and I'm not going to let you get it, no matter what happens."

The nurse paused, narrowing her eyes at June. She was clearly affected by June's comment and, for a moment, June swore she could see the holes opening up on the nurse's face. But Joya didn't transform. Was it possible that the nurse believed her? Maybe June could string her along until she was able to find whatever the thing was, if she lived beyond tonight, anyway. It was still vital that the monsters didn't get their hands on what they were looking for.

"I'm afraid you're going to have to come back for another procedure," Nurse Joya said, and suddenly there were five other nurses behind her, one of them holding a syringe. "Cracking open your girlfriend here didn't reveal anything new to me, but it *did* give me the idea that maybe I'd get better results doing the same thing to you. Time is running out for us, I'm afraid, and we're getting a little desperate."

"No!" June bellowed, rising but still gripping Eleanor's hand. The nurses all rushed forward at once, holding her down while she screamed and kicked, and injected her with something stinging and hot.

"You'll never get it," she slurred as the drugs kicked in. Another wheelchair appeared, and June was lifted onto it. She was promptly pushed away from Eleanor and back into the dark hallway. June cried Eleanor's name, but Joya slammed the door shut midway through.

"Don't be insulted," she insisted at the look on June's face. "She most definitely wasn't able to hear you. She won't be able to hear anything ever again."

When they got to the dark rec room, June saw that all the women from the nurses' station were watching her, their faces unmoving and unkind, angry. Angry at her for getting by them undetected. June wished she had the strength to flip them all the bird.

The door to the doctor's office was open wide, greedily waiting to consume June. She was wheeled through it and the entrance of the laboratory, past the room where she had endured the electroshock, past the hanging plastic partition and into the room that had once held Adie but was now sterile and quiet, and finally beyond another plastic sheet that led to a much larger room, a room with carts, the trays of which held metal instruments, like saws and scalpels and needles, and basins to catch waste.

The doctor stood at the side of an empty bed. June cried out in objection but was lifted onto it anyway, strapped in with heavy buckled leather belts that wound through and around the sides of the mattress.

"The night before you came here," Nurse Joya said, and the doctor's mouth moved silently along, "you were at your

engagement party. You killed the man who was to have
been your father-in-law. I should know, June. I was there.
I saw it myself."

June closed her eyes, concentrated as hard as she could
on making it all stop somehow. "Drop dead," she managed in a hateful but softened slur of words to the nurse,
who looked nervous for a brief moment before overcom-
pensating with laughter.

"You don't even know how you did it," she went on,
tightening the last strap before using a pair of rusty scissors to cut June's hair off a half inch from the scalp. "I fully
believe that now. You don't even understand what's happening. You don't know what we're looking for any more
than you know the name of the character in that story you
wrote."

She didn't have a name, June wanted to say, but was too
drugged. As paralyzed as she was, though, she could still
feel the pain of the dull scissors ripping at her hair, the
discomfort of the straps around her extremities, waist and
neck. She was finding it hard to breathe.

"Area almost prepped," Nurse Joya said, and the doctor
leaned over June so closely that she could smell his sour,
awful breath, startlingly reminiscent of decomposition.

"You had better be right about her," he said, and June
realized that he was addressing Joya. "We cannot afford a
single mistake. They're getting closer. They're laughing at
our efforts."

"I have to be right about this," the nurse said, now
shaving the shortened hair. The blade snagged and tore at
June's scalp, and a tear ran down beside her temple. "The
key didn't work like it was supposed to. She doesn't know
the name of the character in her own novel. There has to

be another way to force the truth to reveal itself. It's dangerous, but she's too weak and fearful to properly understand. It ends tonight."

June felt another nurse inserting an IV into her arm. A strange sensation flooded her, just as there came a shrill whirring that would have made her jump if she'd been able to. She looked as far to the side as she could without moving her head, which was now also bound to the table with a strap tight across her forehead. The doctor was holding a hand-held electrical saw. *That isn't what they use for lobotomies* was June's last thought.

Without pause or a moment of warning, the doctor lowered the saw directly onto June's forehead, right above the strap. She felt blood spray down her entire face, cover her mouth and nose, making breathing even harder, making it impossible to do anything but scream inside. On the outside, her body strained. The saw continued, deeper, deeper, until June's mind was filled with the sounds of ruined bone being done away with, first down, then across her entire forehead, down the side, across the bottom.

It felt like it took hours. June didn't understand how she wasn't dead from the shock or the pain or both. She didn't understand how she was still *conscious* even. It was like the sound of teeth grinding but amplified, multiplied, turned into a gravelly symphony that was only accompanied by the warm rush of heavily flowing blood. She could feel the liquid dripping from her chin and jaw, down her front, and somehow remembered Eleanor and how she'd looked in that wheelchair, gone. At least Eleanor hadn't gone through this.

Finally—*finally!*—the sound stopped. The silence that followed was more foreign than the sound of the saw had come to be, and to be released into it was jarring and unpleasant, but at least there was no more of that saw-on-bone grinding.

"Let's take a look-see," Joya piped up from behind, and June felt the top of her skull get lifted away, felt the air of the place kiss her exposed brain. She heard a sickening sound that could only have been Nurse Joya hastily discarding the scalp-covered skull cap onto the floor.

This is it, June thought in the absolutely unreal haze of doom. *Peace in death at last. I'm sorry, Eleanor. I'm sorry, Simpson.*

I'm sorry, June.

"Ooh," the doctor breathed excitedly, and June knew that they had won. "Something's been tinkered with inside of this one!"

At his words, it occurred to June in a violent jerk of the mind that she had written about this exact feeling before, about being helpless and strapped down and cut into. It had been in her story, the thing that got her through all those mundane and expectant days of living with Mom and Dad before the hospital. She thought about the creatures that had started appearing in her room as the engagement party got closer, how the night Stewart Dennings had died, June had come home and finished her story in a single sitting against her own will.

That's right, she remembered, comforted at the thought. *I finished it after all. How did it end?*

She had sent the heroine back to Earth to fulfill her destiny. The girl was changed by what she'd been through, never to be the same. She'd descended upon her town, barefoot and shaking, and then what?

"What *is* that?" Nurse Joya asked, her voice full of wonder. "I'm not so sure we should touch it."

The girl in her story had only been ten years old, June also remembered something she'd forgotten until now. And she had figured out, only after coming back to Earth, that the creatures who'd taken her and cut her open endlessly weren't scary at all, weren't malevolent, but had been intelligent, had been cunning. Had been...*deliberate*.

June's eyes opened easily, the haze from whatever the IV had delivered completely gone, as though she'd willed it away. She felt blood run over her eyes, stinging, but her head didn't hurt at all anymore. In fact, nothing hurt, and everything was wonderful. Overhead, the lights began to flicker.

"She looks awake," the doctor remarked, worry evident in his voice. "Quickly, quickly! See if it can be destroyed..."

"No," the nurse said, firm. "I don't think we should touch it. I think that would be very bad..."

Something's been tinkered with inside of this one! And then, much like a baby sliding from its mother's body all at once, the memories returned to June, complete, whole, alive.

Awake.

She smiled, a wide and ecstatic and triumphant smile. The key that the nurse had spoken of... June knew what it was, knew exactly why it hadn't worked before now, despite the hospital's clumsy attempts. Simpson's ghost had been right all along: June was indeed able to tell for certain that she had found it—*it*, the thing, the key—without a shadow of a doubt.

June had named the heroine in her book after all. She just hadn't remembered doing it, hadn't remembered making the rash decision to reveal the name on the very last page, in the very last word, compelled and influenced by the unbeatable force that had pleaded with her to finish her story so she could fulfill her own destiny.

June recited in the clearest of voices, and Nurse Joya's eyes widened as she did:

The girl had a new name, one given to her by the creatures in outer space, one meant to awaken her and allow her access to the full potential of what they had given her. And her name was—

"*Stop!*" the nurse screeched, but it was too late.

"*Nightingale,*" June said, and that was when she heard something in her brain literally click, like a trigger on a gun being pulled back, ready to fire. And since it had been her who could use the key properly, and not the monster in the nurse costume, it would be her with the control of the gun.

So June let the gun go off, much to the dismay of the panicked Nurse Joya, who was yelling at everyone to *Get away, get away, get away from her!*

But it was too late.

For June had awakened.

days past

SOMETHING HAD HAPPENED TO JUNE WHEN she was ten years old, something she had pushed from her mind and never refound, not even all those years later when she awakened in front of the monsters at the ill-fated institution.

Before it happened, she had been a different little girl, one who delighted in the simplest of routine pleasures—coloring at the table while her mother cooked, practicing braiding the hair of her dolls so she'd know how to do her own one day, convincing her older brother to let her sit on his back and ride him around the living room like a horse. She didn't like scary stories and wasn't intrigued by darkness or pain like she eventually grew to be.

Everything was how it should have been, unthinking and never ending in its constant state of normal. She was a delight to her parents, to her classmates, to the people at her church. Everyone was always telling Mom and Dad what a sweet, obedient little girl they had raised. And June loved to hear it, loved to have it confirmed for her that she was doing right.

Then one day when she was ten, June woke up with a headache and felt as though an immense amount of time had passed in her mind, but not in the reality of her bedroom, her house, her family, or the planet itself. She'd had an awful, prolonged nightmare but couldn't remember the details, no matter how desperately she clawed at them. In fact, the more she did, the more they dissipated like smoke.

So June stopped trying to remember. She stopped going on her nightly bike rides to the wooded area that looked over her town, suddenly illogically afraid of the entire area. She went on with her life, grateful to be somewhere secure and safe, grateful to have a stupid brother that made her want to punch him, grateful to have food and shelter and comfort.

But new values grew in her after the mysterious nightmare had scared her straight, new hopes and dreams, things she hadn't considered before. June now felt lucky to have a life like hers. Suddenly, things that others thought were scary or distasteful were interesting to her, and she felt that exploring such feelings could teach her something useful, something that could help her protect herself from the deadly bliss that her previous ignorance had offered. She felt obligated to turn this knowledge into something important, was desperate to discover whatever fate awaited her in adulthood and work toward it as hard as she could.

But her parents seemed to be bothered by postnightmare June. No matter what she did or how genuinely open she tried to be, they were suddenly and constantly disappointed in her, giving her puzzled looks, raising their eyebrows and whispering behind her back. *Strange*, she heard them say. *Off.* They noticed right away that June's number of friends had dropped significantly.

Then one day, Mom told June that they were going to the doctor. Nothing ever came from the appointment, but what June heard her mother say about her disturbed June so deeply that she decided to ignore that it ever happened, erase it from her mind forever.

"Something's wrong with my daughter," Mom told the doctor, who looked unconvinced, as the ten-year-old who sat before him seemed perfectly fine. On the counter in the white and sterile room, there was a newspaper with a headline reporting multiple accounts of an unidentified flying object in local skies. "I don't know how to explain it, but you've got to believe me—she's changed. It's like it happened overnight, a little while back."

June didn't feel like she had changed, but if she had, it was in a good way.

"You'll have to be more clear," the doctor said, obviously irritated at the waste of his time, but what did he care as long as he got paid in the end? "How exactly did she change?"

"It's the strangest thing, the most bothersome thing. Her entire personality is different," Mom said, insistent. "It's almost like my daughter was taken away and replaced with someone who looks exactly like her."

awake

JUNE SAT UP FROM THE TABLE, THE RESTRAINT straps falling to pieces on the floor. She was now able to see everyone in the room: the tiny wrinkled doctor, Nurse Joya with her perfect blond hair and cherry-red lipstick, all five of the other nurses who were like slightly varied versions of their master. They all looked at June with wide eyes. They all kept very, very still.

June realized now that those things—Joya, the doctor, the nurses—were all different appendages of the same beast, one big monster capable of many forms simultaneously. She saw them now like a waving hand of finger puppets, each with a different face.

If she cut off the right head, so to speak, June knew that the rest of them would die, too. She remembered how the doctor had sometimes moved his lips along silently while Joya talked during their sessions. June had a pretty good idea who the head was, but it sure would be fun to test the others just to be sure.

There was no reason to rush things.

"Please," the doctor whispered, putting his hands up, and with her mind, June made his fingers fold backward like a flower blooming, his bones crunching as they went, and he began to scream. June froze him so that only his throat gurgled, and his wrinkled face reddened, and then she caused his head to explode all over Nurse Joya and the other nurses, a satisfying wet *pop!* that sent an array of fluids and chunks flying through the air.

The other women tried to run; June made their legs disappear, and blood poured over the concrete floor. Some of them gave in to death immediately, but a few still tried to crawl with their arms toward the plastic sheet. So June made their arms go away, too, and then their eyes, and then their tongues, all within the blink of an eye.

"June," Joya whispered, the only one who hadn't moved, shivering and covered with the doctor's entrails. "Please. There's still a chance."

"A chance for what?" June giggled manically, unable to imagine what the answer could possibly be.

"A chance to beat them," Joya insisted. "You could use their own technology against them! They kept you in the dark, dangled you like a mouse in front of a snake. Doesn't that bother you?"

"Not particularly," June said. "Especially since the mouse was given sharp enough teeth to chew off the head of the snake."

Despite that, June still had a few questions.

"How were you so stupid that you couldn't figure out I had the key the moment you saw me in that tunnel?" June went on. "I created the path to get in there myself, as I'm sure you knew. You deserve to lose."

"I thought *we* caused that!" Joya cried out, pressing her back harder against the wall in her panic as if she could somehow disappear through it. No such luck. "We knew you were powerful. We only wanted to harness that to help us find the real key. Those other girls, they had powers, too—maybe not like yours but it all came from the same source—and we found them so much earlier than you. We thought your role would be…different."

"Different how?" June was still sitting on the awful table they'd strapped her to. She used her mind to keep Joya from running away.

"A scribe of some kind," Joya explained, softly, as though doing so might somehow save her life. "We weren't alerted to your potential until you started writing your story. From the moment you typed the first word, we were able to smell you, smell where you'd been, just like we'd smelled it on Adie and Simpson and Cassy and Jessica."

June didn't miss that she'd artfully left out mention of Eleanor. An attempt not to pour gasoline on the fire, June assumed.

"The Others," Nurse Joya said. "The ones that took you-all at one point or the other…they have a very distinct odor." Her nose scrunched. "Our kind is hypersensitive to the stink."

June knew the smell well, *like warm salt water and form-aldehyde.*

"We began watching you, secretly," Joya continued. "We started noticing that the story was causing a decline in you. And it was riddled with clues. We thought you were the one capable of finding the key, we just didn't know you were carrying it yourself. We didn't even know what we were looking for or what it would do—we just knew that they were coming for us and that there was a way to stop them. We thought having captured you-all was a victory in itself."

Joya paused, and her face reddened in her rage over her own failure. "We thought we were being clever when we set you up to get admitted. We didn't know that those disgusting things were one step ahead of us all along. We figured that having you admit that you'd killed that man with your mind, facing that impossible reality, would enable you to remember whatever it was they'd made you forget. Little did we know they were still in control. They always were. Your story wasn't a side effect of you processing your trauma. It was just bait, plain and simple. And we took it."

So that was why Nurse Joya and the doctor had been so fixated on the night of Stewart's death in June's sessions. They knew they were looking to make something click, they just had no idea what they were really messing with. They had no idea of the true nature of the key that would be used to destroy them. And they made the mistake of taking the repercussions for the other girls more seriously than hers.

Eleanor. Eleanor's gift had been to pass along important messages through Simpson from the land of the dead. The other girls had played different roles at different points that had led to this. June wasn't sure exactly how, but she remembered how Lauren had claimed to be able to see through anyone's eyes she chose. How Cassy had spoken of past lives. How Adie had heard things nobody else could. How Jessica had made sculptures of things that didn't look like humans.

Despite it all, June hadn't been quick enough to figure it all out before Simpson was killed and Eleanor was taken away from her. It was unfair. Each and every one of these monsters deserved to die. June didn't want to disappoint her makers.

"Come with me," June said softly as she swung her legs over the side of the table, her newfound power creating an incredible and terrifying calm within her. There were many things left to do. "Follow."

June didn't have to look to make sure the nurse was listening: she knew it'd be so. In an effort not to slip, she stepped barefoot over the scattered bodies and through the surprisingly hot fluids that had spilled onto and flooded the floor. She stopped in front of a mirror, looked without reaction at the reflection of the blood-smeared face she still just recognized. The top of her head was still missing, her brain still exposed.

There, toward the front part of the pulsating gray matter, closer to her eyes, June could see a single gleaming piece of metal attached to the tissue. A tiny green light on it flashed. *The key.* June smiled and stepped away from the mirror. The monsters hadn't been wrong per se. The code word had always worked. June knew now that it had simply never been activated in the right conditions: with the brain chip from outer space exposed, rather than hidden beneath layers of scalp and bone.

The gift of the stars, indeed. The beings had always known that the monsters would do it to themselves, go to any extreme in order to beat their foes. They had always known that June would be cut open like a cadaver. The key had worked exactly as intended. Everything had gone according to plan.

"Let me free," Joya screeched from behind her, so for now June silenced the monster in a nurse costume. All she had to do was think something to make it happen, and it was wonderful.

Together they walked through the laboratory, through the elaborate office with the trippy carpet and the heavy furniture, into the hallway of rooms where the rest of the patients slept or cried into the night. June's mouth twitched, and all of the doors flew open.

"Run," she whispered, and suddenly girls and women emerged from the open doorways, running to the front of the building, running to their freedom. June spotted Jessica and Cassy, willed them to look at her and raised a hand in farewell. They gaped at her, disbelief painting their faces, and June hoped that they'd remember her in a fond way, hoped they knew how much she had gone through to free them, hoped they understood how much had been lost to bring them all to this point.

June led Joya to stand directly before the nurses' station. The uniformed women inside looked panicked at the sight of June, her brain still exposed, and Joya standing immobile beside her. They rushed to lock the doors, but—those silly nurses!—June had no need for something as minor as a *door*.

They all exploded at the same time, splattering the glass that separated them with blood and tissue. June carried on toward the hallway that she'd snuck into earlier, where she'd lost any and all hope of succeeding. Despite the feeling of failure that had followed, she had been right to have blind faith earlier. She hadn't been stupid or foolish. And there was nothing she could have done to save Eleanor while she was in a coerced, drugged sleep in the room they had shared.

They entered the room where Eleanor still sat, mouth open, gazing into forever. June knew what she had come for, but despite everything that had happened and was happening, she felt afraid. Upset. Angry.

She went to Eleanor in the chair, leaned down to kiss her blood-streaked cheek. "I love you," she whispered, and then she made Eleanor's body die, as quick as a flash, painless, a mercy. Now there was no more suffering in her already-dead body. There was only June and Nurse Joya in the room now.

"You didn't care what any of us felt," June said, turning to the nurse. "What was this place before you became aware of the impending threat? All those women, everyone who came before us…" She reverted Nurse Joya to a state where she could speak again.

"It was our lifeblood," Joya explained, and June was surprised to see tears welling in the thing's eyes. "Our infinite food source. Humans had already done such a good job of herding themselves, lobotomizing each other and worse. We simply…took over. We looked like them, lived like them, lived off them."

"Disgusting," June said, crossing her arms. "The Others were right. You deserve to be wiped clean from this planet."

"We were born of this planet!" the nurse snarled, spitting. "It is *ours!*"

"No more," June said with a little grin. "Maybe if you had handled things differently, I'd be on your side. This is going to hurt very much, I'm afraid."

"I'm sorry!" Joya begged, and June let her drop to her knees. "I'm so sorry! Please, please! I'm sorry—"

"No," June said impatiently, cutting the nurse off. "There are no apologies now. It's much too late for that."

Nurse Joya's eyes filled with genuine fear as she realized she couldn't move again. June took a deep breath and began the nurse's transformation. The holes in her face were forcibly opened, the appendages shivering as they protruded painfully forth from them. Tendons snapped as the monster revealed itself in full, only to have the appendages ripped from their roots, the claws pulled from the fingers, the fangs torn from the mouth.

June let Nurse Joya scream as loud as she wanted. June peeled the skin from the meat, then peeled the meat from the bone, then let the bones crumble and disintegrate until they resembled nothing more than blood-soaked sand. The screaming was long over, but June continued until nothing was left.

When she was through, June walked calmly through the empty institution, hardly processing the sound of the fire alarms, only vaguely realizing that she had started the fire herself with just a look. *Burn it all to the ground. Chew the head from the snake to ensure it will never grow back.*

June finally found the front desk, also empty, and looked out the window that faced the parking lot. For the first time in months, she saw the morning sun beginning to rise. She stepped out of the Burrow Place Asylum, felt the breeze upon her skin, real and clean, felt it lick her exposed brain tissue, felt the blood that covered her face and neck begin to congeal.

She knew just where to go first.

"I'm coming, sweet husband," June sang into the morning as she made her way down the winding road leading to town. "I'm coming home to you now."

She walked the whole way, making it so that nobody could see her. When she passed a bus stop crowded with people, nobody even looked up from their newspapers or books, although for fun she let one random young man see the truth. Nobody could seem to figure out what the hysterical man was pointing at, screaming and screaming, and June was ashamed to know that the screams gave her joy. She shivered, her new gift causing her entire body to buzz in pleasure.

It occurred to June that even though she had just acted as a mere cosmic weapon to wipe out the monstrosities of the institution, she didn't mind one bit. It was nothing like being used by Dad or Mom or Robert or Fred. It didn't take power away from her but rather provided it in droves, made it flow, washing and warm and wonderful through her every vein. She savored her gift from the land of stars and voids. It'd been her destiny ever since she was ten years old. Out of everybody on the planet, June had been the one who was chosen to carry the key. *Imagine what else they are capable of*, she thought breathlessly as she walked.

Surely, *surely*, they only had more greatness planned for June. Surely they would never discard their precious weapon, years in the making, after just one use. Surely their only plan was to cleanse the earth of the monsters, not the humans. They would have done that already...right? June wished she could ask Eleanor.

Eleanor.

June firmly told herself that she didn't have a place in her current state to think about Eleanor. Not one bit, not now, maybe not ever. If she thought about Eleanor, she might accidentally lose control and cause everything in existence to just...go away. She didn't care to face the fact that she was unbearably, unspeakably alone.

There were things she wanted to do, needed to do, and

only *then* would she stop and think about what could possibly come next.

June willed herself to know exactly where Robert's new house was, the one Stewart Dennings had bought as an engagement gift. She made her way to a very well-maintained neighborhood, all lawns and mailboxes and high-end automobiles. Stewart hadn't gone cheap on his son, had kept the image rolling hard and fast. June was glad that she'd killed him, caught deep in a rare moment of brushing her fingers against the power that was hidden in her mind, a flash of ability that had sparked out as quickly as it'd occurred. Joya and the doctor had been truly stupid to underestimate her potential.

June stood in front of the bushes until she saw Robert emerge from the house, dressed in his work clothes. Only after he drove away, oblivious to June's presence, did she go inside. She spent hours exploring every nook and cranny of the building, laughing at the mess, such an immense mess by a man obviously drowning in loss. She saw that he kept a photograph of them together on his nightstand and was truly surprised at the sight of it. Somehow, Robert still held on to the idea of being with her forever, even after everything that had happened. It baffled her beyond belief. She continued to search through the house.

After she had checked all the rooms and seen everything, she clapped her hands together and got to work.

When evening came and Robert's car pulled into the driveway, June was ready. He opened the door, and June was standing right there, holding a fresh bourbon on ice for him, and even though he initially froze and tried to back away, June had him take the drink and sit at the dinner table, which was already set.

"I've been waiting for you to get home, darling," June said, stooping to retrieve a whole roasted chicken from the oven, the juices bubbling, the skin browned to a perfect crisp. "I've been cleaning all day for you, made sure the house was spotless for our first night together."

Robert sat still at the table, his eyes wide with terror, his body rigid with what June supposed was terror. She could feel that he was trying very, very hard to move, to scream, to run. She'd taken the time to wash all the blood from herself and find a fresh dress that showed a lot of leg, but dear heavens, she'd forgotten to do something about her exposed brain. No matter. Robert soon wouldn't mind, she knew.

"What's wrong?" June asked into the silence, as Robert's eyes began to fill, tears streaming down his face. "Isn't this everything you ever wanted, darling? Us, together, in our very own home? Me making you the perfect dinner? My mother is quite the cook, as you know, and of course she was happy to pass those skills along to me."

June, still smiling and holding the steaming roasting pan, made her way over to Robert and leaned in close, making sure to hold his eyes with hers. "Fuck you for thinking that the world owes you something," she whispered. "Fuck you for thinking that I *ever* owed you *anything*."

There came a knock on the door then. Robert's eyes turned desperately toward the sound.

"Now, who might that be?" June said playfully, rising and setting the chicken down on the counter to quickly tent it with aluminum foil. "I know you like to be the very center of my attention, Robert, but—surprise! After a moment to think about it, I've decided that you're not actually going to be the guest of honor tonight after all."

She went to the front door and opened it, where her

brother, Fred, stood with a bottle of champagne in a twitching hand. "Right on time," June beamed, taking the bottle from her brother's hand. "Oh, for me? So polite, Freddie. You shouldn't have."

Fred said nothing. His face was red, and the veins on his neck and temples were bulging with effort as he tried to fight against the force that drove him. June had him step inside, had him hang his own coat up, had him pour his own drink before sitting at the table directly across from Robert.

"How long I've waited for a moment just like this," June sighed dreamily, sitting at the head of the table. "I've got a few minutes while I let that chicken rest. Seems to me like the perfect moment for us all to have a little talk."

She could see Fred and Robert looking at each other, neither able to move their heads or stand or run.

"One of you is a symptom to be treated," June said. "And one of you is a cancer to be cut out permanently."

She loved seeing them try to figure out who was who.

"You were controlling," June said, starting on Robert first. "You were dismally boring, you only cared about yourself, and you only loved me because your mother was dead." Her face darkened. "And you hurt me. You shoved me against a wall when I wanted to follow my whims, all because you believed that I somehow owed you something." A painful nuisance of a lump formed in her throat. "You pretended to care about my feelings on marriage, but you lied. You let our parents play you like a pitiful little puppet. You let them try to force me into the wrong fate."

June took a breath, realized her hands were shaking. "But despite all of that," she kept on, keeping her voice steady, "I can't help but harbor just a touch of pity for you. You

334

see, Robert, I was just as guilty as being a puppet as you were. Live and learn, right, darling?"

June stood and went back to the kitchen, peering at the boys via the pass-through. She cut into the chicken with a sharp knife, made up plates for Robert and Fred loaded with thick slices of breast meat, as well as some mashed potatoes and scoops of a bubbling green-bean casserole topped with toasted cornflakes. She drizzled pan juices over the meat and added two piping hot rolls with fresh butter to the side. It was the first dinner she'd ever made on her own, and judging by the taste of the delicious meat juices on her fingertips, she'd done very well.

"But I'm willing to give you another chance," June said, setting one of the plates down in front of Robert. "Let you discover what purpose lies in store for you. It's much different than what you ever expected, I can assure you that. You're going to find out *exactly* what it feels like."

She allowed Robert to eat then. She let go of him completely for a moment, just to see what he would do, and when he lifted his arms and realized he was back in control, but refrained from running away and instead began eating, pale, sweating and trembling, June knew she had made the correct choice. He was learning to be obedient already.

June set the other plate in front of Fred, but he wasn't able to move to eat it. "Not hungry?" June asked, crossing her arms over her crisp new dress. "Now, my dear brother, that simply won't do."

Fred stared at her, pleading, and June remembered the false hope of protection that she'd granted him when they were young. He had failed her. She let her smile fade, dropped the bubbly demeanor and leaned over the table so that her face was inches from his.

"You made a horrible mistake the night the bus station called," she said.

June knew now that it had never been her real fate to go to the writing retreat in New York and that she'd been meant for something else, and her story had simply been the vehicle that led her there chapter by chapter. But it didn't matter. Fred wasn't aware of any of that. For all he knew, he'd happily taken away the one chance June had to escape her miserable life without so much as a second thought. She remembered the disgusting glee in his eyes when he came into the living room, hardly able to wait to spill her secret to Dad.

You can't train that sort of betrayal out of someone. June supposed that Fred had shown her his true colors in that moment all those nights ago. A sibling that showed such hatred, that was willing to inflict such *damage*, had no purpose being a sibling at all.

Despite feeling it so strongly, June was unable to articulate to Fred why she was about to do what followed. She wanted to so badly, wished that she could make him fully understand, wished that she could slow it down so he *really* knew, but in the end, June got so upset at the memory of the night her dream had been extinguished that she lost more control than she would have liked.

"My patience has simply run out," she murmured to herself, defeated. "It really is a crying shame."

Fred's eyes stayed on June's, at first anyway, but then the blood started to drip down his face and his eyes rolled back into his head, where they stayed.

June never allowed him to scream.

epilogue

JUNE AWOKE IN A BED OF FRESH SHEETS, WITH the sun cascading through the open window. She smiled and stretched, feeling more refreshed than she had in recent memory. The smell of bacon and coffee made her rise and dress, taking care to get her lipstick and mascara just right: it was a big day for June after all. Before heading to the kitchen, she took one last glance at the mirror over her new dresser. Her face was happy and fresh, her dress clean and comfortable, the glass fixture that covered her exposed brain and the blinking piece of metal embedded in it sparkling clean.

She walked down the hall, toward the sound of clinking dishes, and stepped into the tiled kitchen. In the corner, Robert Dennings crouched on all fours, scrubbing the floor with concentrated intensity. He was wearing bright yellow rubber gloves and a filthy apron. His eyes met June's for just an instant before fearfully moving away.

Eleanor stood at the counter, not noticing June at first as she concentrated on pouring cream into each of the steaming coffee mugs before her. June cleared her throat, and Eleanor looked up with a surprised smile.

"Good morning!" she said, and went over to wrap June in a hug. "I thought you were going to sleep forever."

The embrace, for some reason, was especially comforting to June, although she couldn't quite place why. "I did sleep in late, didn't I?" she asked. "I think I was having a bad dream. But I feel great now that I'm awake."

"Another bad dream?" Eleanor's brow wrinkled in minor concern. "Geez, they're really plaguing you lately, aren't they?"

But June couldn't remember if she'd been having bad dreams lately. She felt something pulling inside her head, like a magnet, but she dismissed the sensation. Both girls ignored Robert as he stood to pour the dirty water from his bucket in the sink, then immediately began to wash the dishes that were piled in the twin sink.

"Thanks for making breakfast," June said, looking in delight to the two plates filled with bacon, fried eggs, and toast. "This looks delicious."

"Yes, well..." Eleanor gave her a sly smile as she brought the plates to the table. "We need our strength for today. It's a big day for all of us, isn't it?"

"It is."

They ate and talked and laughed, neither of them addressing the plate of untouched food at the other end of the table, in the spot where Fred had last sat. The plate had a molded pile of something that could have once been roasted chicken and potatoes and green beans but was now rancid and fuzzy. Only when Eleanor got up to clear their own plates did June let her eyes fall on the plate of rotting food. It wasn't until then that she remembered in full.

"The hospital," she said aloud without meaning to, the cloud of her own creation dissipating at last. "The monster nurse!"

And now she remembered everything else, including what had happened to Eleanor before June had realized she could bring her lover back, rewrite the world however she chose. She'd made the decision to make Eleanor forget the truth, to protect her from the pain of the memory. After everything Eleanor had gone through, she deserved never to feel afraid again.

June had simply made it so, and even let herself forget the full truth in between reminders like the plate of rotten food at the table or the ash on the chair before it, where a dead body had been blinked out of existence. Most of the time she even saw through the ever-working Robert, who never ate or slept or took a break from his work. It felt like he'd always been there, with no other purpose than to quietly obey. Whenever she remembered the truth, she remembered all her past reasonings, and they were always good. This was how it should have been.

Eleanor giggled from where she stood at the counter, refilling her coffee. "That hospital story again? For goodness' sake, June, you have such an imagination in you. I wish you'd write it down like you're always talking about doing."

Yes, June thought. Someday she should certainly write a book about it. But her typewriter was at her childhood home, where her parents lived. She doubted she'd be able to catch them on the phone to ask them to bring it to her;

surely they were already on their way to June's and Eleanor's house. She'd have to get it another time, if another time ever came.

"Your mom and dad just pulled up," Eleanor said, looking out the window over the sink. "You packed our suitcases last night, didn't you?"

"I think so," June said, tearing her eyes away from the plate of rotten food and standing. Sometimes, all the power made her mind go fuzzy. "I'll go get them."

Sure enough, there were two suitcases on the bed, which June didn't remember packing, but that didn't matter. She dragged them down the hall to rest by the front door, where Eleanor was greeting June's parents with hugs and exchanges about how everyone's morning had gone. June felt like she hadn't seen her parents in a very, very long time. She hugged them extra hard before letting them go.

"This one slept late," Eleanor said, teasingly motioning to June. "She almost made us miss our flight."

"I'm just so excited for you girls," Mom said, heading into the kitchen to pour herself some coffee. She patted the top of Robert's head like he was a dog before turning away from him again. "Such an adventure you'll have!"

Yes, June remembered suddenly. Today was the day she and Eleanor were going to have the adventure of their lives, going to be with *them*, the ones who had made all of this possible. June told herself that there was nothing sinister in store for them, or for the remaining humans of Earth. That the next step in whatever this grand plan was would allow Earth to stay just as it was, and also allow June eternal happiness in the stars. But deep in her stomach, a seed of doubt was germinating.

June self-consciously brought her hand to the glass that

was protecting her exposed brain. Eleanor saw her do it and gave her hand, and the glass, a kiss.

"It's beautiful," she said, looking into June's eyes with assurance. "And so are you."

"I can't wait to show you," June answered and kissed Eleanor's lips with deep gratitude. "It's going to be wonderful, more awe striking than anything you've ever seen."

"I believe it," Eleanor said, then went to carry their bags outside.

"You folks have everything under control here?" June asked her parents, who sat at the table across from each other while Robert began to dry and put away the dishes.

"We'll take care of the house while you're gone," Dad assured her, his grin warm and gentle. "Although, let's be honest, who knows if you'll ever come back?"

"Maybe we will," June said, but deep down she knew they wouldn't. "In either case, I love you both so much."

"We love you, too," her parents said in unison, each of them shifting their focus to the dissected newspaper in front of them.

"June!" Eleanor called from outside. "Hurry up, darling, or we're going to miss our flight!"

They won't leave without us, June thought, but hurried nonetheless. She hesitated for just a moment at the front door, looking through to the kitchen, where the plate of rotting food was squirming with tiny white worms. In it, she saw every detail of her previous life, all the ever-encompassing sorrows and the anguish, all of those awful years so neatly condensed in the mold and the rot and the worms.

"Goodbye," she whispered to her old life. Then she bid her parents farewell.

She wondered how they'd fare without her, wasn't sure

what would happen to them or the house or Robert once she was far enough away for her influence to wear off. Regardless, it was no longer her burden to bear. June Hardie stepped out into the warm sunshine, filling her lungs with the fresh air, ready for the excitement of a new chapter to begin.

A better young woman, at last.

★ ★ ★ ★ ★

ACKNOWLEDGMENTS

THE IDEA FOR *NIGHTINGALE* CAME TO ME fully formed and charged with inspiration, the greatest kind of idea. Writing it was one of the most enjoyable and creatively fulfilling experiences of my life. I am so endlessly grateful to all of the people in my life who helped me get through the process in one way or another:

To the ever-thoughtful Nicole Brinkley, who asked me one day if I wouldn't mind sharing my feelings on what it was like to be a female horror author. My knee-jerk re-action was that the question was boring and maybe even irritating, because why should it matter if I am a female horror author as opposed to a male one? But while I untan-gled my thoughts on the subject in order to write a proper response, I realized that I had far more feelings about it than I'd previously allowed myself to really explore, and the more I thought about it, the more I had to say. Thank you so very much, Nicole, for sending me down the path of thought that would lead directly to *Nightingale*.

To my truly kick-ass agent Joanna Volpe, as well as everybody on the incredible New Leaf Literary team. It never ceases to amaze me how smart, passionate, and generally rad my agency is, and I am endlessly grateful for them. Jordan Hamessley, thank you so much for understanding my vision and thoughtfully helping me bring June's story to its full potential. New Leaf rocks!

To Joya "Joya Destroya" Schmidt, who is not only my roller derby teammate but also one of my favorite women on the planet. You inspire me with your strength and tenacity and good humor on a daily basis—I am a better derby player and a better writer because of you. The Joya in *Nightingale* wasn't originally intended to play such a pivotal role, but I realized very quickly that in order to properly honor her namesake, I'd need to roll my sleeves up and have myself some fun in creating an exciting, badass female villain. Destroya, I hope you love her as much as I love you.

Likewise, to my entire team at Northern Arizona Roller Derby, also known as The Whiskey Row-llers. The blood, sweat, and tears involved in training to become a better player have unavoidably affected every other aspect of my life, including writing. Thank you, my babes, for welcoming me and for pushing me to always do my very best in everything I do. They are: Juana Ash Kickin', Joya Destroya, Capt'N Jack, Selethal Weapon, Holly Ween, Cleo Patricide, MuZack Morris, Swamp, Hot Tee, Buffy Vanderbush, Lil' Kitty Split, Kaos Katalyst, Professor Pain, Baby Eagle, and DeeStroyer.

To my incomparable crew of writer friends, lovingly known as my hags, being able to chat daily about everything under and above the sun with you ladies has been such a treasured escape in my work and personal life: Kate Hart, Kody Keplinger, Courtney Summers, Somaiya Daud, Stephanie Kuehn, Lindsey Culli, Samantha Mabry, Phoebe North, Alexis Bass, Stephanie Wargin, Kara Thomas, Veronica Roth, Maurene Goo, Debra Driza, Kaitlin Ward, Michelle Krys, Kristin Halbrook, Laurie Devore, and Leila Austin. Thanks for all of the laughs and support, hags.

To Chelsea Stazenski, Alexa Simpson, Cassy Foster, Jessica Crocker, Adie Matthew, and Lauren West: as always, you gals are essential to my happiness. May we continue to have the wildest adventures together, and thank you for letting me use you to build June a girl squad almost as awesome as ours. (Nurse Chelsea may have not been a favorite of June's, but I sure loved her.)

To T.S. Ferguson and my wonderful team over at Harlequin TEEN—thank you so much for enabling me to live my dream.

And last, but certainly not least, to my love Edmund. You are the chainsaw to my Ash.